SALTING THE WOUND

A captivating romance set in nineteenth-century Dorset

Charlotte Honeyman jilts her long-time swain, and on the spur of the moment marries a stranger. His pride damaged and his matrimonial plans upturned, sea captain Nick Thornton threatens to take revenge. Charlotte's younger sister, Marianne, takes pity on Nick and secretly boards his ship, where she meets with an accident. Nick regards Marianne as the perfect tool with which to get his own back, but in the process falls in love...

*Janet Woods titles available from
Severn House Large Print*

BROKEN JOURNEY
CINNAMON SKY
THE COAL GATHERER
EDGE OF REGRET
HEARTS OF GOLD
WITHOUT REPROACH

SALTING THE WOUND

Janet Woods

Severn House Large Print
London & New York

This first large print edition published 2011
in Great Britain and the USA by
SEVERN HOUSE PUBLISHERS LTD of
9-15 High Street, Sutton, Surrey, SM1 1DF.
First world regular print edition published 2009 by
Severn House Publishers Ltd., London and New York.

British Library Cataloguing in Publication Data

Woods, Janet, 1939-
  Salting the wound.
  1. Ship captains--Fiction. 2. Revenge--Fiction. 3. Dorset
  (England)--Social conditions--19th century--Fiction.
  4. Love stories. 5. Large type books.
  I. Title
  823.9'2-dc22

ISBN-13: 978-0-7278-7968-4

Severn House Publishers support The Forest Stewardship Council
[FSC], the leading international forest certification organisation. All
our titles that are printed on Greenpeace-approved FSC-certified paper
carry the FSC logo.

MIX
Paper from
responsible sources
FSC® C018575

Printed and bound in Great Britain by the
MPG Books Group, Bodmin, Cornwall.

To Jill Lawson and Pat Hornsey.
With my appreciation and thanks
for a job well done.

One

Nicholas Thornton stepped ashore and took a deep breath of his native English air. His hand closed around the pistol under his coat, his glance sought out any danger that might be lying in wait in the shadows. Under his arm was a length of rare exotic silk safely packaged in a satchel made from sailcloth. The silk was a gift for Charlotte Honeyman, from which she could fashion herself a wedding gown.

It was a fairly quiet night for the quayside town of Poole, except for the faint hum of voices coming from the taverns, the occasional spill of light and noise when a door opened and spat out a drunk or two. A pair of cats exchanged insults in an alley.

The summer air was as cool and soft as a whisper of satin against his face, the dewed stillness of it broken only by the impatient slap of the rigging against the masts, the creak and squeak of timber against timber and the lap and splash of water against the hull of the *Samarand*.

Square-rigged and with a sharp rake to her stern *Samarand* averaged only twelve knots in the right conditions. She'd been built eight years previously but would be lucky if she lasted till she was fifteen, when she was due to be sold for scrap. Already she was full of worm. Nick hoped he wasn't on board when the bottom dropped out of her.

He jumped when the cats' argument became a full-blooded skirmish and the pair exploded out of the alley into the circle of light left by a gas lamp. Ears flattened, they spit and slashed at each other with ferocious cries and shrill growls. He chuckled when one broke off and ran back into the alley, the other one in hot pursuit.

Much as he liked life at sea, and much as his uncle wanted him to, Nick had no intention of sailing the world's oceans forever. There were easier, less dangerous ways of earning a living. He'd also like a bed that didn't pitch and toss, unless he happened to have a woman under him and the pitching and tossing was of his own creation. If he stayed in the career he'd grown up with he'd end up like his great uncle. No woman wanted a husband who was rarely home.

In vain he'd argued with his uncle some three months ago, which had been the last time he'd tied up at the company berth in Poole.

'We could warehouse the goods we import, open a shop and sell them ourselves.'

Erasmus Thornton had scoffed with some disgust at his suggestion. 'You want to become a shopkeeper? I suppose you intend to settle down with the eldest Honeyman girl, as well? After a few weeks with her you'll be glad to get to sea again. You're thinking with your balls.'

He grinned. Didn't most men? 'Being a shop-

8

keeper is nothing to sneer at; I know some damned wealthy ones. Neither is having a wife and children. If Charlotte will have me, and there's no reason why she shouldn't, I'll marry her. I've known her all my life.'

'You'll come to regret it if you do. She hasn't shown any inclination to wed you so far, though she's good at keeping you on the hook. You'll be damned if she agrees, and she'll be cursed if she doesn't. Still, if you want to marry and produce a family I'm not against that. God knows, the Thornton family is thin on the ground now and you might as well choose a woman with some looks and backbone to her. But Charlotte Honeyman is as bad-tempered and as stubborn as they come. It will take a special kind of man to handle her. She'll probably need a stick around her backside now and again to point out to her who's the boss. But mark my words – it damned well won't be you!'

Nick had roared with laughter at the thought of Charlotte marrying anyone else but him.

Erasmus smiled at him. 'The younger one is more your style. She has the looks and softness of her mother.'

'More your style, Uncle, since it was your liaison with their mother that caused the split between the families.'

Nick couldn't recall the younger girl's name, or even what she looked like come to that. She'd usually been out on the heath when he'd visited, or helping the maid around the house. Besides, when set against Charlotte, everyone else paled into insignificance for Nick. He'd wanted

Charlotte ever since he'd been old enough to introduce lust into his life. Her refusal to co-operate had only added fuel to his fire.

Erasmus had sighed and passed a hand across his forehead then. 'It's a great pity that their mother died. Take my advice, lad. Never fall in love with a married woman, like I did. I'll be taking possession of the *Daisy Jane* soon, so you won't get me working in a warehouse or shop. We'll work both clippers for a while, and you can have command of the *Samarand*. She's still got some life in her. I daresay you'll enjoy life better without having me breathing down your neck.'

That fact had improved both his life and his temper. Nick had now completed his first voyage with *Samarand* under his command. His uncle has been right. He'd enjoyed being out from under his critical gaze, and was proud that his seamanship skills had brought his ship safely back to harbour.

He took another perfunctory look around. The shadows were still, except for a seaman rolling back to his ship. He respectfully touched his cap as he passed, grunting, 'Evenin', Cap'n. She's a fair one.'

'Indeed she is.' Nick gazed around. There had been no sight of the *Daisy Jane* as he'd entered harbour and docked, though his uncle was due in at any time now. Erasmus had named the ship after his sister, who kept house for them.

'It might sweeten her up a bit,' he'd said. 'Though anyone who looks less like a daisy I've yet to meet.'

Looking over her glasses at her brother, Daisy had then snorted.

Nick had been raised by his uncle and aunt from the age of three. He couldn't remember his parents, but his father had been Dickon Thornton, who'd been an adventurer. His mother was a Greek woman. According to Erasmus, she'd been encouraged by her new husband and her stepsons to lose interest in her bastard child.

It had been a strict upbringing. Blood was thicker than water with both of them. Aunt Daisy had been fond of using the stick to keep him under control when he misbehaved, but he loved her. Erasmus had always treated him as though he was his own son, instead of the son of his much older half-brother, whom he'd never got along with. Nick had been left in no doubt that Erasmus was proud of him, though. As expected of him, he'd set sail with Erasmus at the age of twelve to learn his trade.

'I imagine the Honeyman girl will have you eventually. She has nobody else to turn to and no money with which to attract a man,' his uncle had pointed out the last time they'd been in port together, and after Charlotte had turned Nick down once again. 'I'll give her an ultimatum. If she doesn't stop prevaricating I'll have her out of that house on the next tide. I don't want the upkeep of it any longer. I'm a seafarer not a builder, and the place is falling down.'

Nick smiled to himself as he stepped confidently forward. It had been a long time between ports and there was time to find a willing woman for himself before the morning. There was a

11

whore called Nancy who always gave value for money. He'd seek her out. And he'd visit Charlotte in the morning and propose marriage. If Erasmus had delivered his ultimatum to her, this time she'd agree.

His smile faded as he remembered the last time he'd proposed to her. She'd been in a fine fizz of a temper and had stamped her foot. 'I've told you that I don't love you and I'll never marry you. Don't you listen?'

'My uncle has promised to give us the house if you wed me,' he'd said, then in a fit of generosity, 'I intend to put it in your name so you don't have to worry about not having a roof over your head any more.'

'I loath Erasmus Thornton. I'd rather die than take anything from him, even the house I grew up in. He ruined my mother and impoverished my father.'

'Your mother loved him. As for your father, he was a drunken gambler. Nobody made him wager the house. It was his own idea. Erasmus doesn't want the upkeep of Harbour House. At the moment he's of a mind to sell it out from under you. Agree to marry me and it will always be yours.'

'If he attempts to turn me out I'll burn the place down. As for becoming your wife, you'd make a terrible husband. You're always away ... though that would prove to be a plus rather than a minus. You have no manners and you probably have a girl in every port.'

He'd grinned at the truth in that. 'I can learn some manners, and I intend to remain ashore in

12

a year or so and open my own emporium.'

'Hah!' she'd thrown at him. 'You're too arrogant to learn any manners now. I want to love and respect the man I marry. And I want him to love and respect me. You're incapable of either.'

Anger had risen in him then, because he'd done both and for several years now. 'You don't know me if you think I've got no feelings, Charlotte. But if you want pretty words and gifts to prove that I care for you, then you won't get them. To my mind, love is a damned fool notion that weakens a man. But I'll be faithful to the woman I marry. I'll be back, and I won't take no for an answer. Make up your mind to it.'

She heaved a sigh and told him again, talking slowly, as though he was an idiot. 'It won't make any difference, Nick. I won't marry you.'

'Charlotte, you promised yourself to me in childhood and I'm going to hold you to that.'

'That was before I discovered who caused the death of my mother.'

He sighed then. 'You can't blame me for what somebody else did. Besides, it was only a rumour.'

He watched her eyes begin to despise him when she quietly said, 'One you believe yourself. I don't want you and I won't marry you. Come here again and I'll shoot you dead.'

He'd retreated to lick his wounds, confident she'd come round eventually. Two days later he'd taken the *Samarand* to Shanghai, but now he was back with a cargo of tea and exotic silk, which he intended to sell at a huge profit. Despite his vow that he wouldn't prove his regard for her with gifts, he'd set a length of the precious silk aside for Charlotte's wedding gown and intended to take it to her as a peace offering. By now she would have come to her senses.

It was the middle of the night. Even if his Aunt Daisy had seen the ship coming into harbour, Nick decided not to rouse her from her bed by going home and letting himself in. Instead, he paid Nancy for the night, for he had a raging need on him.

As it turned out, if he'd gone straight home he might have saved himself from a wasted journey.

The next morning Nick went home in time for breakfast. He kissed his aunt. 'Uncle's not home yet, then.'

Aunt Daisy snorted. 'That's a damned fool question if ever I heard one. Can you see him? Go and get yourself a bath and shave before you sit down at my table. You smell like a whore's petticoat.'

He gave a slightly shocked grin. What did his maiden aunt know about whores, let alone what their petticoats smelled like? Then he realized it was one of his uncle's expressions.

The bath was kept in the back room, where the laundry was done. Aunt Daisy already had water heated for the exercise. Soap and his shaving gear were on the marble washstand and his robe hung over a chair.

He had himself a bath and a shave, then tidied up after his ablutions, because shipboard life had taught him to be tidy. Dressing in his best shore

14

suit he went down to breakfast.

Aunt Daisy looked him over, then smiled. 'There's handsome you are. Are you meeting someone?'

He avoided her eyes. 'Could be,' and he tucked into his breakfast of bacon, eggs and sausages, and two pieces of toast covered with thick yellow butter.

'You'd better take her some flowers,' Daisy said, just as he was about to leave.

'Take who flowers?'

'You know who.'

He kissed her cheek. 'Mind your own business, Aunt Daisy.'

He bought Charlotte a posy anyway, and hiring a black horse from the stables, he set out towards the heathlands that bordered the harbour. There was a faint flush of dawn in the sky that deepened in colour and reached down into the water as he rode.

Red sky in the morning sailor's warning, he said under his breath as the horse stepped out along a path worn through the undergrowth to the chalky soil beneath.

A man emerged from Harbour House before he reached it and pulled on his jacket. He stood alone as though he was waiting for him. When Nick neared the man he saw that he had a straight, taut bearing while seeming relaxed, grey eyes and light brown hair.

'I'm Seth Hardy,' he said. 'Is there something you want with me?'

Seth Hardy? He'd heard of him. Erasmus had said the man had come into a legacy, and had

15

talked about him as being interested in the clay and gravel pits that had belonged to Charlotte's father. But he'd wanted the house as well. What was he doing here?

He'd soon find out, Nick thought as he dismounted and held out a hand. 'I'm Nicholas Thornton.'

Hardy gave his hand a brief shake. 'I know who you are. State your business.'

There was a feeling of dread growing inside Nick. His uncle must have gone ahead and sold the house from under Charlotte. He wondered where was she?

'Is Charlotte Honeyman inside?'

'It's early. My wife is still in bed.'

'Wife?' Nick said harshly, and his heart plummeted into his boots. 'Charlotte is married to you?'

'Two months, since I bought the house.'

The man was about thirty, five years older than himself, Nick thought. There was a quiet strength about Hardy when he informed him, 'Charlotte doesn't wish to see you, Captain Thornton.'

'She married you ... a man who's a stranger to her. I don't believe it. I'll hear it from her own lips.'

A shot kicked up a spurt of dust just in front of him, the report making him jump. Automatically he reached for his own pistol.

'There's no need for that, Charlotte, put the gun away,' Hardy said.

Nick's hand stilled when he heard Charlotte's laughter come from the upstairs window. 'Per-

16

haps that will convince you, Nick.'

She was still in her lacy chemise, and her hair tumbled gloriously around her shoulders. His eyes narrowed. So she was married ... yet she still had a look of innocence about her. Surely this was a trick to get rid of him.

'I thought you were going to shoot me dead if I came here again,' he scoffed.

'If that's what you want.' The gun came up steady in her hand as she lined it up on his head. He remembered that she was an expert shot.

'Stop this,' Hardy shouted in alarm, then he shrugged, and relaxed.

Time slowed as Nick watched her finger tighten on the trigger. His mouth dried and he gazed at the man who'd said he was her husband, but mostly with bravado because his heart was thundering in his chest. 'I see you are a man who hides behind Charlotte's petticoat.'

He was about to pull his pistol out the rest of the way and give the man a scare for poaching his woman when Seth Hardy chopped his hand across Nick's wrist, causing a momentary paralysis. The weapon dropped to the ground and Seth gave him a tight sort of smile. 'Think again, Captain. Her pistol—'

'Say your prayers, Nick,' Charlotte threw at him.

The contrary little witch! She meant it, and he still had some living to do. He threw himself to the ground just as the hammer clicked on an empty chamber, crushing the posy of flowers beneath his body. He'd forgotten that her father's pistol only had one shot, and Hardy reminded him as he finished, '–only has one shot, which has already been discharged.'

Hardy offered Charlotte a grin that locked him out. She held the man's gaze for a moment, fluttered her eyelashes and blushed. Nick was well aware of the signs. Charlotte's blush and enticing little smirk said it all. Her new husband was giving her her head before he closed in for the kill. Jealousy tore him to shreds, until he thought, Charlotte was doing it to make him jealous.

Nick scrambled to his feet, his face flushed with anger ... and dare he admit it, feeling humiliated beyond measure. Charlotte had always known where to stick her pitchfork so it hurt him the most. And this time it was straight into his heart.

Seth said quietly. 'You've scared him enough I think, Charlotte. I think Captain Thornton got the message.'

'Did you, Nick?' Charlotte said.

'For God's sake, Charlotte, have a heart,' Nick pleaded. 'We practically grew up together.'

'No we didn't. I was forced to play with you when you visited with Erasmus Thornton. You were always an arrogant bully who wanted your own way and wouldn't take no for an answer. You broke my toys, scribbled over my books and frightened my sister and made her cry. And our father always took your part.'

Nick wasn't responsible for the way her father had acted, or his uncle come to that. But had he done all those things? He couldn't remember her sister. He searched his memory and recalled her

18

as being a pair of years younger than Charlotte. She'd clung to her sister's skirt like a whimpering grey mouse. He couldn't remember frightening her. Not on purpose, anyway. 'I'm sorry for everything.'

'It's too late, you worm. I don't want your apology, and neither does Marianne.'

Ah yes, that was the sister's name, though he'd always called her by another name ... one he'd given her himself, since she'd liked to sing, and it was short for Marianne. He remembered turning her round and round, then when he'd let her go she'd staggered around on her plump little legs and crashed into the furniture while he laughed and teased her. Aria is in a dizzy tizzy, he thought, and tried not to grin.

Behind Charlotte in the shadows, the form of another girl appeared, a shawl covering her shoulders. The girl's hand lay against her throat in fright, her eyes were wide and her mouth an astonished oval in a heart-shaped face. Dark hair was pulled back into a braid that hung like a rope over her shoulder. She reminded Nick of a startled rabbit before she quickly shrank back. He grinned. That must be Aria, and he hadn't even said boo to her yet. She didn't possess the spirit or looks that her sister had.

He recalled the window as being the bedroom the sisters had always shared. It looked as though they still shared it. Seth Hardy hadn't had his length of Charlotte yet.

Nick's gaze shortened back to his adversary and his grin became a frown. He'd known Charlotte would have put up some resistance to his proposal, but found it hard to believe that she'd have thrown him over in such a callous manner. Their eyes locked, but the expression of disdain in hers defeated him.

She belonged to another man. He could have no claim to her now. It crossed his mind that he could always challenge Seth Hardy to a duel, then throw Charlotte over his shoulder, take her aboard the *Samarand* and sail off with her into the sunrise.

But then what? He'd be forced to settle abroad, and so far he hadn't seen anywhere he liked better than the land of his birth.

His thoughts were interrupted when a child came running from the house.

Charlotte called out with unnecessary anxiety, 'Come away from him ... come back inside, at once.'

The boy stopped, then gazed from Seth to him, then back to Seth again, for all the world as though he was a rabbit caught in a trap. Uncertainty danced in his mossy green eyes. 'Pa?'

Seth stepped between them, creating a barrier. He didn't look at the boy but said quietly, 'John, there's no need to be alarmed. Do what your stepmother says.'

'Yes, Pa.' The boy returned to the house with some alacrity.

So, Charlotte had saddled herself with a stepson. Did Seth Hardy imagine he'd harm the brat? Did Charlotte? The fact that she thought so little of him was wounding in itself. It also angered him. But there was no point in making a fuss now. Seth Hardy could have the shrew.

There were other women, just as beautiful, much softer and more willing to please him than Charlotte had ever been.

He'd always loved her, he admitted to himself.

Bah to such tomfoolery! There were other women in the world, and he'd learn not to love Charlotte. It would serve her right. She'd miss him when he was gone. Under the watchful eyes of Seth Hardy he retrieved his gun and, checking the safety catch, shoved it back into his belt. He had no intention of blowing his own balls off.

'Put the pistol away, Charlotte. Captain Thornton is leaving.' Hard grey eyes came up to his. 'Isn't that right, Captain?'

For the first time in his life Nick had been denied his own way. He didn't like it much, but he didn't blame Seth Hardy for taking advantage of what was on offer. He ignored the man, turning instead to the woman who'd betrayed him. 'You've had your fun, Charlotte, but you should know me well enough to realize that you might live to regret this.'

It was a face-saving remark. Nick wouldn't damage a precious hair on her head, no matter what she'd done to him.

He left the sailcloth satchel in the low gorse where it had fallen, then mounted the black. He rode away without a backward glance, his self-esteem in tatters and feeling like a dog slinking off with its tail tucked firmly between its hind-quarters.

Charlotte and Marianne stood at the window on the landing and watched Nick Thornton's retreat, a lonely, dejected figure in black.

Marianne had tears in her eyes. 'Stop snivelling, he deserved it,' Charlotte said.

But her final triumph over Nick hadn't given her the pleasure she'd expected, and had left her feeling strangely diminished in her own eyes. Nick had always loved her, and Charlotte had held a sneaking regard for him until the death of her father had revealed the extent of the debt owed to Erasmus Thornton, and his involvement with her mother. It had offended her, and she'd simply refused to be the payment to settle the debt. Once she'd refused, her pride had not allowed her to go back on her word.

'You shouldn't have humiliated him so,' Marianne said.

Charlotte shrugged. 'It was no more than he deserved. You're never to speak to him again, do you hear? If it wasn't for his uncle—'

'I'm old enough to make up my own mind to whom I speak, and I refuse to blame Nick Thornton for something that's not of his doing.'

Charlotte abruptly changed the subject, as she often did when the conversation was not going her way. 'You're not wearing that awful brown gown and shawl are you?'

'It merges with the colours of the heath, so if you keep still the animals mistake you for a plant and don't take fright so easily.' Marianne pulled on her scuffed boots. 'I promised John I'd take him up to the copse, and I'm going to teach him about the heath birds today. We'll probably be out all morning.'

'Seth was brave standing up to Nick,'

Charlotte said softly. 'Do you think he's handsome?'

'Nick has never been fearsome, he only pretended to be. So no, Seth wasn't that brave, since he's been trained to fight and Nick hasn't. And Nick has always been handsome, in a dark, tough sort of way. He has a nice smile and I love it when he laughs, it's usually a soft sort of chuckle.'

Charlotte glowered at her in the mirror. 'I meant Seth, you idiot. Besides, what do you know about Nick Thornton? He was my friend, not yours.'

'Oh Seth ... yes, I suppose he is handsome, I haven't really noticed. I must go, I'm starving and I want to get some breakfast.'

Her sister dashed off, calling down the stairs, 'Good morning, Seth. Have you seen John anywhere? I'm taking him out on the heath today and want to make sure he eats a good breakfast first.'

Charlotte laughed before she whispered, Aria is always in a dizzy tizzy. Then she remembered that was what Nick used to tease her sister with. Spots of colour flared in her cheeks and she had a moment of regret about the way she'd treated him. She picked up the brush and began to furiously attack her hair.

'You'll pull it out by the roots. Give me the brush, I'll untangle it.'

'Seth!' She automatically reached out for her robe, which was on a nearby chair.

He stilled her hand. 'Leave your robe where it is, Charlotte. I've seen a woman in her chemise

23

before.'

She retorted, 'You may have, but a man hasn't seen me in one before.'

'No? It didn't seem to bother you when you were at the window.'

She had no answer for that. He began to pull the brush through her hair, stopping to gently tease out the knots. It was relaxing and she forgot she was so lightly clad and closed her eyes.

'Tell me about Nicholas Thornton,' he said after a while.

'I've told you about him. He's a persistent rat.'

'I didn't expect you to react the way you did to him. Who taught you to shoot?'

'My father. He could shoot the eyes from a frog, even when he was drunk. I was tempted to wing Nick.'

'I'm glad you didn't. Enemies are something I'd prefer not to have. Has there ever been anything serious between you two?'

'We were playmates when we were small, that's all.' She gave a faint smile. 'By now he will have got the message that he doesn't have any claim to me on the strength of that.'

'Which is the main reason why you married me in the first place, I imagine. To teach Nicholas Thornton a lesson.'

She shrugged, and decided that truth was better than deceit with Seth. He was no fool. 'It was one of the reasons. I thought you were a decent enough man and John needed a mother. What was the boy's own mother like? Did you love her?'

'Aye, I loved her. Mary didn't have a mean

bone in her body. John was only young when she died. I promised her I'd look after him and I brought him back to England.'

Envy slithered through her body like a cold worm at the thought that her husband had genuinely loved another woman. She knew she was selfish, possessive and stubborn, and she hated knowing it. 'You lived abroad? You didn't say.'

'You've never been interested enough to ask before.'

'I'm asking now.'

'I was an officer in the army, and my regiment was attached to Port Arthur, which is the penal colony in Van Diemen's Land.'

'Where's that?'

'It's a small island off the south coast of Australia. I met Mary there. She was widowed and destitute, and she had a small baby to care for. When she died I sold my commission and returned to England. John missed his mother for a while then he seemed to forget about her. I wish I could forget her as easily.'

The woman was dead and of no risk to Charlotte, yet still she experienced envy. The wistful tone in Seth's voice said he still thought fondly of his former wife. Charlotte had avoided discussing it with him before. 'Didn't you mind taking responsibility for another man's child?'

'Of course not. I always regarded John as my son. I still do. I hope you'll accept him as such in time.'

She nodded. 'Your mind can be at rest about that, Seth. John and I get on well, though I think he prefers Marianne to me.'

'That's because she's more easy-going, and plays games to keep him occupied. He's learned to respect you over the past two months.'

'About Nick Thorn—'

'I would have preferred to have known about the situation with him beforehand.'

'You did. I told you yesterday when I saw his ship come into harbour that he'd proposed and I'd turned him down.'

'You should have told me about it before then. And you should have left the situation for me to handle, Charlotte. I don't like to see a man humiliated like that, especially when his intention towards you appeared to be entirely honourable.'

'Nick hasn't got an entirely honourable bone in his body. He's always thought he owned me.'

'Now he's aware that it's me who owns you ... but what's more important is that you should realize that. I bought you with the house and business.'

Her temper flared at that. 'I'm not a slave to be bought and sold. I only married you because you wanted a mother for John.'

'Not quite correct, Charlotte. You're not that altruistic. You asked me to marry you for your own reasons. I thought it was for the house, but now I learn that the marriage was also a weapon to use against Nicholas Thornton. I weighed up the drawbacks as well as the benefits of marriage to you, very carefully, for John's sake as well as my own. That one wasn't part of the equation.'

'What drawbacks?'

'You have a mulish disposition. I can understand why, but I'm hoping marriage will cure
you of that, since I'd rather not make an enemy
of my wife, and it wouldn't be wise for you to
make an enemy of me. Let me make one thing
very clear. I will not be treated with the same
lack of respect you offered Nick Thornton.'

She gave a small huff of annoyance. 'What of
the benefits of being married to me? I suppose
there are some.'

'There will be in the future. You're beautiful to
look at and can cook well ... and you're an
intelligent and amusing conversationalist when
you put yourself out to be. Also, you're of child-
bearing age.'

'The likelihood that you'd wed a woman who
wasn't is rather remote, since she'd be either too
young or too old.'

He kissed the spot between her neck and her
shoulder, and she stiffened, then shivered. Her
eyes flew open to encounter his and her mouth
dried. She'd never seen his eyes so predatory.
'What do you think you're doing, Seth? When
we married you agreed to wait until I was ready.'

'Did you think I would wait for ever, even
though encouragement was not forthcoming?'

Outside, John and Marianne were chattering
and laughing as they left. Charlotte was tempted
to call her sister back on some excuse, but
something stopped her. Cowardice was not one
of her many faults, nevertheless she could feel
her face flaming. 'No, of course not. Damn you,
Seth! You've embarrassed me. Didn't it occur to
you that I wouldn't know when I was ready to

become a wife in that way? I've never been one before. The longer a union between us was avoided, the harder it's become for me. I thought that you ... didn't find me attractive.'

His grey eyes softened and he smiled. 'I find you exceedingly attractive, which was one of the reasons I accepted your surprising proposal. And perhaps we should have discussed this before. Even so, I've decided to claim what I bought with the house.'

'Please don't regard me as a commodity you bought ... it doesn't endear you to me.'

'I'm sorry, Charlotte. Suddenly discovering that I've got a rival for your affection has added a little spice as well as some urgency to the situation.'

'Nick's not a rival.'

'Ah, but he is. His regard for you is such that he's prepared to give his all for you. Yet still you profess to hate him. A man who brings such a strong reaction from a woman is a rival, and I'd prefer that passion to be expended on me.'

Her heart began to flutter. 'You might as well know, Seth, I hold you in no affection ... I haven't even decided if I even like you yet.' She shrugged. 'Well, yes, I do like you, but if I'd just wanted the house I could have married Nick and had it all back. Erasmus Thornton intended to give it to us if we wed. And Nick would have given it to me as a wedding present. He couldn't get it through his head that I didn't want him along with it.'

'Yet you took me—'

'On the spur of the moment.' When Seth

winced, she smiled ruefully, 'and for better or worse. Remember that you've been warned, when my worst comes out.'

Seth chuckled. 'It matters not if you feel affection for me, and I'm sure I'll find a way to handle you, since I didn't imagine that you'd fall instantly in love with me. However, I'll expect you to respect our marriage and remain faithful. From now on you'll spend your nights in my bed, but I intend to show you exactly what to expect from your marital duty now, so you needn't wonder about it any more.'

Her blood chilled. 'I didn't think you'd go about it in such a cold-blooded manner.'

'I promise you it won't be that. I've sent Alice into town on an errand and we're quite alone, so there's no danger that we'll be disturbed.'

'You planned this right from the start, didn't you?'

'Your seduction? Yes, of course.' He gave a regretful sigh. 'I'd intended to give you six months in which to get used to me. After your gentleman friend left I decided to bring it forward.'

'How many times do I have to tell you. Nick is not my gentleman friend. He's not even a gentleman, and after today he certainly won't even be a friend. Stop being tiresome. Better we wait until the six months is up.'

'Hush, Charlotte, I will not be manipulated.' Seth slid his hand under her chin, tipped her head back and kissed her. He kept her face there when she tried to turn away, his mouth caressing an eventual response from her. Sneakily, he slid his other hand over one of her breasts, his thumb brushing the nub to a response.

Charlotte wanted to push it away and fought the sensations jostling inside of her. Further down his caress went, over her thigh to her knee, where he gradually bunched up her chemise and drew the filmy material back up and under.

She stiffened at first, especially when his touch became more intimate, but she didn't struggle, and resigned herself to what now seemed inevitable. She just hoped it didn't hurt too much.

Against her back she experienced the hard, urgent nudge of his arousal and nearly panicked.

She felt at odds with herself, and her feelings embarrassed her with their sheer unexpectedness. All at once she was lethargic, helpless and filled with the need to cover up, or leave her body exposed to his gaze.

Even while she struggled to contain what he was making her feel, she knew she was fighting a losing battle and would have to surrender to it eventually.

And she did, easily dispensing with her initial inhibitions when she allowed her instinct to take over.

Sensing her surrender Seth pulled her to her feet then to the comfort of her bed. She lay there without averting her eyes, watching with curiosity as he divested himself of his clothes. His body was lean, muscular, and beautiful in its manly angles, so she wanted to reach out and touch him, take his arousal into her hands and into her body. But she didn't dare. He would think her immodest.

He gazed at her, smiling when she blushed, as if he could read her thoughts. Her heart began to pound too fast to count when he joined her on the bed. He kissed her mouth, her eyes, each taut breast and then whispered against her ear, 'Now, Charlotte, let's put that passion of yours to good use.'

A short while after that Charlotte forgot to pretend that Seth was Nick Thornton.

Two

Now Charlotte had become a married woman and Seth had joined the various business associations open to him, many more invitations came the way of the Honeyman sisters. As well, more people took the trouble to visit the occupants of Harbour House. Charlotte was becoming a good hostess.

Seth was the perfect escort for them. He was good-looking, especially in an evening suit, he was mannerly and he could dance well. Marianne had never seen him lose his temper over anything.

He had taken over their father's study, and spent most of the early evening poring over the company books. 'The clay and gravel pits are making a profit,' he'd told them with some satisfaction.

Charlotte hardly ever tore her eyes away from

Seth. Sometimes she fussed over him, and he'd give a small grin as he allowed her to; sometimes she had a soft, dreamy look in her eyes when she looked at him; and sometimes they exchanged glances that were entirely personal.

Marianne thought that her sister might have fallen in love with Seth, though she never mentioned it, and she hoped some man would look at her that way, one day ... preferably Lucian Beresford.

Tonight they were going to a Christmas ball at the assembly rooms. Seth had urged them to buy a new gown apiece, and he'd hired a couple of rooms at the inn, which was just a few steps from the assembly hall, so they wouldn't have to cross the heath in the dark.

'I've got a beautiful woman to wear on each arm and I want to show them off,' he'd told them with a smile.

Charlotte was in dark blue silk with a fringed, tiered skirt. For herself Marianne had chosen an unfussy white muslin with a pale blue stripe, blue embroidery and ribbons. A lace collar matched the flounce of lace at her elbows. Their gowns had been made by a local dressmaker.

Charlotte finished fussing with her own gown and turned her attention to Marianne's. 'That gown is prettier than I first thought. It's simple, but it suits you.'

'Are you saying I'm simple, Char?'

Her sister laughed. 'Certainly not, in fact, you are more complicated than you know. You grow more beautiful by the day, Marianne, and even if you wore a flour sack you'd look wonderful.'

'What a horrible thought ... though that would set the rumour mill going. As for you, Char, you're positively glowing with health. Marriage seems to suit you.'

Her sister's glow took on a pinker tinge. 'Oh, I'm happy enough. Seth is a good husband. He isn't overbearing like most men.'

Marianne wondered if she was thinking of Nick Thornton, but decided not to mention him and possibly spoil the evening. She missed Nick coming to the house because he'd been so much fun. Not that he'd even noticed her when Charlotte was around, except to pull her braid or tease her. He'd always spent his visits arguing with Charlotte about the most ridiculous of things.

She twisted a lock of Charlotte's hair around the curling tong. 'Ouch,' Charlotte said, 'that's too tight and it's burning my head.'

'Sorry.' Hastily she loosened it, rewinding another lock of hair. This time she was careful not to overheat the curling tongs, less she frizzle Charlotte's side ringlets. It was a perfect ringlet, and she smiled as she dealt with another. Long hair was a nuisance, Marianne thought, and she wished she could wear it short like a man. But then she'd have to shave her chin and wear a moustache, like Seth did. That must be worse than fashioning the odd ringlet.

'I wonder if Lucian will be there tonight?' Marianne said, keeping her voice casual.

Charlotte caught her gaze in the mirror and laughed. 'You've always wanted Lucian to be your sweetheart.'

'I have not. I was just making conversation. He wouldn't want me anyway. I haven't got any money.'

'Not all men marry women for their property. Seth didn't.'

'He did in a way. You told him you'd burn the house down rather than allow Erasmus Thornton to kick you out and sell it from under you – and if he wanted the house he'd have to marry you and provide us both with a home. Lor ... how Seth laughed. I was so surprised when he said yes that I nearly fell over.'

Half laughing and half protesting, Charlotte said, 'So did I. I can't believe I did such a forward thing, now. You must have been eavesdropping at the door, you wretched girl!'

'I've always thought that it was a good way of finding out what's going on. I hate it when I'm left out of things.'

People thought that she and Charlotte were alike, and they were to a certain extent. But her own hair was darker, her face less oval and her mouth differently shaped and a fraction wider. Too, she was finer boned and smaller than her sister. Their natures were different too. Charlotte was intense, and she worried about things, whereas Marianne knew she was more accepting of people and events. She didn't see the sense in fretting about something that had already happened, because it couldn't be changed. She'd rather make the best of it with good grace.

She finished creating Charlotte's remaining ringlet, then tugged on it. 'There, now it's my turn.'

They swapped positions.

Seth was waiting for them downstairs, made not at all impatient by the fact that they were late, but talking amiably to two other men. Snatches of music drifted across from the hall. His gaze went to Charlotte first and he smiled as he stepped forward and offered her his arm. 'You look lovely.'

'Thank you, Seth,' and she sounded slightly flustered. Then their eyes met and Charlotte gave a breathless little laugh.

'Marianne, you too. I'll be the most envied man here tonight. Put me down for the military polka. You're the only woman I've met who can gallop as fast as I can.'

'Must you, Seth, it will make Marianne all hot and bothered.'

'But it's such fun, so it's worth it. You'll never know how much we suffered to create this effect. Charlotte nearly burned my ear off with the tongs. Oh...' she whispered. 'Do look at Mr Miller, he's absolutely round, as though he's swallowed a cushion.'

'Shush, Marianne. Somebody might hear you,' but Charlotte laughed anyway.

A few minutes later they were part of the crowd of merrymakers. Marianne saw Lucian heading towards them in the crush. She smiled, pretending not to see him, then began to speak to Charlotte. She turned when he tapped her on the shoulder, looking surprised. 'Why, Lucian, how wonderful to see you again after all this time.'

'Miss Honeyman. May I compliment you on your appearance?'

'You may. Have you forgotten my first name then?' she said with a smile.

The smile he returned was pleasant. She noticed that he'd grown a golden brown moustache to match his hair. Even though they were the latest fashion for men, Marianne thought they looked silly on most men, like furry spring caterpillars. Eyes of a light ice blue gazed into hers. 'How could I forget your name, when we grew up together? But we're adults now, and must observe convention.'

She groaned. 'Must we? How exceedingly tedious being grown up is.'

'One gets used to it. May I have the pleasure of the next waltz?'

'Certainly, Mr Beresford.'

'In the meantime perhaps you'd take a turn with me around the floor.'

She took his arm and they threaded through the throng, talking politely together like a couple of strangers.

'I thought I saw an osprey on the heath yesterday,' she told him.

'Isn't it a little late in the year for osprey?'

'Yes, I suppose it is. They usually migrate through in September and October. Perhaps it was injured and is wintering here to recover before the flock flies back through in the spring. It could have been a Merlin, I suppose, though it looked like a bigger bird altogether. How are your medical studies progressing?'

'I've graduated. After Christmas I'll be a fully trained physician and working for my father.'

'Already? Goodness, Lucian, it seems like

36

yesterday that you went away to medical school. How very exciting ... congratulations.'

The music began and they went out on to the floor. Lucian was light on his feet, and he was a good dancer. She followed his lead and allowed him to guide her through the other dancers without mishap.

Lucian kissed her hand when it ended, his moustache tickling her wrist. She felt dizzy with delight when he wrote on her dance card, 'the Lancers'.

The Lancers? It was obvious that Lucian had been taking dancing lessons, as had she and Charlotte. At Seth's insistence they'd been instructed in the steps of the various dances at the academy run by Alicia Bottomly and her sister Hattie. Because of their father's excesses, it was a part of their education they'd missed out on.

Alicia and Hattie had become ballerinas to earn a living. They were both upright, graceful and elegant, and far superior in their manner than anyone else in town. They went to London twice a year to learn the latest dances and bring them back. How fortunate that they'd just brought back the Lancers, which was a relatively new dance – and one more intricate and pretty than the normal quadrille.

There was a whiff of scandal about the sisters that titillated the society ladies of Poole. It was said the sisters had aristocratic blood on the wrong side of the blanket, and had been married off to twin brothers in their youth – minor peers who'd lost their fortunes at the gaming tables and their lives in a duel.

As well as the dancing academy, they ran a salon where writers and artists gathered for conversation once a week. For a shilling one could gain admittance and hear the latest poetry recited – and because everyone knew that such intellectuals were poverty-stricken and needed to earn a fee, the event was always well patronized.

Marianne's card was soon full and she was kept dancing until supper was announced. Goodness, her feet ached, and she hadn't even danced the polka with Seth yet.

She tried to gaze over the crush to find Seth and her sister. The room was warm and she spread her fan.

'If you're looking for your sister and her husband, Miss Honeyman, they're over by the door talking to the Wilmotts. I'd escort you over, but I don't think my presence would be welcome.'

At first Marianne thought it was Nick's voice, but when she turned it was to find it was his uncle, Erasmus Thornton. She gazed at him over her fan. He was a handsome, neat-looking man with greying brown hair and steady brown eyes. They were not as dark and as liquid as Nick's.

So this was the man her mother had been in love with, she thought, unable to recall being so close to him before. She smiled at him, liking the hint of danger in their encounter. Charlotte would be furious if she saw them together. 'Captain Thornton senior, I didn't expect to see you here.'

He gave a bit of a grin. 'Neither did I, but my

sister Daisy wanted to attend. It's Christmas, after all, and she rarely gets the chance unless Nick or myself is home to escort her. She's off catching up on the gossip.'

Cautiously, she asked him, 'How is Nick?'

'Keeping busy.' He raised an eyebrow. 'Would you risk going into supper with me, Miss Honeyman?'

She giggled nervously at the thought of what Charlotte would say, but her sister seemed to be fully occupied. 'Thank you, Captain, that's most kind of you.'

He looked surprised for a moment, then his grin became a slow smile. 'I'll be damned, I didn't expect an affirmative answer.'

'Why not? There's no quarrel between us.'

'No, there isn't, unless you seek to make one. You're very much like your mother, you know,' he said as they began to thread their way through the crush of people into the relatively empty supper room.

'So I've been told. But I'm not her, Captain Thornton. Remember that.'

He gazed at her for a moment, a pulse twitching in his jaw. If her words had angered him, he didn't show it, but simply nodded. 'Warning noted. Sit here. I'll fetch us a plate and some punch. Or would you prefer lemonade?'

'Thank you, I would. Punch makes me lightheaded, and lemonade quenches the thirst better.'

They sat and chatted, talking of trivial things. He was a man with a taciturn persuasion and Marianne could see he was bored with her chatter. Desperate to draw him out and lead him round to what she wanted to know, she said, 'Do you waltz? I have a free dance now.'

'Well now ... could be that I remember how to waltz, though it's been a long time. You know that you'll get a lecture from your sister when she learns I've been talking to you, let alone dancing with you.'

'Would my mother have disapproved, Captain Thornton?'

His smile came, lightening his eyes to reveal a glimpse of something hidden behind them ... a precious memory perhaps. Unexpectedly, he touched her face and said softly, 'I reckon she wouldn't have, at that.'

'Then that's good enough for me.'

When he smiled and offered her his arm she took it. He was nimble of foot and she enjoyed dancing with him. The people twirled around them in a colourful blur. Faces she knew. The Bottomly sisters, Seth, and her sister looking horrified. She wanted to giggle when she saw Daisy Thornton, her eyes as round as saucers with astonishment. She was wearing a drab grey gown that made her look older than she was.

Seth appeared at her elbow with Charlotte in tow. 'Our dance next, I think Marianne.' He nodded to Erasmus. 'Captain Thornton.'

'Colonel Hardy, Mrs Hardy.'

Charlotte turned her back on him, a deliberate snub.

'Thank you, Captain Thornton. I enjoyed our dance,' Marianne said.

'It was my pleasure, Miss Honeyman.' He

turned and walked away.

She and Seth danced the polka with plenty of dash and verve. It was fun, and so was Seth, who twirled her around, marched her about and tossed her into the air with confidence. The music was noisy and the laughter noisier.

Shortly afterwards, Lucian claimed her for the Lancers. A buzz of excitement went up as the couples formed their sets. People hung back, even though there was a caller for those new to the dance.

Lucian smiled at her when the music started and the caller said, 'First lady and gentleman turn in centre ... partners cross over ... dancing couple to rejoin partner and lead back to place...'

Soon they were all dancing in union. 'Basket right ... basket left ... promenade...'

When they finished the set she was returned to Charlotte, who drew her across to where a pink draped and fringed curtain concealed a rather ugly square window. Rather crushingly, she said, 'You're making a show of yourself, Marianne.'

'For dancing the Lancers with Lucian?'

'You know exactly what I mean.'

'The polka?' She smiled. 'Seth was very dashing and energetic. You know, I'm sure Seth would rather have danced it with you.'

'Oh, do shut up, Marianne. You're deliberately setting out to provoke me. You know very well I'm talking about Erasmus Thornton.'

'All I did was to take supper with him, and dance one dance. He's awfully difficult to talk to, you know. But when he answers it's straight to the point. He's quite sweet really. He came to

41

the ball so his sister could socialize.'

'Daisy Thornton is such a sad creature. That gown she's wearing is dreadful, and she looks like a grey owl.'

'Don't be so cruel. I don't suppose she needs an extensive wardrobe, since she mostly keeps house for her brother and Nick. Several men danced with her apart from her brother. The reverend and Lucian's father, to name two. She dances very gracefully, I thought, especially when she danced the Viennese waltz with the reverend. Even the Bottomly sisters beamed at that.'

Charlotte signed heavily. 'Stop trying to change the subject. You know how I feel about Erasmus Thornton. You're not to dance with him again.'

Up until then Marianne had been enjoying herself enormously. 'Nobody is asking you to dance with him, or even talk to him. But the way you turned your back on him was the height of rudeness. Oh ... don't be so stuffy, Charlotte. Your quarrels are not my quarrels, and I shall dance with whomever I want to. And if you throw one of your sulks I shall pretend I don't know you.'

'Marianne,' Charlotte said faintly as she began to walk away.

She turned back. Her sister's face was pale and her forehead was dewed with perspiration. She was at her side in an instant. 'What is it, Char?'

'I feel a little faint.'

A woman obligingly gave up her seat and Marianne began to fan her sister's face. The

42

woman went off to alert Seth, who came back with a plate of supper for her and a drink. He looked concerned. 'You should have eaten some supper,' and he beckoned Dr Beresford senior over.

'I'm sorry, I forgot. I was too busy talking.'

Lucian's father declared the episode to be no more serious than a faint. He had drunk more than his fair share of punch so he was quite jolly and he whispered, 'You young ladies shouldn't lace your corsets so tight. You haven't got a little surprise for your husband under that bodice, have you, Mrs Hardy?' To which question the blood ran into Charlotte's face and she nearly fainted away all over again.

In a short while Charlotte had recovered, and although she'd assured them that it was just a faint and she was perfectly all right, Marianne spent most of the remainder of the evening in her sister's company, just in case it happened again. Seth didn't dance any more, but spent time talking to his fellow clay producers.

Marianne saw Lucian dancing with many other women. How they simpered when he looked at them. He was so correct, keeping them at exactly the right distance. When he'd lifted her up at the end of the Lancers and set her lightly back on her feet their bodies hadn't even touched. She smiled, wondering if she'd looked just as simpering. Probably.

The reverend went past with Daisy Thornton. Was that how she'd end up herself, a lonely spinster who supervised her nieces and nephews and lived on her family's generosity? Would she be trotted out now and again at an occasional social occasion, wearing a gown that had long since died, and be called an old grey owl behind her back by some young woman who'd forgotten how to be kind? She sighed at the prospect. Perhaps Lucian would ask her to marry him, even though she was poor. They'd always been friends, and since he'd become a man she'd felt a strong yearning inside her to be more than friends.

She voiced her thoughts. 'Will I end up an old maid, Charlotte?'

'You're too pretty to become a spinster. When I have children I want them to have cousins so they can grow up and play together.'

When Lucian caught her eyes and smiled at her, Marianne's happiness nearly bubbled over. The next moment she murmured as a black dog of doubt leaped against her chest, 'What if he doesn't ask me?'

'Oh, don't worry so much. It's simple. I shall make it my business to find you a suitable husband of your own.'

Not if she could help it! Marianne wanted to be in love with her husband, or at least be able to like and respect him. She didn't want to marry a man for the sake of convenience. Some of the speculative looks she'd received from men tonight had almost made her shudder.

A marriage of convenience had worked for Charlotte, she conceded, but lightning didn't strike twice in the same place.

It wasn't the first time that Nick had been in a

bad storm. So far *Samarand* had weathered everything the sky could throw at her. Nevertheless he wondered if the masts would take it. He'd shortened sail to take the strain off both ship and the exhausted crew, but it had slowed them down.

He hunched in his sou'wester as lightning zigzagged out of the sky and snicked across the water. There were two of them at the wheel, using all their strength to haul her round and keep her steady on course. He was nursing the ship along at a comfortable seven knots, allowing her sharp prow to cut through the water.

The roaring forties had lived up to its name and rounding Cape Horn was proving to be a nightmare so far. But the laboured shuddering was beginning to lessen, or was it his imagination? He said to the first mate, 'Is the wind dropping, James?'

James Mitchell was a solid, unflappable Scot who'd been at sea since he'd been weaned from his mother's teat on to a whisky bottle, or so his uncle had told him. It was comforting to have a man of his experience by his side, but there was no doubt that his uncle had put him there to keep an eye on him. Nick didn't mind.

'The command of this ship should have gone to you, James,' Nick had told him once.

'Aye, lad, but that would have been unfair, since I joined the Thornton company after you, though you were nae more than a bairn yourself and wet behind the ears at the time.'

Now James smiled. Licking his finger he held

45

it up. 'Seems so, Captain. At least the wind is blowing in the right direction. We'll soon be around the Horn and homeward bound.'

But it was another twelve hours before they got into calmer waters. Even *Samarand* seemed to sense the respite. He knew the exact moment when she stopped fighting the water and capitulated, when her shudders became quivers and her hull settled into her own comfortable and particular rhythms. He sent seamen into the rigging to restore a full set of sails, and the ship surged eagerly forward on the regular roll of the homeward bounders.

There was relief in him that the ship had survived the most hazardous part of the journey once again. Having the crew relying on his seamanship didn't always sit easy on him. It was a responsibility he didn't want.

Sending James Mitchell below to get some sleep he placed the wheel in the capable hands of the bosun and a seaman while he calculated and adjusted their course. They'd drifted off, but not too far. Adjusting it would make the most of the prevalent currents and save several sailing days. Time was money, his uncle always said.

His cabin boy looked a bit green around the gills when he brought his coffee up at dawn. 'I've roused Mr Mitchell. He'll be on deck to relieve you as soon as he's had his breakfast.'

Cupping his hands around the mug Nick warmed his palms as he sipped at the bitter brown liquid. 'I'll be glad when we get home.'

'Me too, sir.'

'Rough night was it, Sam?'

'It's been a rough few weeks.' Sam managed a wry smile. 'I was all right for most of the time, though.'

'Of course you were. It happens that way sometimes. The weather is as unpredictable as a woman.'

'Yes, sir, I'll go and get your breakfast. Cook said the chickens took fright and laid half a dozen eggs, and there's some smoked ham to go with it. He's baking some fresh bread while he's got the chance.'

The weather was also as unpredictable as a man, he thought, as Sam made himself scarce. Who'd have thought that he'd get over Charlotte Honeyman so quickly? Fickle creature that she was!

There had been a few weeks of feeling sorry for himself, a few bottles of whisky, a few nameless women to restore his own belief in his masculinity and – apart from the occasional hurt feeling making it to the surface – he was beginning to think straight again. He'd had a relapse, of course. He'd woken up one morning in an alley in Melbourne, his pocket picked and a monumental hangover squeezing his brain. A woman had screeched at him and she'd sounded like Charlotte. Suddenly he'd experienced a strong a sense of freedom, and knew that her loss would never bother him again.

He was thinking now that he was nearly old enough to take control of the legacy his uncle held in trust for him, and it was about time he and his uncle talked seriously about the establishment Nick wanted to open.

Three

Poole, Dorset, 1851

It was near noon.

On her way home, from the top of the rise Marianne saw Lucian, his rig pulled by a placid grey horse that plodded along the pale ribbon of a track winding through the tough heathland plants.

'Lucian!' Marianne waved, losing her grip on her apron in the process. The fragrant early blossoming heather she'd picked to decorate the hall tumbled to her feet. Neither shout nor wave was effective. She was too far away to be heard and the wind was taking her voice in a different direction, pushing the sound across the sweep of tossed grey wavelets shivering across the water and on towards the bustling harbour town of Poole.

Marianne adored Lucian. Retrieving the heather and holding it against her body, she began to make her way towards her home. Harbour House was a solid building of weathered stone clutched in the grip of bony fingers of ivy. It stood on the next rise, defying anything the weather threw at it and affording the occupants a sweeping view of the sheltered haven it overlooked.

The wind flattened her skirt against her buttocks and loosened some of her hair from its bun, sending dark strands streaming. It was hard to keep tidy at the best of times. The management of her long curls depended entirely on the weather, and the skills of her sister. She began to run, leaping from tussock to tussock and startling the birds, which noisily scolded her as they exploded in splashes of colour from under her careless feet.

'Lucian!'

They arrived at the house together, she dishevelled and panting, he perfectly calm. He watched her come, his mouth grave and his astute eyes filling with laughter when she skidded to halt in front of him.

He put out a hand to steady her, his palm warm under her elbow. Lucian didn't know it, but she'd hankered after him ever since the Christmas ball nearly seven months previously, even though she'd seen him rarely. Now he was a fully trained physician in partnership with his father she adored him even more. He was so handsome. The trouble was, half the unmarried women in the district also adored him.

'Are you here to visit us?' She dropped her skirt, using her free hand to fuss with her hair.

Lucian messed it up again. 'Stop fidgeting with it. You look exactly the same as the first day we met. I think you were about seven when you came running out of the heather with a bird's nest tied to your head, including eggs, and the mother bird fluttering over the top and twittering in alarm.'

'Oh, you,' she said. 'You were a horrid young man at the time, and you laughed and laughed until I kicked you on the shin. And you know very well that I bought it from a gypsy on the heath who tricked me into believing it was a hat.'

'I think she got the better of the bargain, since you handed over your silver locket in exchange as I recall.'

'And my father stayed sober long enough to go after them and get it back, then he spanked me so I couldn't sit down for a week – but not because I'd handed over the locket. It was because I'd gone on to the heath all by myself to visit the gypsies.'

The maid jumped down from the rig and grinned. 'Shall I take the heather and put it in water for you, Miss Marianne?'

Marianne's glance went to Alice in alarm as she handed over the heather. She hadn't seen the maid earlier, she'd been shielded from her sight by Lucian's body. 'Is something amiss, Alice? My sister hasn't fallen, has she?'

'Mrs Hardy thinks she's having her baby. She sent me to fetch the doctor.'

Marianne's heart leapt. 'But the baby is not due for another four weeks. Charlotte didn't say anything this morning before I went out.'

'No, Miss, but she was still in bed and that was at the crack of dawn.' Alice gazed at the doctor and lowered her voice. 'Her waters broke ... could be she's had it by now.'

Lucian smiled. 'It would be highly unlikely for a first baby to arrive so quickly.'

Marianne watched Alice walk off towards the house and sighed. 'Oh, Lor! I told Charlotte not to do all that cleaning work yesterday. She was a hive of industry all day.'

'Don't worry, Marianne, it's normal for a baby to arrive a little early. We'd better go in so I can examine her and see if everything is progressing as it should.'

Her sister was composed, but there was a spark of relief in the blue depths of her eyes when she set eyes on them. 'Nothing has happened yet, except I'm a bit damp.'

'No pressure?'

Charlotte shook her head.

Lucian nodded. 'Marianne, would you arrange the sheets so I can do a physical examination on her stomach?'

Together, Marianne and Charlotte had read a book about midwifery, and they knew exactly how the birth would progress. They'd even practised the event, laughing with excitement at the thought of having a baby in the house, and they'd sewn little garments that looked too small to believe anything but a doll would fit inside them.

Marianne wanted Charlotte to have a girl. Charlotte wanted a boy. John said he wanted a brother. When pushed, Seth had simply grinned and said he'd like one of each, and had remarked that if the infant looked like its mother then he'd be contented with whatever its rear end resembled.

Charlotte had blushed at that, and Marianne had giggled and wondered – and not for the first time – if her sister had fallen in love with Seth. After all, it had been a marriage of convenience for both of them, but more so for Charlotte who had entered into the union to keep a roof over their heads, and to save that same roof, and herself, from falling into the hands of Nicholas Thornton.

Harbour House had started out as an inn owned by Marianne's ancestors. The family fortunes had fluctuated over the years and the Honeyman name had fallen into disrepute several times, including during the lifetime of their own father, who'd been described as colourful by various of his debtors. Their father had taken several years to drink himself to death after the demise of their mother in childbirth. There had barely been enough money left to pay for his funeral.

Now Charlotte was about to contribute a new member to the family. Excitement squeezed at her. How wonderful to have an adorable child ... one who resembled Seth.

Marianne smiled at the thought of Nick not getting what he'd wanted, even though she had a sneaking regard for him. Nick had been a persistent, if demanding suitor, who'd taken Charlotte's eventual acquiescence to a marriage between them very much for granted. It must be wonderful to have a suitor besotted by you, and she wished Lucian was more forceful in going about such matters. At least she'd then know where she stood in his affections.

While they waited for the maid with the water, Lucian chatted to Charlotte, putting her at ease.

Even so, Charlotte caught her breath when he performed the intimacies of the examination, his hands probing the outlines of her stomach. But he was professional and remote from them, his mind on the job at hand, his voice soothing with reassuring phrases. Marianne couldn't help but admire the detachment with which he conducted himself, something that was designed to cause his patient the minimum of embarrassment.

Finishing his examination he turned away and moved to the window. There he deliberated while Marianne tidied the bed and Charlotte composed herself.

Marianne nearly exploded with impatience and said to his impassive back, 'Well, Lucian! Is Charlotte having this baby, or isn't she?'

'She is.' He turned, the lack of a smile on his face somehow ominous. 'There's a problem. It appears that the infant is in the breech position.'

'What does that mean?'

'That it will be harder to expel the child because its rear will present itself first, instead of the head.' He came and sat on the side of the bed, taking Charlotte's hand in his. 'You're a healthy young woman, Mrs Hardy, but I want you to get as much rest as you can before the contractions start. They shouldn't be long in coming. I don't want to alarm you, but I do want you to know what to expect. This appears to be a large infant and it will not be an easy birth. You'll need all the strength you possess to deliver the infant safely.'

'Will my baby be all right?'

'At the moment its heart is beating strongly. If

you can bear the pain without panicking then the infant will have a much better chance of survival. But in any case, I'll administer some chloroform towards the latter stages of labour. It will help ease your discomfort.'

'What's that?' There was alarm in Charlotte's voice and Marianne took her hand.

'It's a liquid that gives off a gas, and will lessen the pain considerably. It's dripped on to a pad and held to the patient's nose, where it's breathed in.'

It sounded as though Lucian was reading from a set of instructions, Marianne thought. 'Have you used it before?'

'Not in practice, but I've been trained in its use.' For a moment his eyes blazed with enthusiasm. 'I've seen a man operated on under the influence of the drug. He went to sleep and didn't feel anything until the operation was all over.

'Why can't Charlotte have the coliform earlier?' Marianne asked.

'Chloroform,' he corrected, giving a faint, but rather superior smile at her mispronunciation. 'It's dangerous if too much is used, and not good for the baby. It could slow down the contractions.'

Charlotte nodded, but there was a twinge of fear in her eyes. Knowing she was thinking of their mother's death during childbirth, Marianne took her sister's hands. 'I'll be with you every minute, Charlotte, I promise. In the meantime I'll make you comfortable so you can better relax.'

'Should we let Seth know? He went into Poole

early this morning to discuss business with the pottery owners he supplies clay to. He was going to attend a meeting and luncheon of the Clay Producer's Association before picking John up from school.'

Taking out his watch Lucian gazed at it. 'He'll be home in plenty of time. I'll alert the midwife, then go about my rounds and come back later. But anyway, the infant is not going to arrive in a hurry.'

Marianne followed Lucian's tall figure down the stairs. 'Charlotte will be all right, won't she? Our mother died in childbirth, and I know it's on her mind.'

For the first time Lucian looked troubled. 'It's better if she knows what to expect, then she can prepare herself. Breech births can be gruelling, and I cannot guarantee anything. The midwife knows her job, and I'll do my best if any complications occur. Try not to alarm your sister in any way.'

'That's something you've already succeeded in doing, Lucian.'

He became distant. 'Nonsense. I don't need advice on how to do my job, Marianne.'

The reprimand was spoken so severely that she was shocked by his change of manner towards her. Tears sprang to her eyes. 'I'm sorry, Lucian. It's me who is rattled, I think. Will you forgive me?'

'It will be my pleasure.' He held her close for a moment, then kissed her on the forehead. 'Be brave, Marianne. I'll be relying on you to help to keep your sister calm.'

His body was warm and firm and her instinct was to snuggle up to him. But Lucian didn't invite any intimacy and was moving away from her, both physically and in spirit.

'You know, Lucian, you've changed an awful lot. 'You've become really serious since you've become a doctor ... and remote.'

Her observation seemed to startle him, but he smiled. 'Have I?'

'You know you have. Sometimes I feel as though you're trying to push me away. Don't you like me any more?'

'Of course I do, Marianne Honeyman ... I've always liked you.'

'I've grown up, you know,' and she felt slightly sick at the thought that their friendship must be put aside for the sake of propriety.

'I've been trying not to notice.' His smile sent her pulses fluttering, then her spirits plunged when he added. 'But we're both adults now, and I have to be careful not to invite too much familiarity from my patients, or cause any conjecture by my actions.'

'First of all, I'm not your patient I'm your father's, though I haven't seen him on my own behalf for some time. The last time he saw me he made me hang out my tongue as far as it would go for inspection, then told me it nearly reached my feet and that was a sign that I'd live for ever.'

Lucian chuckled. 'Then you probably will. My father is an expert diagnostician.'

Fitting a sprig of heather into his buttonhole she smiled up at him. 'That's to bring you luck, Dr Beresford.'

'Thank you.'

As he turned towards the rig, she said, 'Second of all, you're in danger of becoming a stuffed shirt, Lucian.'

A smile flirted around his mouth. 'The devil I am.' He climbed into his vehicle, took up the reins and gazed down at her. 'Miss Honeyman, I'd appreciate it if you didn't attempt to flirt with me when I'm working. It takes my mind off the job at hand.'

'I only see you when you're working.'

'Quite.' Clicking his tongue at the horse he turned the rig and moved off in the direction of town. Marianne was left gazing with uncertainty after him. Had he paid her a compliment, or had his remarks been designed to put her in her place? she wondered.

Remembering Charlotte, Marianne's smile faded. She hurried back upstairs, to discover her sister in tears.

'Hush,' she said, taking Charlotte into her arms. 'Lucian said you must relax as much as you can to conserve your strength. A gypsy gave me a bunch of white heather to tie over your bed to keep you safe.'

'You're so gullible, Marianne, but I don't suppose it will do me any harm.'

'She tells such wonderful stories of far away places, and she says you will have an easy birth.'

'That's not what Lucian indicated. I have an odd feeling inside me, Marianne. As though things will not be as we expect.'

'You're afraid of the unknown, that's all. Be brave. You can be if you try. Look how you held out against Erasmus and Nick Thornton.'

'That was easy, because I didn't love Nick in the way that he wanted me to, even though I thought I did to begin with. And I loathe his uncle. If it hadn't been for Erasmus seducing our mother the child he planted in her womb would not have killed her, and our father wouldn't have drunk himself to death.'

'Hush, Charlotte. We don't know that it's true about the baby.'

'Pa said it was true. He said the child was a girl and she looked like Erasmus Thornton, with her dark hair and eyes. And Nick said he thought the story was true because his uncle had told him that he adored our mother. I know I shouldn't have punished Nick for the action of his relative, but I don't want to be part of the Thornton family. I will never be able to reconcile myself with the events surrounding the birth of that child.

'Nick said he was just as much in love with me as his uncle had been with our mother, and his intentions towards me had always been honourable. He wouldn't believe that I didn't love him, and it was pride talking. The last time I saw him he said he'd never forgive me for marrying Seth, and will find some way to take his revenge. That was nearly a year ago, just before he sailed off on the *Samarand* with a cargo for Australia. I wasn't with child then. Seth and I were not married ... well we were, but not...'

'...a proper wife, you mean,' Marianne finished for her, grinning at the blush that rose to her sister's cheeks. She remembered the day exactly,

58

and of coming home from the heath with John to find a very rumpled and pink-faced Charlotte in the process of moving her belongings into the master bedroom, and who, after that day, no longer treated her husband as if he was a guest in her house.

Marianne began to busy herself getting out the list of objects that the book stated her sister would need for her confinement. Thank goodness the place had been thoroughly cleaned yesterday, she thought, tying a freshly laundered white apron round her waist.

'Yes ... properly married, and I don't know why I feared becoming a wife, in truth.' Charlotte smiled. 'I'm worried that Nick might do something foolish when he hears about the baby. If anything happens to Seth I'd never forgive myself.'

'It won't. Nick knows when to surrender. It was just foolish talk, Nick's hot blood coming out. Besides, Seth looks as though he can take care of himself. Nick will find someone else to fall in love with, then marry her and have several baby Thorntons waiting for him on the quay each time he comes home from a voyage. They'll all look like him and be handsome little devils, because they wouldn't dare look and act like anyone else. Just you wait and see.'

Charlotte chuckled at the picture her sister painted. 'I suppose I should apologize for humiliating him when I get the chance.'

'It wouldn't hurt. Now, let me prepare everything for the birthing. If you swing your legs around I'll help you to the chair, then I'll prepare the bed with a rubber sheet, some padding and clean linen, like the book said. Would you like something to eat? Some broth perhaps.'

Charlotte shook her head. 'I'd probably end up being sick.'

'Are you cold ... shall I light the fire?'

'It's the middle of July,' her sister reminded her. 'Stop fussing.'

'Just imagine, soon you'll have your very own infant in your arms. Seth will be so proud.'

But Charlotte wasn't listening. Her hands had cradled the bottom of her stomach, her eyes widened and she gave a small groan. When the pain subsided, she whispered, 'I think it's started.'

Charlotte was right, the birth didn't go as expected. The labour pains came thick and fast. An hour later, a tiny red backside put in an appearance, followed by legs folded back on a skinny body, followed by a head. The crumpled little creature gave a wavering whimper of protest with her first breath. It strengthened to an outraged warble with her second.

Marianne was fascinated by her. 'Lor, listen to it, Char, I don't think we need to smack its arse,' she whispered. She wiped the infant's squashed face with a flannel and wrapped her in a linen cloth to keep her warm. 'It's such a tiny baby. I don't know what all that fuss was about from Lucian.'

Charlotte gazed at her. 'What is it?'

'A girl,' and Marianne's puzzled gaze went to the mound that was Charlotte's stomach. 'But you don't look any thinner.'

'I don't feel any thinner ... oh, my Lord,' Charlotte groaned.

'Having a girl isn't that bad, surely?' Marianne said, feeling the need to defend her slightly squashed-looking, but altogether adorable new niece.

'More pains ... I think there's another one coming.'

'A pain?'

'No ... another baby ... you idiot.'

'Alice,' Marianne shouted out in sudden shock to the maid, who was fluttering like a demented moth outside the door. 'Take the cart. Go and see if you can find us some help. Tell the doctor or midwife to hurry if you can find them. Mrs Hardy has given birth to one baby and there's a second infant on the way.'

She returned to Charlotte, who gave a painful little yelp. It turned into a prolonged groan. When it subsided, Charlotte cried out, 'the pains ... are coming one on top of ... the other. I'm frightened. I can't stop them.'

'You're not supposed to stop them, and you're beginning to panic. Remember what the book said. The pains won't last forever. You have to suffer them bravely. Take some deep breaths.'

'That book was written by a man. How would he know about childbirth? Let him bravely suffer, then we'll see how clever he is.' Charlotte's voice rose to a scream. 'Ouch, ouch, ouch, it hurts! I'm going to die ... like our mother did.'

'If you say such a wicked thing again I'm going to smack you. You have a daughter who needs you, and another child on the way. Now

Charlotte, I don't mind the odd groan and curse, but don't you dare scream. It's deafening and it doesn't help, and there's enough of that coming from little Miss Hardy. Lor, this is a messy business. What did the book say about cutting the baby from the umbilical cord?'

'It didn't say anything.'

'Then we'd better leave it. It might drop off by itself.'

There was a cough at the door and Marianne turned to see the gypsy woman from the heath standing there. She wore a scarf over her hair and her face was weathered from being out-doors. 'Can I be of help, Miss?'

'I didn't hear you arrive, Jessica. How did you get here? Who let you in?'

'Your maid left the door wide open. You don't need to fear, Mrs, I've closed it behind me.' She crossed to the squalling child and said, 'Now there's a fuss, like a gale coming off the harbour, you are,' and she caressed the child's face with a roughened finger. 'There, there ... dear, your legs will soon straighten out and you'll be like every-body else ... though prettier than most with that flaming hair. Now let's cut you free. We'll need some twine to tie the cord with.'

Marianne went to fetch some and a few moments later the infant stopped crying and fell asleep.

Marianne told the gypsy, 'There's another one coming. The doctor said my sister was having a breech birth and it would take a long time, but everything seems to have gone wrong and it's happening too fast.'

A pair of earth brown eyes gazed into hers. 'Nay, Miss, there be nothing wrong. But what do doctors know about womanly things? Let me take a look at you, lady. I've birthed several infants of my own and delivered many more.'

Charlotte quieted when the woman gently felt around her distended stomach. The gypsy smiled and said calmly, 'This lad is the right way round. He's a good size and has pushed his sister out like a cork from a bottle, so to make room for himself. Good that he did, since she didn't have to struggle. Now he be settling himself in before he follows her out. Could be your pains will stop for a while, lady. Then he'll get his strength up and it won't take long. An hour or two, perhaps. In the meantime I'll see to your sweet little daughter and you can put her to your breast so she can know her mother's smell and voice.'

The woman took a small bottle from her pocket and handed it to Marianne. 'Add this lavender oil to a bowl of warm water, my lovely. We'll wash your sister in it, and the fragrance will help calm her.'

Marianne did as she was told, and the birth happened as the gypsy said, with Charlotte grunting and groaning a bit but not too painfully. The transformation in Charlotte was marked when the boy emerged with a rush and a lusty fanfare. He was detached, wrapped and was put to her other breast. There, he began to suck strongly. The afterbirths came away from her.

Charlotte laughed, her earlier pain and fright having obviously been put aside. 'Look at him, so much like Seth. How on earth am I going to feed two of them?'

'I daresay you'll manage.' The gypsy gathered up her things. 'I'll be going then, lady.'

'Wait,' Charlotte said. 'My sister called you Jessica. Is that your name?'

'Yes, lady, and my mother's name before me, and my grandmother's before that.'

'Then I'll name my daughter after you. Jessica Hardy she'll be called.'

'Thank you, lady.'

Charlotte must have noticed her own disappointment for she added. 'Her second name will be the same as yours Marianne, and you can be her godmother.'

Marianne followed the gypsy downstairs, smiling because she was to be her niece's godmother. 'I must pay you something for your help.' She pressed two shillings into the gypsy's rough hand. 'I can't thank you enough. My sister was so scared. We both were.'

The woman pocketed the money. 'Bless you, dearie, I was glad to be of use.'

The gypsy had not long left when the sound of wheels and horses took Marianne to the window. It was Lucian with the midwife. After him came Seth astride, and a long way behind him, the maid with John in the cart.

But beyond them, coming round Brownsea Island was the *Samarand*, her sails grey and shabby and flying a pale blue pennant with the Thornton Company emblem of entwined black initials flying from her mast. She looked as though she'd been sailing through a storm.

Closing her eyes Marianne breathed in the soft

July air. It smelled of the sea, the mud, and the perfume of the heather just coming into bloom on the heath.

She imagined Nick standing there on his deck, his feet planted firmly astride – a slightly menacing figure in black. He would be able to see the house from the deck, could be looking at them through his telescope. She felt sorry for him. Opening her eyes she caught a flash of sunlight on glass, and waved.

'Who are you waving to?' Charlotte said, momentarily looking up from the wonder and admiration of her babies, who were tucked up next to her now.

Marianne smiled, for she'd never seen her sister look so soft and loving. Her eyes were filled with the miracle of her two perfect infants. It had been a special day. Both Charlotte and the babies had survived the birth without too much fuss, and the infants were making little baby noises. Charlotte was responding with her own little baby noises, the secret language between mother and child, soothing them as though she'd always been a mother.

'I'm waving to your husband and to Lucian, of course. They're all coming. I'd better go down and let them in.'

'Don't tell Seth what the babies are. I want to surprise him.'

Marianne wondered how Nick would take this news as she went down the stairs. She remembered the length of silk she'd found after the last time he'd visited. Had that been nearly a year ago? It would give her an excuse to visit him if she took it back it to him. Then she could gently inform him that Charlotte had become a mother.

Four

London, 1851

Charles Barrie's house was situated on the north side of Bedford Square and indistinguishable from its neighbours. Built of donkey-brown brick relieved by the addition of Coade stone trim, the reserved facade, with its oblong windows and a solid door crowning a rise of four steps, served to remind passers-by that, although hidden from their sight, the occupants were not only well heeled but usually well bred.

Amongst the professional classes residing around the square was the occasional aristocrat. Justice Sir Charles Barrie was one of them. His money was inherited, wisely managed and invested. As well, he lived comfortably on his earnings as an eminent judge. But money and good breeding didn't necessarily buy happiness. Now, some twelve months after his eldest son and heir had succumbed to cholera, Charles was sorely troubled.

Coffee cup cradled in his hands he gazed at the man seated on the other side of his fireplace. 'I'm fifty-five next month, Edgar. I need to find my surviving son and bring him home.'

'When did you last hear from Jonathan?'

'Several years ago, at least six, so he'd be twenty-seven now. We parted on bad terms. He wrote to me from Van Diemen's Land shortly after he arrived, to tell me he'd married a governess he'd met on board ship. You know how impulsive Jonathan is. It was probably somebody unsuitable with her eye on the main chance.'

'You told him that?'

'To my eternal shame. He also asked me to forgive him for disobeying my wishes. I bitterly regret not doing so now.'

Edgar Wyvern, barrister, gazed at him over his glass. 'Tell me about the disagreement you had with him.'

'Oh, you've heard it all before I daresay. Jonathan gave up his legal studies when I fully expected him to join his brother in the firm. He said he wasn't cut out for it. He wanted to become a botanist, travel the world and devote some time to his art.'

'Surely that's not so bad a profession.'

'It wouldn't be if one didn't need to earn a living. But I thought so at the time, since he was halfway through his law studies and he had a position in a fully established practice waiting for him. Jonathan asked me to give him the legacy his mother left him. I refused, since I had control of it until he was twenty-five. He stormed off and bought a ticket on the next ship leaving England with only the courtesy of a short note. It advised me that I was wrong and he

67

certainly knew what was best for him.'

Edgar chuckled.

'It wasn't funny. I was more furious than worried.'

'I'm sorry, Charles. I was amused by his similarity of nature. Admit it, it's the same sort of thing you would have done in your youth ... tweaked your father's nose.'

Charles's shrug was accompanied by a shamefaced grin. 'Thank goodness I've learned a little wisdom since.'

'Hmmm ... that's a debatable point. Wisdom doesn't necessarily come with age, or with the donning of a judge's wig and gown. Consider what has happened between you and Jonathan.'

A shamed expression settled on Charles's face. 'You're right of course, Edgar.'

'What was his reply to your letter?'

'He again requested the legacy. I hurled the letter into the fire and wrote back to tell him to ask for it when he was of legal age to inherit it. He didn't.'

'You've tried to contact him since?'

'Yes. Four years ago. In the first letter I offered to transfer his legacy in case he was in straitened circumstances. When he didn't answer, after a year had passed I wrote again. Both letters were returned recently, unopened and with addressee not known scribbled on them.

'I wrote again, advising him of his brother's death. There has been no answer so far. Now I am worried. Jonathan wouldn't have carried a grudge this far. He wouldn't have ignored news of the death of his brother or moved on without leaving a forwarding address. I need to know that he's all right. Damn it, Edgar, I miss him, and I need some counsel on this. You've always had a good nose for ferreting things out and coming up with something fresh.'

'Did Jonathan mention the name of the woman he married?'

'Yes, but I've forgotten it ... it was something simple, so I'm sure I'll remember it in time.'

'It might jog your memory if you check the shipping lists for the day he left, especially if he met her on board. We need to have as much information as we can before we involve anyone else.'

'I'll do that this afternoon.'

'We'll do it together, then it will take only half the time. When we know the ship they sailed on we can put the matter in the hands of an investigator. There is one I know of by reputation. He is young, but has a wise head on his shoulders I believe, and had contacts in Van Diemen's Land. Do you have a likeness of Jonathan?'

'There's a photograph of us together ... but it's the only one I've got, and I'm loath to part with it.'

'Can you find someone to copy his likeness from it?'

'That shouldn't be too hard.' He sighed. 'If only communication didn't take so long.'

'One step at a time, Charles. Be patient. That's the best you can do for now, unless you wish to make the journey to Van Diemen's Land yourself.'

'I'm not that adventurous, and neither am I a

69

good sailor, but if the journey becomes necessary, I will.'

'You've considered the worse result, I suppose.'

Pain ripped through Charles. He stood, moving to the window, which afforded him a view across the Bedford Square gardens. Of course he had taken a pessimistic approach, and often. For now though, he'd put it aside. 'Yes, Edgar, I have. But if that proves to be the case, wondering about it will be worse than knowing. Besides, surely his wife would have contacted me by now, unless she cannot write.'

'The woman must have been well educated, otherwise she wouldn't have been employed as a governess. But a governess to whom?'

A visit to the shipping office enlightened them a little. The ship's records showed that Mary Elizabeth Ellis had been travelling alone. There was no mention in the ship's log of a marriage taking place on board the ship, which, as luck would have it, happened to be in port at the time. Her former master was retired, and living with his daughter in Chiswick.

Charles's visit to him proved fruitless at first, for the man was old. Captain Forrester, his eyes a faded blue and his skin grizzled from years at sea, was seated in the corner of the local inn.

Charles brought him a tot of rum and took it over. 'Good day, Captain Forrester. I'm looking for a young man who sailed to Australia on board one of the ships you captained. May I join you?'

The captain was happy to talk about his years

at sea, but he couldn't remember Jonathan or Mary Ellis, and he didn't pretend that he did.

'The memory isn't what it used to be. It comes and goes like the tides, you see. I could say a prayer over the dead and bury bodies at sea, and I could hold a service on Sundays and sing the praises of the Lord, but I wasn't licensed to marry passengers. Not proper like.'

'A pity.'

'Sometimes we might have a reverend travelling with us who would say the words over people, but any marriage that took place would have been entered in the ship's log. More likely they would have waited until they were ashore so they could take their vows proper and legal like in front of a minister in a church.'

Charles handed him his card when they'd finished talking. 'Thank you, Captain, if you remember anything about them I'd be obliged if you could let me know. I'll be quite happy to pay for the messenger.'

Captain Forrester called out when Charles was leaving, 'This Jonathan Barrie you're looking for ... he didn't have reddish hair, did he?'

'No, Captain. My son's hair was a dark brown.'

He cogitated for a moment, his forehead creased into a frown. 'Ah yes ... I do remember now. It was the girl who had red in her hair. I forget her name, something to do with the bible. They were shipboard sweethearts. Smitten with each other they were.'

'Mary Elizabeth Ellis her name was.'

'Was it? Was it indeed? A lovely girl, she was,

and sensible with it. She was going out to be a governess, even though she had no job to go to. I thought she was a bit on the skinny side, and she didn't seem to be very robust to me. Why couldn't you be a governess in England? I asked her. She gave me a smile, as if she had a secret inside her. Captain Forrester, she said, life is short. I had never seen the ocean before now, and I wanted an adventure. Now I'm having one, and for as long as I live I'll never forget it.'

The captain smiled at the thought. 'Your lad drew pictures. The passengers bought them from him, drawings of their children, their husbands and wives. Good he was ... did one of me. That's how I remembered his name. He signed the drawing on the bottom. Jonathan Barrie. Yes, he was a nice young man and you can be proud of him.'

'Be certain that I am. Do you know what happened to him?'

'No, sir. Once the passengers disembarked at Hobart town they were no longer my responsibility.' He cleared his throat. 'Happens that all that talking has made me thirsty. A pint of ale wouldn't go down badly.'

'Of course it wouldn't. How very remiss of me. You've been very helpful.' Charles bought the man his ale then took his leave. If nothing else, the visit had revealed something of Jonathan and the woman he'd married. He was relieved that he'd been wrong about Mary Ellis ... though if they'd wed he must start thinking of her as Mary Barrie.

Five

Two babies made an awful clamour. In the past two weeks Jessica had developed a high-pitched trill that she could turn on in an instant. Mitchell, who'd been named after Seth's father, a man who'd also been a soldier, had a warbling cry that intensified as it worked its way up the scale to a full-throated roar. Marianne had playfully added his grandfather's rank to his name, and the boy was now referred to as Major Mitchell by all of them.

When one baby began to cry it was a signal for the other to join in.

Donning a dark blue bonnet that matched the colour of her eyes, Marianne grimaced at her sister. 'How can you stand it? I haven't slept properly for the last week.'

Neither had Charlotte by the looks of her, even though Seth had hired a wet nurse to help out.

The noise stopped abruptly when Charlotte put Jessica to her breast and the girl started to suck, making satisfied little mewing noises. Charlotte gazed down fondly at her daughter's golden head. Major Mitchell gulped greedily from the wet nurse. They would swap children halfway through, because, although Charlotte's milk was thin, she didn't want her children to get too used

73

to another woman's milk.

'Is there anything you want in town?' Marianne asked her.

'No ... Seth has a list. You should have gone in with him when he took John into school.'

Marianne offered Jessica a meaningful look. 'Your babies were quite determined to keep me awake last night and I overslept. I'm thinking of taking up residence in the stable with the horses until the twins learn how to sleep through the night.' She stooped to kiss her niece's golden head to take the sting from her words. 'It's a nice day, I'm happy to walk.'

'So am I. I'm sick of staying in bed.'

'Lucian said you must stay there for at least another week.'

'I won't tell him if you don't. I've heard that gypsy mothers squat to give birth, then just get up and get on with it.'

Marianne grinned. 'I thought you didn't believe gypsy tales.'

'I do now, since Jessica came to my rescue. I'll just walk around the room to stretch my legs.'

'Well, don't overdo it.'

Sparing her a moment, Charlotte glanced up from her admiration of her baby. 'Why are you going into Poole?'

'I need a new sketching block, and I thought I might pay a visit to Jeannie Beresford. She's to become engaged shortly and I'm hoping I'll get an invitation to her ball.'

Charlotte smiled. 'Are you sure it's not Lucian you hope to see?'

Marianne was not about to tell her sister that

74

the real reason for the visit was her intention to visit Nick Thornton aboard the *Samarand* afterwards. He might show her around the ship now he was the master, which was something his uncle would never allow. 'I imagine Lucian will be doing his rounds.'

Detouring to her room, one she'd shared with her sister when they were growing up, she picked up the sailcloth satchel that contained the silk Nick had dropped on his previous and last visit to propose to her sister. She'd looked after it carefully. Placing it with her beaded reticule in her basket she set out into a shining day. As usual, Marianne covered the ground fast. She'd always loved striding out when she walked, even though Charlotte said it was unladylike. And sometimes she ran just for the joy of it. Around her the heath was alive with flowering plants, birds and bees, and the air coloured with gaudy butterflies.

To her right was the harbour, and beyond that, the small island of Brownsea. She shivered when she looked at the well-wooded but gentle slopes, remembering that two years previously the owner had taken his own life in a fit of depression. She'd been told that the man was in the diplomatic service, and had been responsible for the war between England and America. Even there on the uninhabited island, he could find nowhere to hide from the remorse he felt, so he'd cut his own throat. Now it was said that the castle on the island was haunted by the man's ghost.

The tide was out, exposing the rippled mud.

The breeze lifted a slightly acrid sea smell from the surface, as piquant as pickles. It reminded her that she'd promised to take John to dig for cockles at the weekend. He was looking forward to it, so no doubt he'd remind her.

She lifted the skirt of her gown to negotiate a patch on the path where water seeped from a low bank of heather, exposing the dusty half boots that she always wore outside on the heath. Anything more delicate on her feet was impractical. She didn't usually wear her crinoline hoop around the house, only when she was visiting, and found it a nuisance in the wind.

But she wore her newest gown, fashioned from cornflower blue cotton damask. Around her shoulders she wore a cream Kashmir shawl, pinned by a pearl brooch that had once belonged to her mother. Seth had given the shawl to her, a gift for Christmas from himself and John.

Jeanne Beresford was out visiting, and so was Lucian and his father. The Beresfords lived a few houses away from the Thorntons, whose house was situated halfway up Constitution Hill and had a fine view of the harbour. Perhaps she should take the silk there. But no, Daisy Thornton was a tartar by all accounts. Marianne retained a vision of her gracefully dancing the Viennese waltz with the reverend from the church, and couldn't connect that image with the concept of the woman being a shrew. But Marianne wanted to see over the ship. She turned back towards the town.

The harbour was a bustling place today. Even the wind bustled in unexpected and short little gusts, like an infant with sudden and erratic bursts of energy. It set the ships swaying in unison, the masts pointing into a silver sky. Seagulls squabbled and squawked in the rigging.

On the quay vendors smoked eels over braziers. There were cockles, oysters and fish fresh from the sea. Provisions were lined up on the shore, waiting to be taken on board various ships. Crates of live fowls clucked and craned their necks nervously amongst the barrels of water and sacks of this and that, along with coiled ropes and tools.

Marianne found the *Samarand* at her usual berth. She was fairly low in the water, her deck level with the quay wall, which meant she was fully cargoed. Nick probably intended to sail on the next ebb tide.

Oddly, there was nobody about to challenge her on deck when she stepped aboard, but she could hear men's voices. She had no idea where Nick's cabin was. She stepped around the open hold to the back of the ship.

The deck moved gently beneath her feet. There was the shriek of a gull from above and a man swearing at it. She gave a soft giggle and her gaze moved up the mast. There was movement right at the top.

She tipped her head right back to see more clearly. The deck suddenly lifted in the wash of a passing boat, then it plunged. As she staggered and took a couple of steps backwards a gust of wind took her unawares. It found its way under her wide skirt and lifted her from her feet. Her legs caught on the edge of the hatch and she fell, tumbling down into the darkness.

The breath left her body as she landed on her side, one arm out to break her fall. She bounced up and over. Flung forward, her head collided with something hard enough to rattle her teeth, then she slid down between two bales and the light faded.

A noise brought her round. Stunned and dizzy she looked up towards the light, and tasted blood in her mouth. The light began to disappear as she called out, but her voice went unheard in the rumble of the hatch cover being pulled across and the shriek of gulls.

No! she thought, and reached out to try and pull herself up from between the bales. She cried out when she tried to lift her arm, and was met with excruciating pain that exploded dizzily into her head before she pitched headlong into a denser darkness than the one surrounding her.

Marianne didn't know how many times she fell asleep. When she was awake her exhausted calls went unheeded. Gradually she found enough strength to pull herself out from between the bales, and scrambled on to the top. Her mouth hurt and she gently touched a finger against it. Her lip was swollen, but thankfully, her teeth were still intact.

They were at sea, and any romantic notion she'd clung to about sailing, quickly evaporated in the face of her fright. It was dark and smelly in the hold, and she daren't move in case she fell further. The only comfort was that she could sometimes hear noises from above, and knew she wasn't alone. The ship creaked and groaned, water sloshed along the side. She didn't know if it were day or night, and huddled under her shawl for warmth.

Footsteps pattered overhead and she shouted. But they went past without a pause. This happened several times. Hunger attacked her, but the thirst was worse. Her mouth became dry and her lips cracked, and much to her embarrassment her body relieved itself and her skirt was damp. Despairingly, she knew that she'd die if she wasn't rescued from her predicament soon. If only there was a light.

Reaching out in the darkness, her fingers encountered a wooden pole. She felt along it. There was a hook at the end, and it had been tied to a bale. Painfully, she edged it out with her one usable hand. The effort exhausted her.

For a moment she gave into tears, then tried to remember how far she'd fallen. Not very far. She'd just landed awkwardly. She stood, legs apart, balancing herself on the pitching cargo. At least it was well secured, even if she wasn't. Taking in a deep breath she reached up with the stick. Nothing! Knowing she was taking a risk she jumped, stick still outstretched. It banged against the underneath of the hatch. The pain shooting through her encouraged her to drop it, and she heard it go bouncing off into the darkness.

'Help!' She screamed, and sank to her knees when there came the sound of footsteps.

The footsteps stopped.

'Help,' she screamed out again. 'Please help me.'

Someone knocked on the hatch top. 'Is someone down there?'

'Yes, someone is down here. It's dark and I've hurt myself. I'm scared.'

'Don't move. I'll fetch some help.'

Nick had just enjoyed his dinner when the mate knocked at the door. 'There appears to be a stowaway in the hold, Captain.'

Nick swore and said in annoyance, 'But we're two days out. Get him out and bring him to me. Send one of the crew down on a ladder to bring him up, then find him a hammock. Make sure he's got no weapons about his body first. When he's recovered from his fright he can work his passage.'

'Yes, sir.'

The cabin boy had just cleared the dishes away when there was another knock. The door swung open and Nick blinked. A woman stood there, her hair all over the place. She was bloodstained, covered in dust and supported by the mate, whose hand had slipped to rest an inch away from one of her breasts.

Her elbow pressed warningly into the mate's ribs and she frowned. 'You can release me now. I can stand perfectly well by myself.'

Nick gazed at her in astonishment as she swayed back and forth, proving her lie.

She said. 'Is that all you're going to do, stare at me with your mouth hanging open, Nick Thornton? Haven't you seen a woman before?'

'Plenty of them.' He smiled, thinking that whichever of those women this one was, he must have been mad to have overlooked such a delicious peach. The girl was a sight for sore eyes despite her state.

'I came on board to look for you. I fell down a hole in the deck and banged my head. Now my shoulder hurts.'

'No doubt it does.' He shrugged. 'Now you've found me, what exactly is it that you want me to do for you?'

'I don't know.' He wished he hadn't said it when she burst into tears and they tracked through the dust on her face. 'I could have died. And that man ... touched me. He said he was looking for weapons and it was on your orders.'

'It was ... I thought you were a man, and you most certainly could have died. Nobody would have noticed until we reached America.' With concern he noticed the way she was supporting her arm. He stood, gazing over her misshapen shoulder to where several of the crew stood, ready to support her if she fell. 'The woman's injured. How did that happen?'

'She must have done it when she fell. She said she were a friend of yours, Captain, and she'd kill me stone dead if anyone laid a finger on her. A right little tiger, she was. Wouldn't take any help. She went up the ladder in a single-handed huff, then stamped her foot and demanded to know where Poole Quay had gone. Then she fainted dead away and banged her head all over again. She were lucky she didn't fall back down into the hold.' He placed a basket on the chair. 'These belong to the young lady, I think.'

'You meant tigress. Tigers are male and I'm a female,' she thought to point out to the seaman.

'Yes, miss. You certainly are. I can see that now. I apologize for making such a mistake.'

'Apology accepted.'

The men shuffled their feet and gazed at each other, grinning.

Nick gave a pleased huff of laughter when her identity suddenly dawned on him. He crossed to where she stood, gazed down at her and smiled. 'It's little Aria Honcyman, isn't it?'

'Of course it is. I haven't changed that much, have I? You know, you're the only person who had ever called me that, Nick.'

His mind waxed lyrical. Miraculously, Charlotte's young sister had changed into an exquisite sprite. More beautiful than her sister even with her delicate high cheekbones. Her mouth, although swollen, was almost overwhelmingly kissable. His expression must have said it all.

'You can wipe that smile off your face.' She'd hardly got that out when the ship hit a trough. Propelled forward, she cried out with pain when she cannoned into his body and his arms closed around her. Colour drained from her cheeks and there was a moment of reproach in her blue eyes before they began to go out of focus. Her knees buckled, but he had her held safely against him. Sweeping the papers from his table he lifted Aria Honeyman gently in his arms and laid her there. Her hoop went up in the air, displaying the mystery of what was underneath.

He moved between her and the men, and nodded to the mate. 'Send the cook up. Tell him to bring his doctoring bag. The rest of you can go about your work.' He said to the cabin boy,

'Sam, fetch some water.' As soon as the men dispersed he removed her shawl, then untied the hoop from under her skirt. He began to battle with the ties fastening her bodice.

Her shoulder was definitely dislocated. He folded a towel and placed it under her head, frowning when blood immediately soaked into it. Head wounds bled a lot, but on investigation he knew this one would need stitches.

She opened her eyes, her dark eyelashes fanning a couple of times while she tried to focus on him. 'I'm embarrassed because I'm so dirty.'

'I know, but it can't be helped. Try not to think about it. You have a dislocated shoulder, and that needs to be manipulated back in. And there's a deep gash on your head that will require stitches.'

Her cornflower blue eyes never left his. 'Will it hurt?'

'I'm afraid so. I'll give you some laudanum, it will help to ease the pain.'

'Thank you. I'm thirsty, Nick. Can I have a drink, too, please?'

'I'm not surprised, since it's two days since we left Poole.' He poured some water from a jug into a glass, supported her head and held it to her lips. 'No ... don't gulp it. Sip.' Halfway through the process he held a vial of laudanum to her lips. 'Swallow this before you have the remainder of the water. Tell me, how did you manage to fall down the cargo hold?'

'There was a seagull up the mast and someone swore at it. It was too high for me to see properly so I took a couple of steps back to get a better

83

look at it and tipped my head back. A gust of wind found its way under my skirt and lifted me off my feet, then something knocked my legs from under me. I overbalanced. I'm sorry.'

'It's not your fault, though wearing a crinoline hoop aboard certainly contributed to the accident. The hold should have never been left unguarded with the hatch open. You were lucky.'

Nick smiled at her when the cook arrived. 'This is George Fisher, commonly known as Red. He used to be a barber surgeon before he took up cooking. He doubles as a doctor for the crew.

'How d'you do, Miss.'

Aria smiled dreamily at Red, who had obviously garnered his nickname from his shock of ginger corkscrew curls. 'Am I floating?'

'Yes, Miss. You most certainly are, so just you lie there and enjoy it.'

Nick drew Red aside. They'd dealt with dislocations together before. 'I've given her a good dose of laudanum and that seems to be taking effect. Which task would you rather do, anchor her or manipulate the shoulder?'

'Anchor. She's only a little thing and won't put up much of a fight, so use feel rather than force, Captain. One click should do it. Afterwards, you can hold her down when I put the stitches in her head. My embroidery is neater than yours.'

Nick turned back to her. 'You need to be very still, so Red is going to hold your body to steady it, while I fix it. It won't take long.'

'You haff lice flies, Nick,' she slurred when he lifted her arm. 'Lack ones.'

He chuckled. 'Black flies, or did you mean eyes?'

'Swat I said ... black fires and fleas.' She giggled. 'You're mixturing me up.'

'Aria's in a tizzy lizzy,' he teased, and his eyes shifted to her face. She was nice and relaxed now, unsuspecting. Gently he probed around the arm socket and said quietly, 'Now.' When Red applied his weight to her body Nick twisted the arm socket in with a satisfying click. He winced when she screamed. Her body went rigid and she jerked against the restraint of George's arm a couple of times. She screamed again, but more out of temper this time. The wounded expression in her eyes condemned him, and the tears trembling on her lashes made him want to cry himself.

'You hurt me.'

Even though it was the only cure for her injury, he felt guilty. 'I had to be cruel to be kind. It doesn't feel as painful as it did before though, eh?'

'S'better,' she said with some surprise.

'You must be careful with it for the next few weeks, while it heals. We'll put it in a sling. We're going to have to shave some of your hair off now, so we can see to that cut on your head.'

Her brilliant smile made him ache, because he knew there was more pain to come and she was trying to be brave.

'Cut it off,' she said.

'You have lovely hair, so certainly not.'

The only sound she made was a small moan now and again, though she bit her lip. When the stitching was done she turned her face against the blanket and cried, giving small snuffling sobs. Eventually, she fell asleep, and Nick knew the laudanum would keep her asleep for some time.

'Are we turning back to port with her, Captain?' Red said.

'Like hell, we are. It's too much trouble. I'll have to re-provision and questions will be asked.'

'Somebody's going to miss her.'

'It serves them right. They should have looked after her better. Oh, don't worry, Red. I know her family.' And Charlotte will be furious, he thought with some satisfaction.

'Where will the girl sleep? *Samarand* is already stuffed to the gills with cargo.'

Nick looked around his cabin, and his eyes settled on his cot. 'In there, she won't take up too much room. We'll rig a canvas across the cabin on that side of the door to give her some privacy. I'll have one side for my cabin, and she can have the other. As for sleeping arrangements, I'll share and share about with the first mate. After all, we're rarely on deck together. Thanks, Red. Make some nice broth for when she wakes. You may go now.'

Sam came in with the water and Nick set about cleaning the blood from his unwanted guest. Aria was fair-skinned where she was usually covered, but wore a light tan on her face that supported a drift of freckles – as though she threw off her bonnet whenever she got the chance. She was attractive. Hell, she was more than that, he thought.

Placing a blanket over her he slid the blood-stained chemise and gown down over her dainty feet. He moved her to the bunk, nodding towards the soiled garments. 'Put those to soak, Sam, but don't expect to get rid of the bloodstains altogether. Clear my things away from this side of the cabin. We'll make our guest as comfortable as we can. Rig up a rope so she can hang her things up. Make sure there's a bucket and a jug of clean water at all times. You can empty her slops along with mine every day. I'm making you responsible for her comfort, Sam, and I don't want her to feel embarrassed by her situation. It won't be easy for a woman to live amongst men. They have different feelings and needs. You have five sisters and you know what females are like.'

Sam said quite seriously, 'Yes, Captain ... like a coop of quarrelsome hens.'

Nick laughed at that. 'And don't get any ideas about Miss Honeyman. I know what lads of your age are like, and how they think. I used to be one.'

Sam's face turned a fiery red.

Charles Barrie was entertaining Edgar Wyvern and some other guests when a manservant came in with a card on a silver tray.

Charles nodded. 'Give the gentleman a brandy and ask him to wait in my study.'

When the ladies excused themselves and went into the sitting room to socialize, Charles sent his male guests into the billiards room then beckoned to Edgar.

'You'll excuse us for a short while, gentlemen. Some business has come up that I need to attend to.'

The man in the study was in his early twenties. Placing his brandy on the table, he stood when Charles and Edgar entered. A pair of astute grey eyes gazed at them.

'Adam Chapman ... you have brought news at last?' Edgar said, and the three of them shook hands.

'Forgive me for arriving unannounced, especially since you are entertaining, Sir Charles. I have this evening received a comprehensive report, and felt you should be informed of it as soon as possible.'

The three men settled themselves, then the two gazed at the younger man expectantly.

He cleared his throat. 'I'm afraid the news is not very promising. Jonathan Barrie was wed to Mary Elizabeth Ellis in Hobart. A year later he was clearing some land and met with an accident.'

Charles was filled with an uneasy dread. 'What sort of accident?'

'There's no easy way to tell you this, Sir Charles, and I'm sorry to be the bearer of bad news, your son was killed by a falling tree branch. By all accounts, death was instantaneous.'

Charles gave a distressed murmur.

Edgar poured his friend a brandy, and handed it to him. 'I'm so sorry, Charles. Be consoled by the fact that he didn't suffer.'

'There is more, sir.'

'How much more bad news can there be?'

'I didn't say the news was entirely bad.' The man gave a small, cautious smile. 'Sometimes the Lord provides us with hope. Jonathan and Mary Barrie had a son ... born just a month before your son died. He was christened John Charles after his father, and after you, I presume.'

Charles gave a faint smile as he glanced at Edgar and told him the obvious. 'If Jonathan named a grandson after me, he no longer bore any anger towards me.'

'That's true, of course,' Edgar said gently.

Charles turned back to Chapman. 'Where is my grandson and his mother? Are they with you?'

'No, sir. There is a trail of sorts to follow. After your son died his wife became destitute, and with the child still at her breast was forced to ... beg on the streets.'

Charles gasped. 'My daughter-in-law had to beg?'

The man gave him a pitying glance. 'There is worse, sir. Mrs Barrie came to the notice of an army officer, who befriended her. He rented accommodation and she and the boy moved in with him. One can only suppose—'

When Charles gave a shocked cry Adam shrugged. 'Women are born with an instinct to sacrifice themselves for the sake of a child. We must not blame them for it.'

'Only the men who take advantage of it, eh.'

'And sometimes a situation can be misread,' Edgar said firmly. 'Not all men are predatory.

The relationship could have been quite innocent.'

'Quite,' Chapman said. 'A couple of years later Mrs Barrie died after a lingering illness. She had consumption, brought about, no doubt by the privations she was obliged to endure on the streets. She is buried next to your son. The soldier resigned his commission shortly before the event.'

'So the scoundrel ruined my daughter-in-law and stole my grandson,' Charles cried out. 'We must hunt him down and make him pay for his crimes.'

Edgar gave a deep sigh and reminded him, 'You're making out a prima facie case against him Charles. The soldier saw Mary decently buried next to her husband, which reveals some sensitivity of character on his part. Perhaps she had relatives who took the boy in.'

Adam Chapman consulted his notes. 'According to someone who shared a cabin with her on the voyage out, Mrs Barrie said she had no kin ... previous to her marriage to your son, of course.'

'The soldier who gave her a home may have placed the boy in an orphanage or given him to a barren couple to be loved and cared for,' Edgar said. 'After all, a child needs a mother to nurture him in the proper manner. Then again, the boy may have died and have been buried with her.'

Charles prayed that Edgar was wrong. 'Do you have the soldier's name, Mr Chapman?'

The man consulted a paper in his hand. 'He is Colonel Seth Hardy, and he had an exemplary military record before he came into a legacy and surrendered his obligations to the crown. There the trail ends, for there's no mention of him taking a child on board the ship that brought him back to England.

'So my grandson is still in Hobart Town.'

'So far there's been no trace of him. A neighbour saw Colonel Hardy go aboard the ship that brought him to England. He was alone. I'm here to see if you wish the search for him to be continued.'

'What other choice do I have? The boy is the only relative I have left.'

'Sir ... Hobart Town is small. The advertisements, even those with the offer of a reward for the return of the child, have produced no results, and the bill is mounting up. There is nowhere else to look there. My contacts will, of course, keep their eyes and ears open for any news of the boy.'

'I've got nothing else to spend my money on, Mr Chapman. If you present your account I will bring you up to date as well as pay you a further retainer before you depart. What do you suggest we do?'

'At this point it might prove to be of use if we try and find Colonel Hardy. If we can find him in England, we can simply ask him what happened to the boy.'

Charles wished he'd thought of that himself. Jonathan was dead ... and had been for a long time. And his grandson, a boy he'd never met but who Charles now already felt the loss of keenly, was missing. Although Charles had strongly suspected that something untoward had happened to his son, it was still a shock. It was his fault. If only he'd allowed Jonathan his head. He must find his grandson. He must! Jonathan would expect nothing less from him.

Edgar rose to his feet. 'Charles, with your permission I'll go and inform your guests that you've received bad news while you settle your business with Mr Chapman. I'll rejoin you in due course.'

Charles nodded. 'Thank you, Edgar. Perhaps you'd tell the butler as well. He can inform the staff.' A few minutes later he heard their muted voices as his guests departed, closing the door quietly behind them.

He dragged in a breath and gazed at the man. 'Mr Chapman, please spare no expense in finding me this soldier, Colonel Seth Hardy.'

'And when I do?'

Charles liked Chapman's positive attitude. Young as he was, the man believed in his own ability, and that made Charles believe in him too. 'Do not approach him on my behalf, or alert him in any way. I'd prefer to do that myself. I can usually tell if a man is honest or otherwise when I meet him face to face and look into his eyes.'

The eyes of the man he was looking at were grey with dark flecks, and they didn't waver from his as they shook hands.

'I'll place advertisements in the main newspapers and we'll see if anything turns up,' Chapman said as Charles escorted him to the door.

'Offer a reward.'

'It will attract confidence tricksters.'

'It can't be helped. Follow all leads Mr Chapman, and keep me informed.'

Despite his disquiet over the news of his son and daughter-in-law's deaths, Charles had been given something to hope for by news of his grandson's existence, he thought, as he bid the inquiry agent goodnight.

'Would you like me to leave, Charles?' Edgar said as he returned to the drawing room.

'No, old friend. Stay and share a brandy with me. My own company will be too miserable at the moment.'

'Jonathan's death must be a hard pill to swallow so soon after that of his brother.'

'Yes it is, but I half expected it. And the pill has a sugar coating.'

'Don't get your hopes up too high, Charles.'

'We'll find my grandson, of that I'm certain,' he said calmly.

'And when you do?'

Charles smiled. 'John Charles will become my reason for living.'

Six

'My chemise and gown is tied to the rigging?' Clad in one of Nick's shirts, her shawl wrapped around her to serve as a skirt, Marianne put her hands against her burning cheeks and said faintly. 'Oh ... how embarrassing.'

She caught the quick grin Nick gave before he said, 'It's the quickest way to dry it. Besides, most of the men on this ship would have seen a chemise before. Eat your breakfast.'

'Broth ... for breakfast?'

'Red made it especially for you. How was I to know you'd wake with the appetite of a starving wolf? Most people would have been seasick by now.'

'I don't see why. The movement of the ship is quite pleasant when you get used to it. And fun.'

'Wait until we hit an Atlantic storm if you think that.' He slapped a piece of smoked bacon on a thick slab of bread and butter and held it out to her. 'Here, eat this instead.'

Nick's patience was wearing thin, so she smiled and bit a chunk from one side. 'Thank you, Nick, but I'll eat the broth if you don't mind. It smells delicious.'

'Contrary little madam,' he growled.

Nick was like a cauldron. Turn the heat up

under him and he began to boil. Turn it down and his temper subsided like a charm. 'Stop being in such of a grumble with me,' and she bestowed her most charming smile on him. 'When will we get back to Poole? Charlotte will be sick with worry about me.'

The smile Nick gave her was altogether smug. 'In approximately seven weeks' time, since we're going there via Boston.'

'Seven weeks!' She closed her eyes for a moment, hoping it was all a dream. When she opened them again Nick would be gone, the ship would be gone and her aching head would be gone. Though, better an aching head that not having a head at all. The trouble was she could still hear the wind and water, ropes slapping, timbers creaking, and other marine sounds. She'd have to use guile on him, though she didn't think she'd be very good at it. She opened her eyes to their fullest, dipped her eyelashes once, then gave him her best smile. 'I don't suppose—'

'You suppose right, Aria. Turning back would cost Thornton Shipping a great deal of time and money, and it would put our schedule out.' His mouth took on an amused curve. 'Why are you blinking, have you got something in your eyes?'

'You know I haven't. I'm being alluring.'

'I assure you, you're not.'

She giggled when he chuckled, and opened her purse to gaze at the contents. She closed it again, saying hopefully, 'I have two shillings, will that get me home?'

He whooped with laughter. 'That won't even

pay for your provisions.'

Picking up her spoon she scooped up the broth, in case it proved to be her last meal. It was filling and had barley in to thicken it. She sighed when she finished it. 'That was tasty. Is there any fruit?'

He plucked a couple of purple plums from a dish and offered them to her. 'They're a bit sour. I was waiting for them to ripen.'

The first one was extremely sour. Her jaw clenched as the acidity sent multiple shudders skittering into her ears. She handed the second plum back to him. 'Yours, I think.'

'Next question, Aria?'

'Where does one get a bath on this ship of yours?'

'We haven't got enough fresh water on board to take baths. Sam will supply you with a bowl of water every day, in which to wash.'

'I never thought,' she wailed. 'My hair desperately needs washing. It's sticky with dried blood and I can't get it untangled.'

'Red said that if you wash it in salt water it will help the wound to heal, even though it might sting. Sam will bring you some. We have an abundant supply, with or without fish.' He smiled. 'Last night you asked Cook to cut your hair. I prevented him because you were rambling a bit. It's too pretty to cut off. If you'd like I'll act as your maid until your shoulder heals properly, and braid it into a queue for you in the morning. It will be easier to manage like that.'

She nodded. 'Thanks.'

Sam came in and placed a jug of coffee on the

table. There was no cream to go with it, but plenty of honey to sweeten. Sipping at the brew she made a face.

'Too strong?'

When she nodded he tipped half of it back into the pot and added hot water from a second jug to her cup. 'Try that.'

She smiled after she'd sipped it. 'Much better, thank you.'

'Now, Aria. Tell me why you came aboard my ship in the first place.'

'Firstly, to deliver a satchel of fabric you dropped the last time you visited my home.'

His eyes sharpened and his smile faded; he was obviously remembering the occasion. 'That was a year ago,' he said harshly. 'You could have left it with my Aunt Daisy. What's the real reason? Has something happened to Charlotte? Is her husband ill-treating her? If so, it serves her right.'

But he looked as though he'd turn the ship around and go back to Poole to rescue Charlotte straight away, she thought with a sigh, and he'd probably come off worse in an encounter with Seth, who was a trained soldier, after all.

She placed a hand over his. Best to tell him now. 'You must reconcile yourself to the fact that Charlotte appears to be happily married. In fact, just a week ago she gave birth to twin babies. A boy called Mitchell and a girl named Jessica.'

Nick didn't say anything straight away, but slid his hand away and stood, his eyes narrowed as he informed her briefly, 'My Aunt Daisy has already acquainted me with the fact.'

'Oh.'

'Thank you for returning the length of silk, but you needn't have gone to the trouble. I'd intended that for Charlotte's wedding gown. It's yours if you want it.'

'But—'

He laid a finger across her mouth. 'The conversation is at an end. Heed my instructions. You are not to come on deck by yourself. I'll be down later to braid your hair and take you up for some air. In the meantime you can rest. If you behave yourself we can watch the stars come out. If you need anything, ask Sam. He has five sisters, so is an expert on women. Aren't you Sam?'

'If you say so, Captain.'

'You'll have to make do for about three weeks, until we reach Boston. We'll arrange a time between us when we can both have private use of the cabin for a short time each day. We can buy you some new clothes once we berth.'

'For two shillings?'

'I'll make you a loan.' He smiled. 'Sam has enough clothing to outfit the gentlemen queuing in a whore's parlour for a month. He might lend you something.'

She giggled at his colourful phrase.

He shrugged and offered her a shamefaced grin. 'Accept my pardon. I'm not used to having women on board. I'll try and watch my tongue from now on. Let me rephrase that. Sam's mother sent him to sea with an outfit for every occasion. Sam's not much bigger than you at the moment and he might lend you a pair of trousers. What say you, Sam?'

'Yes, sir. Miss Honeyman can have my best set, the ones my mother told me to keep for Sundays. The trousers are too short now, and there's that shirt with the frills on. I've never worn it, and I've grown out of it. My chest has got bigger, see.' He filled his lungs with air to expand it.

Amusement danced over the dark surface of Nick's eyes. 'That's enough of a demonstration, Sam. We don't want Miss Honeyman to swoon. I had noticed your growth into manhood and was about to comment on it. And frills on the shirt certainly don't suit you. I'll replace the outfit when we get to Boston with something more manly. The trouble with mothers is that they don't want their sons to grow up, eh lad.'

Marianne remembered that Nick had grown up under the care of his uncle and the fearsome Aunt Daisy, so perhaps it was wishful thinking on his part. Nevertheless, Nick was good with Sam, and she had a sudden vision of the captain sprawled in a chair with a couple of dark-eyed sons on his knees, both gazing raptly up at him with adoration while he told them a story.

But for that he'd need a woman he loved, and one who loved him. There was a sudden ache in her throat that she found hard to set aside. He'd been constant and loyal in his affection for Charlotte, and had made no bones about it. But her sister was unavailable to him now. When he reached the door, she said, 'Nick? I'm so sorry ... about Charlotte.'

Nick knew exactly what Aria was thinking ... that he was broken-hearted and pining for her sister. It was true that Charlotte's betrayal had come as a shock, and he'd be the first to admit that he'd survived a period of some serious soul-searching in the bottom of a bottle.

He'd discovered among the dregs that most of his anger had risen from his own vanity. His relationship with Charlotte had always been one of combat, and at that moment when they'd last met, she'd had no choice but deliver him the coup de grâce.

The wound she'd inflicted on him no longer dominated his thoughts. It was healing, as surely as that ugly gash on Aria's head would heal. Thank goodness she'd whacked her head and not her pretty face, for it would leave a scar.

The humiliation of sprawling face down in the dirt still rankled though, and he doubted if he'd ever get over that particular dent to his pride. Sometimes he considered retribution for that cruelty she'd inflicted on him. The smile she'd exchanged with Seth Hardy had nearly broken his heart, and he'd reached the conclusion that if she'd ever loved him, she didn't now. And if she'd never loved him, then she'd never pretended otherwise. He'd been suffering from a delusion of his own making. More shattering was the knowledge that he'd needed her to fill a space in his life.

Earlier in the cabin, when Aria had smiled so beguilingly at him in an effort to persuade him to return her to her family, it had dawned on him that he'd been handed the perfect tool with which to take his revenge on his former love. He was tempted to, but could he do it, and would he like himself afterwards?

'I daresay I'll get over Charlotte eventually,' he said, and closed the door behind him. When he was outside, Nick leaned against it for a moment and his eyes narrowed as he completed his train of thought with a soft laugh. If he did decide to take his revenge, it would be in Aria Honeyman's best interests to watch out.

The next time Nick set eyes on his unwanted guest, was at dinner. She'd brushed most of the tangles from her hair with his brush and had managed to tie it at the nape of her neck with a ribbon she'd pulled from her bonnet.

Red had made a stew with dumplings. And there was a tart made from dried apples and raspberries.

Aria wore a pair of moleskin trousers, which clung becomingly to the curves of her behind. Over the top she wore Sam's despised frills, the cuffs turned back to the length of her arms. Her hair was a dark and stormy tumble of curls. He gazed at her, savouring her appearance and wondering why he'd never seen her through the eyes of a man before.

She caught him staring. Anxiously she said, 'Do I look all right?'

An exquisitely provocative sprite, indeed, he thought, and cleared his throat before he forced out a laugh. 'The ladies of Poole would foam at the mouth and lash their tongues if they set their eyes on you looking like that.'

Her face fell. 'Is it that bad?'

'My dear Aria, have you looked in the mirror lately? If so, you must know how perfectly ravishing you've become.'

A blush suffused her cheeks. 'You shouldn't say such things to me, Nick.'

'Why not?'

She looked away. 'Because I'm afraid.'

'That I might ravish you?'

'No, I'd never think that of you,' she said quickly. 'You were always a gentleman around me. It's because I love someone. I would not like that to be spoiled.'

The mere fact that she was standing here on his ship meant it was already spoiled. 'Who is it you love?'

'Oh ... someone.'

Curiosity filled him. 'Does the man love you in return?'

'I don't know ... sometimes I think...' She shrugged. 'Then again, he has such a fine, up-right and professional manner. It's hard to tell. He says he likes me and I've known him a long time. Almost as long as I've known you.'

He sounded like a self-important prig to Nick. Longevity didn't breed loyalty or love if Charlotte's example was anything to go by. What a little innocent Aria was. Hearing the yearning in her voice, he asked, 'Has the man tried to kiss you yet?'

She looked shocked. 'He wouldn't. Lucian is a gentleman.'

With water running through his veins. Poor little Aria, yearning for the kiss of a man she'd never be able to have, Nick thought. Lucian Beresford was a handsome man with a charming manner, and he was good at his job. But he was dispassionate and ambitious. If he married at all he'd marry into wealth, and by all accounts he'd set his sights on a woman recently widowed. Aria deserved better than him, and even if she didn't, Beresford wouldn't want her once she was surrounded by scandal. She needed someone with passion, someone who would cherish her and who she could adore in return.

Someone like Nick Thornton, perhaps? He gave a wry smile. Now that would set the cat amongst the pigeons, and it was worth consideration. Aria hadn't realized her slip of the tongue, as she hadn't considered the ramifications of coming aboard his ship unaccompanied. Once she returned home, and they'd realized where she'd been, the gossips would set to work and she'd be like a lamb to the slaughter. Poor Aria.

Still, that wasn't his problem ... unless he decided to make it his. He slid her a sideways look. He'd never met anyone so refreshingly ingenuous, and she was feminine to the core. 'If I were Lucian I'd have kissed you by now.'

'I'm sure you wouldn't take such a liberty.' Her eyes flicked up to his, alight with curiosity. 'Were you always a gentleman with Charlotte?'

'I wouldn't be if I discussed our relationship with you, now would I? If you want us to remain friends mind your own business, Aria.'

Her laughter rode astride the goose bumps prickling down his spine. 'On the strength of that I know I can trust you, Nick.'

'It would be wiser if you didn't assume any-thing.' He gave a soft laugh and held out his best jacket for her to wear, easing it on to her sore shoulder first. Her hands disappeared into the sleeves and stayed there. He folded it around her from behind so she was in his arms, then left a kiss, as light as a butterfly, where her shoulder joined her neck. Her skin quivered against his mouth, but she didn't attempt to move away.

'Can you still trust me?' he whispered against her ear.

She turned to gaze at him, giving a delectable little laugh that set his hair on end as she held out her arms. 'It tickled. Turn the cuffs up please, Nick. Or should I call you Captain Thornton in front of the crew?'

'You can call me any name you consider suit-able.' He folded back the sleeves. 'There, that's better. Here, put that arm back in the sling. You forgot to answer my question, Aria.'

'I didn't forget. Some questions are better left unanswered.' When she gently touched a finger against his bottom lip he wanted to grab her hand and scrape his teeth across her palm. His uncle had been right. This was a woman who made a man feel like a man without even trying. There was nothing in her of the shrewish nature her sister had. Aria was all softness and laughter, but had a fine touch of mettle about her when she needed it, he suspected.

Lightly, she said, 'Let's go up on deck and watch the stars come out, like you promised. I'll expect you to tell me the name of every one.'

'Pick one out for yourself and I'll prise it out

of the sky for you.'

'It would be lonely separated from its companions and wouldn't shine so brightly.' She slid her hand trustingly into his. 'Lead the way, Captain Thornton.'

They sat on the hatch cover, and the crew walked casually back and forth, stopping to ask how she was. The crafty load of buggers, he thought. He allowed them to take a look at her, to smile and be smiled on and beguiled, then sent them sharply about their business.

Overhead the stars peppered the sky one by one, then by their hundreds as the sky darkened, until the whole sky was a blaze of twinkling lights. Now and again a star would shoot across the sky. Marianne seemed enchanted by it, so her voice was hushed in reverence of the show when she said, 'It's magical, Nick.'

His hand closed around hers and her pulse beat against his palm.

In the crew's quarters someone began to play a fiddle. The men began to take it in turns singing the sailor's alphabet, their voices gruff. A is for the anchor that hangs on our bow. B for the bowsprits through the wild sea do plough ... as they neared the end Aria softly joined in the chorus 'So merry, so merry, so merry are we. No mortals on earth are like sailors at sea. Blow high or blow low as the good ship sails on.'

'Give a sailor his grog and there's nothing goes wrong,' Nick finished with the rest of the voices when they were raised with great gusto.

She laughed as a cheer went up. 'Tell me about the stars now.'

It was a balmy night and the ship rode the swell as smoothly as a rocking horse in a child's nursery. All that could change in a moment, but he'd know if the wind changed direction and if the sails needed to be trimmed.

He was showing off, extolling the glory of the heavens to her when he felt the slight weight of her head pressing against his shoulder. He gave a wry smile. 'So much for stargazing, kitten, I've sent you to sleep.' He slid an arm around her for support.

'Mmm...' she murmured and turned her face against him to snuggle against his chest. The breeze caught her hair and a multitude of flying strands reached up, to cling to and caress his face. It smelled of salt and seaweed, like the ocean she'd washed it in.

Her long lashes quivered against her skin. She had a neat little nose and her slightly parted mouth had a relaxed curve. He wanted to kiss it, and gave a bit of a grin. Now, who was beguiled by her? Then and there Nick decided he'd be doing himself a favour if he threw her overboard. At least he'd get some sleep. Then came the afterthought – he might be doing her a favour too.

He woke her with a gentle shake. 'Time you went to your cot, I think. I'll take you down.'

Her eyes were fuddled for a moment, then they cleared. 'Did I fall asleep? It must have been the sea air.'

'I thought it was because I'd bored you.'

'I've never known you to be boring, Nick. As for the air ... it's wonderful air, with a mind all of its own.'

He appreciated her sentiment, and the way she expressed it. She looked at things differently from most women he'd known. He stood, assisting her to her feet. 'I wish there was some way I could make you more comfortable, Aria.'

As they made their way to the cabin she said, 'I realize that being on board ship isn't ideal for a woman, but it's my own fault I'm here. You're doing your best, and I appreciate that, Nick. I'm sorry to put you to so much trouble.'

'What will you tell your sister when you get home?'

She shrugged. 'I've put off thinking about it. Probably the truth.'

'You think Charlotte will believe it?'

He sensed rather than saw her grimace. 'To be honest, I imagine she'll blame you, and be furious with me. We'll both get a tongue lashing I expect.'

He chuckled. 'Perhaps she'll really shoot me this time.'

'Me as well.'

'You know that people will talk about us, Aria. Whatever is said, it's not going to be believed. I'm a man so I can get away with it, but it's your reputation that will be ruined.'

She looked troubled for a moment, then forced a wry smile to her face. 'You shouldn't make it your concern, Nick. It's not your fault.'

'I'm well aware of that.' His eyes narrowed. 'I'll try and think of something.'

'What?'

He laughed as he opened the cabin door. Sam

had lit the lantern, and it swung back and forth making the shadows interchangeable with the light so it was a constantly shifting scene. 'Give me time ... throw you overboard and pretend I never set eyes on you, perhaps.'

He was rewarded by a peal of laughter that brought a wide grin to his face. Perhaps he'd wed her, because he was pretty sure that Lucian Beresford wouldn't.

Charlotte was frantic with worry. 'I don't understand it, Seth. I know Marianne called on the Beresfords because she left a calling card. She couldn't just disappear.'

'Perhaps she was invited to stay with friends.'

'She would have let me know. Besides, she's been gone for several days now and she would have needed her clothes.'

Seth shrugged. 'I've informed the authorities, and they're making enquiries. She was seen by several people on that day, heading towards the quay. They have a list of ships that left the harbour. The crews will be questioned the next time they berth, if she doesn't turn up in the meantime.'

'Most roads lead towards the quay. That doesn't mean Marianne has sailed off on a ship.'

'That's only one line of enquiry. She might have eloped to Gretna Green.'

'Why would she do that when she was enamoured with Lucian Beresford?'

'Perhaps she's eloped with him.'

Smiling at the thought, Charlotte said, 'If she had it would be a blessing. But he doesn't seem as interested in her as she is in him. She spends too much time out on the heath. I hope she hasn't taken it into her head to travel with the gypsies. What makes you think that she eloped?'

Seth sighed. 'I don't think that. It's just that we've been over and over this and I'm running out of ideas. The clay diggers are going to search the heath later on in case she fell into one of the bogs.'

Placing her hands over her ears Charlotte gave a little scream. 'Don't even think such an awful thing. Besides, Marianne knows the dangers of the heath like the back of her hand.'

John came in and tugged at Seth's hand to claim his attention. 'Is Aunt Marianne coming home? She said she'd help me with the jigsaw puzzle.'

Seth smiled down at his stepson. 'Of course she's coming home. Try not to worry, John. Marianne might have decided to visit friends for a while.'

Jessica began to stir. John moved to her cradle and gazed down at her. 'She doesn't look squashed any more, but her hair is a funny colour.' He moved on to Major Mitchell, grinning at him, then at Seth. 'Can I touch him, Pa?'

'If that's all right with you, Charlotte?'

She nodded. 'I'm going to get up. I can't lie around in bed all day, especially when I'm so worried about Marianne. You don't think that someone has kidnapped her, do you? What if someone demands a ransom?'

Seth took her by the shoulders. 'I think they would have let us know by now.'

'What if she's been stolen? She might have been sold into slavery or something worse.'

'Enough, Charlotte. I'm sure she'll turn up before too long and have a perfectly reasonable explanation. She might have banged her head and forgotten who she is.'

She stared at him for a minute, then whispered, 'Do you think it possible that Nick Thornton has taken her prisoner out of revenge? She might have fallen overboard and drowned. We'd never know.'

John had been listening to every word, and now gazed at Charlotte, his eyes wide and confused. 'Aunt Marianne won't drown because she can swim, and was teaching me how to swim too.' He gazed from one to the other. 'I'm not supposed to tell anyone because ladies aren't supposed to be able to swim and she goes in her petticoat and I'm not supposed to tell anyone about that either because she said that everyone is fuddy-duddy about such things and it will cause an awful stink. But I've looked where we usually swim and her boots, skirt and bodice isn't where she usually leaves them. She won't get into trouble, will she?'

Seth grinned and shook his head.

Charlotte's expression of surprise was followed by one of shock. 'I didn't know Marianne could swim. And in her underwear!'

John persisted with his own theory. 'Anyway, if Aunt Marianne fell overboard she'd have swum to an island and become a castaway, like Robinson Crusoe. She might be castaway on Brownsea island, Pa.' His eyes widened even more, 'And Pa, there's a ghost living there.'

'I'm sure your aunt could manage a ghost, especially in her underwear.' Seth chuckled at the thought. 'And I do think that your imaginations are getting the better of both of you. But it won't hurt to go over to the island and search it, if it will put your mind at rest. I'll ask the revenue men to do that.'

'John, go and eat your breakfast, else you'll be going to school hungry. Charlotte, I know staying in bed when you don't feel ill is tedious. I also know that if I tell you to stay in bed that you'll rise as soon as my back is turned.'

She gave a little smile, but he hadn't finished.

'By risking your own health you could jeopardize the health of our infants, who mostly rely on you for their sustenance. Dr Beresford said the lying in period should be at least three weeks. If you show no sign of fever you can take some exercise every day then. And I'm going to ask the wet nurse to stay on as nursery maid.'

'Without asking me?'

'You'd expressed satisfaction with her, Charlotte. You told me yourself that you're unable to feed the children sufficiently. I've talked it over with Doctor Beresford, and am acting under his advice.'

'But I wanted to feed them myself, Seth. I wanted to feel close to them.' They were precious to her, part of her heart. She'd never expected to feel such love for her children. It was different to what she felt for John, or even Marianne. Their birth had brought her closer to Seth, for it was something they shared.

111

'I know. But it seems that you can't, and the welfare of our children must be put before our own needs. They will still love you, Charlotte. You're their mother, and you'll always put their welfare first.'

She gritted her teeth. Trust Seth to appeal to her conscience. Even so, what he'd said was true. Another week wouldn't do her any harm, and it would be a lesson in patience, a grace she knew she was sadly lacking. 'I promise to behave myself, and I will feed them myself, you'll see. Are you going to the clay pits?'

'I'm going to join the clay men in searching the heath after I've dropped John off at school.'

'Make sure you don't get lost yourself. I'd miss you.'

He grinned and kissed her cheek. 'Thank you for those encouraging words, are there any other instructions?'

'Yes,' and her smile faded. 'If you see the gypsies let them know that Marianne is missing. Ask them to keep watch for her, though I imagine they'll know by now. Marianne is friendly with some of them, too friendly at times, but they trust her and they'll keep a watch out for her. We could offer a reward.'

'That's a good idea. I'll think on it.'

'And, Seth...?' she said when he reached the door. 'If you see the gypsy called Jessica ... you could ask her...' She shrugged. 'I don't really believe it myself, but Marianne told me that the woman can see into the future.'

Seth didn't laugh, as she'd expected him to. 'Then I'll ask her if she can throw some light on

112

Marianne's disappearance. Is that what you want?'

She nodded.

Seth was more worried about his sister-in-law than he'd let on to Charlotte. Later, he strode off at a pace designed to cover a lot of ground quickly, his gaze on the cart track that sent chalky dust powdering his highly polished brown boots.

Marianne was impulsive as well as gullible. Charlotte had assumed the responsibility of her younger sister from too young an age, and she now found it hard to relinquish that grip.

It was natural that Marianne would resent that, especially now, with her sister's attention being claimed by their own children. But Marianne usually had an open and sunny disposition, and she loved Charlotte. Seth seriously doubted that she'd have run off without a word. She wasn't that thoughtless.

Unless she'd fallen in love, he thought, watching the path come up to meet his feet as he headed for the arranged meeting place. That particular emotion tended to leave one bereft of sense or reason. Why else would he have provided for Mary ... a woman whose fate had been sealed the moment she'd been forced to live on the streets. Starving to death to maintain a perceived respectability might have been the preferred option in the eyes of many, but it was hypocritical, unless they were willing to provide an alternative way of living for the victim.

But that was something John would never

learn. Mary hadn't possessed the coarseness and the determination to survive that a common whore needed. She'd been delicate, courageous and loving. He'd found her with her son in her arms, standing on the side of the river in utter despair, trying to pluck up courage to end it all for both of them.

Seth had just been informed of his legacy. Compassion had made him share that good fortune, and provide them with a home while he arranged to sell his commission. Little by little he'd learned her story of the shipboard romance, of the idealistic husband who was talented, but who didn't have the practical skills to earn enough to keep them. He'd never probed further.

When they'd exchanged vows over the bible, with nobody to witness the ceremony, she'd been grateful that he'd given her back some respectability. Seth had never made any claim on her body because she'd needed to conserve the little strength she had to provide her son with nourishment. For that small concession, as well as the roof over her head in a small isolated cottage he'd rented, she was grateful. There, he'd looked after her until her strength had given out, allowing her some time to watch her son begin to grow and flourish. In the process he'd fallen in love with her. He'd wept as he'd buried her next to the husband she'd loved.

'Promise me you'll look after John, you're the only father he's ever known,' Mary had whispered with her dying breath. And he'd promised, for by then her will had been made and witnessed, and he regarded the child as his own.

Charlotte reminded him of Mary. She had the same courage and pride, though not Mary's soft helplessness and vulnerability. He didn't love Charlotte, but he had a healthy regard for her. She'd been resigned to submit to her wifely duties when he'd brought her to bed, ending up surprised that the physical part of the relationship could be participated in with enjoyment. She'd not been too shy to admit it. Charlotte was a good manager, sensible and intelligent. Mary's child, as well as his own, would have a good mother.

Deep in thought he came to a sudden halt as he nearly walked into somebody in his path. 'I beg your pardon.' He doffed his hat when he saw a skirt and his heart leapt.

But when he raised his gaze it wasn't Marianne, it was a gypsy woman.

'Cross my palm with silver and I'll tell your fortune, soldier.'

She had a careworn, secretive face and her outstretched hand was mapped with lines. He knew who she was and he smiled. 'You must be Jessica.'

'That I am.'

'Then I have you to thank for helping my wife safely deliver our babies.'

'Your missus wouldn't have had any trouble. There will be two more sons for her in the future.'

He dropped a shilling into her palm. 'I'll gladly cross your palm with silver for telling me that, but the fortune-telling can wait. I'm on a mission. I'm looking for my sister-in-law, Marianne

Honeyman.'

When he moved to one side to step around her, the gypsy moved to block him, and her eyes took on a distant look. 'The girl is far away now and you won't find her on the heath. She fell down into the darkness ... and is surrounded by water.'

His heart thumped. 'Are you saying she's drowned?'

'No, sir, she is not dead. There's a man.'

'A man?' Tall, dark and handsome, he supposed, giving a wry grin. Instantly he thought of Nick Thornton. He shook his head. Thornton was no fool. In fact, the man and his ideas had impressed him when they'd met on a social level. Thornton wouldn't invite trouble like Marianne into his life so blatantly.

The gypsy detained him with a hand on his arm. 'Listen to your instinct, soldier. Miss Marianne won't be harmed, but she'll come back, changed.'

She was talking nonsense. 'Sorry, I haven't got time to listen to this, Jessica. If you see my sister-in-law tell her that Charlotte is worried sick, and she's to go straight home.'

Seth pushed past her and picked up speed. He'd gone several yards when there was a whisper against his ear, as if the gypsy was right next to him. 'Beware, soldier, there's a hunter with a cage behind you.'

He slewed around, his hand reaching for his pistol, and goose bumps crackling on his body. There was nothing behind him except the track. Even the gypsy had somehow blended into the landscape.

A hunter with a cage, she'd said. What the devil had the woman been talking about?

For a moment the sun faded, as though the molten gold light of morning had become tarnished. The air grew quiet and menacing, the water in the harbour was still. Then a seagull screamed, and the day brightened again.

Giving a little shiver Seth continued on his way. Finding Marianne seemed a little less urgent now.

Seven

Colonel Hardy's trail hadn't been too hard to follow. He'd disembarked from his ship in London three years previously, had travelled to Edinburgh then moved into the house left to him by his mother's cousin until probate had been finalized. In fact, Hardy still owned the house, though it was now leased out to the family of a minister of the church, who was negotiating a purchase price.

From there, Adam Chapman was guided toward the solicitor who'd acted on Seth's behalf in the matter, and who had administered his relative's will.

Alistair Matheson gazed at Adam's card, then at the young man himself. A pair of sharp grey eyes met his. 'A detecting agency, is it? What exactly is your business with me?'

'I'm looking for a gentleman who goes under the name of Seth Hardy, former army Colonel. I'm given to understand that he's a client of yours.'

'Are you, then.' The solicitor tapped the card on the desk. 'I'm afraid I cannot help you.'

'Cannot, or will not?'

'My dear Mr...' and he gazed at the card. 'Chapman? Will not, because I have no proof that you are who you say you are – whom you are working for, or why you are working for them. And cannot, because of ethical considerations. My client's business is his own. No solicitor worth his salt would hand over information that should be properly kept confidential.'

'Even when that client has broken the law?'

'In what way has Colonel Hardy broken the law, sir?'

'It concerns a child, one John Charles Barrie, who he took into his care without the permission of the child's grandfather. You may have seen the notice I placed in the papers inquiring on his whereabouts.'

'I'm afraid not.'

Adam took a letter of introduction from his satchel and laid it on the desk. 'I'm representing Justice Sir Charles Barrie in this matter, who is the boy's grandfather and his only blood kin. The boy is also his heir.'

Shock came into the solicitor's eyes. 'Is there a warrant out for the Colonel's arrest? If there is that will be a different matter altogether.'

'No, sir, there is not. Judge Barrie is concerned that the man might flee abroad with the boy,

118

should he get wind of the search.'

'And if he sees the notices.'

'That's a risk we had to take, in the hope that the offer of a reward will prove to be effective.'

'A reward, you say. May I ask the sum involved?'

'It's a substantial one.'

Opening the letter Alistair Matheson scrutinized it, drumming his fingers on the desk. The smile he gave was shrewd. 'I'd like to confer with a colleague on this matter. Can you return next week, Mr Chapman?'

'I'm afraid not. I have another line of enquiry to pursue and I depart tomorrow.'

Matheson wasn't easily fooled. He raised an eyebrow, said, 'Another line of enquiry, is it? I wish you luck with it, sir. May I enquire what that line is?'

An out and out lie was sometimes justified. 'I have the address of someone Colonel Hardy soldiered with. They returned to England on the same ship.'

'Ah, I see.' The old man gave a faint smile. 'I have to say that I never saw the Colonel with a young boy, and neither did he mention one. Our relationship was one of business, and I found the man to be a little standoffish, if truth be told. I had very little to do with him, in fact, and he discouraged personal interaction between us.'

Something that rankled by the sound of it, Adam thought.

'I was friendly with his mother's cousin. We grew up together, so the Colonel's attitude towards me was rather surprising. His relative always talked fondly of the young man, and he fully expected him to sell the Edinburgh house and return to the English county where he was born and grew up. That has proved to be the case.'

'Which is where?'

'That I have yet to inform you of. Exactly how much did you say the reward was worth?'

Adam wrote a number on the solicitor's blotting pad, an indication of the reward offered for information received.

Matheson nodded, then took a card from his desk and placed it face down. He kept his finger on the card as he slid it gently across the polished surface of the desk. 'The address.'

He released it when Adam took a packet from his pocket and handed it to him. Adam sat patiently while the man counted the contents.

'All seems satisfactory.' The solicitor consulted his gold watch then looked up at him. 'If there's nothing else, good day to you, Mr Chapman.'

Adam didn't as much as flicker an eyelid as he was dismissed. He had no reason to linger, even if he'd liked the company he'd found himself in, which he didn't. Standing on the pavement outside the building he patted his other pocket. The information had only cost half of what he'd expected.

He gazed up at the castle looming over the city, and beyond that, the lowering sky that had begun to turn the remaining daylight to a leaden grey. He sniffed the air and smiled. Edinburgh smelled like rain. Indeed, the first heavy drop plopped on his face, quickly followed by another.

Upping his umbrella he headed down Princes Street to where his hotel was situated, a leisurely fifteen-minute walk from Leith Harbour. From there he intended to book a passage round the coast to Southampton – or on to Poole if he was lucky. He was in no hurry to repeat the interminable train journey.

His present case was interesting. Normally Adam wouldn't consider the objects of his searches as anything more than felons, and invariably they were. But he couldn't help wondering why a respectable law-abiding former army officer with means would lay himself open to a charge of child stealing ... unless he was the father of the boy, a possibility that had occurred to Adam before. Or perhaps the soldier had a certain behavioural weakness. Adam frowned at the thought. First he must make sure that the boy was living with Colonel Hardy, then he would judge what that relationship was. He'd rather take his client some encouraging news.

Adam arrived in Poole three days later. It was a compact town with bracing air and a colourful history of fishing and smuggling. The harbour was large, but pretty, with an island in the middle of it. The quay, which was a tangle of ships and masts bustled with activity, and supported the Guildhall with its elegant curving staircases at either side. The countryside surrounding the town was tinted with the shades of autumn and the climate was much more temperate after chilly Edinburgh.

He sought directions to Harbour House of a fisherman who was mending his nets, and who introduced himself as Rob.

Rob pointed. 'The heath be in that direction, Mister. You can't miss Harbour House, it be the only house there for miles. Used to belong to smugglers.'

'Do you know who lives there now?'

'Can't rightly say. Used to be the Honeyman family. But someone married into the family. I can row you there for a shilling. All you'll need to do is step ashore.'

The last thing Adam wanted was to step ashore on a deserted part of the heath, where he'd be conspicuous.'

'Thank you, but no. I don't intend to visit today. Is there anywhere I can hire a dinghy for tomorrow?'

'I reckon there is, at that. You can take that there old dinghy of mine. She's seaworthy enough for your purpose, but don't go out beyond the island. Five shillin' for the day. Do you reckon you have enough strength in your arms to row her?'

Adam grinned. 'I'm not quite as useless as I look. Nor am I stupid. Let's make that three shillings, I've already checked on the tides and will be here at ten.'

The fisherman looked surprised. 'Done. A deposit would be a sign of goodwill.' The fisherman's face puckered into wrinkles as he palmed the shilling Adam offered and slipped it into his pocket. He cackled before he went back to his mending.

The next day Adam used the tide to manoeuvre himself into the required position without too much effort. There was a cold breeze blowing off the water and he wore the fishy smelling windproof sou'wester and jacket the fisherman had offered him for an extra sixpence. If nothing else, it was a good disguise. Opening his bag he allowed the dinghy to drift, oaring it back into position every now and again. Then, making sure he wasn't observed, he took out a telescope and trained it on the house.

An hour later someone came in a gig. He carried a doctor's bag. The maid let him in. Adam saw him at an upstairs window a couple of times, and he came out fifteen minutes later, turned his vehicle round and headed back towards town.

Nothing was moving, and a lazy scribble of smoke rose from the chimneys. Taking out a sketching block, which was a good thing to have when carrying out surveillance work, he made a quick sketch of the house in its setting, admiring its solid lines. He was a competent artist. He was even better at detecting. He liked the hunt.

The sky was a seamless, even grey, with patches of blue. The wind lifted a haze from the surface of the water. He hunched into his smelly jacket, then glanced at his watch. Another hour had passed. He took an apple from his bag and bit into it, savouring the tart juice against his tongue. When he'd finished munching the fruit, he placed the glass against his eye again.

To his left a man appeared. He had an upright bearing as he strode along the path, his arms swinging. Adam knew a trained soldier when he saw one, and he certainly matched the description the Scottish minister had given him. But there was no boy with him. The man went into the house. He saw him come into the upstairs window, and for a moment he seemed to be staring straight at him. Then he stooped, and straightened, cradling a bundle in his arms. A baby! The man had a family. Considering the doctor's visit to the same room and the size of the bundle it was a fairly recent event. If there was a boy living there, he was most likely at a dame school.

Adam hesitated for a moment. What if he'd got the wrong man? It would be needless cruelty to get his client's hopes up. But he had to make sure.

He turned and rowed back towards the quay, relishing the task he was giving his back and arm muscles. The sun was directly overhead. By the time he'd got the dinghy back to its owner and had settled up, two hours had passed. The fisherman was leaning against his boat, puffing on his pipe. 'You didn't sink her, then.' He cackled at his own joke.

'And neither did I get stuck in the mud. Is there a school hereabouts?'

'It's up the road a way. It's owned and run by the merchants for their own children. Verger's wife runs a dame school for the poor. Then there's the grammar school for older boys. Thinking of moving your family here, are you? It's no good looking at Harbour House. It's been in the hands of the Honeyman family since it were an inn. The old man were in debt to a sea captain when he died, but the eldest daughter, Charlotte her name is, refused to move out. Said she'd shoot his ratty Thornton eyes out if he tried to evict them. 'Tis said she married the man who bought the clay pits, so she could stay there.'

The man's breath smelled of ale, which had obviously loosened his tongue. Adam let the fisherman ramble on.

'Year ago I recall it was. I hear tell she gave birth to twin babbies a week or so ago.'

'Twins?'

The man straightened up. 'If you want to keep women from interfering in men's business keep them pregnant, I say. I do hear that the younger girl has run off. Saw her myself, going aboard the *Samarand*. Pretty as a picture, she was.' He touched his hat. 'It's been right nice talking to you, sir. I'd best get off home to my woman. She do nag if I'm late home.'

The fisherman deserved a reward for the information, and Adam dropped a couple of florins into his hand. 'You've been most helpful. Here, buy your wife a ribbon or two for her bonnet.'

Staring at the coins in astonishment, Rob murmured. 'Thank you kindly, young sir.'

Adam made his way to the most likely of the schools, just as the bell was rung. The boys went off in all directions, punching each other and laughing. A couple of them were met by parents, and a bunch of four boys were chattering and laughing together, pushing and shoving at each other in the way boys did. He took up station in

125

a handily placed lane opposite when a gig arrived, driven by Hardy, who appeared to be a few years his senior.

'Pa!' one of the four boys shouted out, then waved and smiled. Seth Hardy jumped down from the cart.

Adam wanted a better look at both of them. He crossed to the opposite side of the road and, pretending to stumble, dropped his bag in front of Hardy and the boy. Pencils and other bits and pieces scattered across the ground.

'My pardon,' he said.

Both Hardy and the boy helped him pick the pencils up.

Adam offered a hand to Seth. 'My thanks.'

'I'm Seth Hardy ... this is my son, John Hardy.'

The boy held out his hand, saying politely, 'How do you do, sir.'

Adam shook it, thinking that the lad looked nothing like Seth Hardy, but he did resemble Charles Barrie to a certain extent, and had the same green hazel eyes. He also had a ready smile, and an easy manner that said he was perfectly at ease with his guardian. 'I'm very well, young sir, thank you.'

As Hardy lifted John into the gig, he said. 'Can I stand between your knees and take a turn on the reins, Pa?'

'When we get out of town, perhaps.'

'Did you find Aunt Marianne?'

Seth's smile was replaced by a worried look, and the boy's smile faded when he said, 'Not yet, but we will.' He nodded at Adam, flicked the reins and they moved off.

Adam watched them go with sadness in his eyes. There seemed to be nothing inappropriate in the relationship between the pair. It was obvious that the boy had a good home. The soldier also had a new family to support. For the first time in his life Adam felt guilty about what he was about to do. But child stealing was a misdemeanour, not a felony, so he'd probably get away with it if he had a good excuse, and he expected that he would have.

But it was not his job to judge Colonel Hardy. In fact, he rarely offered an opinion to his clients unless they asked for one. His task had been to find the child. He had, and would be paid well for both his time and expertise. While their faces were still fresh in his mind he quickly sketched both man and child, then turned and walked away.

The boy's question stuck in his mind, and the way both their smiles had faded.

'Marianne,' he whispered, and connected it to the fisherman mentioning that there were two sisters. Marianne Honeyman must be the younger one.

He was tempted to catch the man up and tell him what the fisherman had said, but it was really none of his business. No doubt they would know soon enough when the ship returned.

But what if she was kept on board against her will and disposed of?

Later, Adam wrote a note and signed it with a name he used sometimes. Just before he headed for the railway station, he placed it in the hands of a messenger to deliver to Harbour House.

Dear Colonel Hardy,

We are not acquainted, but yesterday I overheard that a young lady called Marianne Honeyman is missing from her hearth and home. A fisherman, in the course of a conversation, mentioned quite incidentally that he saw her go aboard a ship called *Samarand* on the day the young lady disappeared. I cannot, of course, verify that the information is correct, but for what it's worth, you may wish to question the man yourself, and indeed, follow this line of enquiry up. The fisherman's name was Rob.

Sincerely,
Henry Smith

'*Samarand*,' Charlotte cried out, and Major Mitchell jumped and gave a startled yelp. Gently massaging his scalp with her fingertips she shushed him, then lowered her voice. 'There, I knew Nick Thornton had stolen her away. I'll shoot him dead when he gets back. Just see if I don't.' She began to weep. 'My poor sister. Nick has ruined her to spite me, and it's all my fault. If I'd only married him in the first place, then this wouldn't have happened. We must ask a magistrate to issue a warrant for his arrest, and we'll have him thrown into jail when he returns.'

'Charlotte, this isn't about you, or about you taking revenge. For Marianne's sake it would be better if this business is hushed up. As for Thornton, there's no proof that he was involved in her disappearance in any way.'

Eyes furious she gazed up at him, prepared to argue. 'But the letter—'

'It was written by a stranger, and could be a mischief. Until we know for sure what has happened to Marianne we cannot accuse anyone of anything. What if Nick Thornton is innocent of wrongdoing?'

Charlotte wanted Nick to be the villain, it would give her a reason to keep hating him. 'Why are you always so reasonable, Seth?'

He laughed and ran a finger down her nose. 'I've learned to keep control of myself, and so should you.' He picked up her hand and bore it to his lips. 'Don't worry, I'll go and see this fisherman in the morning. If it were Marianne he saw going aboard, he should be able to remember what she was wearing.'

'It was her blue gown and bonnet and her Kashmir shawl.'

Jessica began to make agitated little noises. Seth picked her up and gently rocked her, saying softly, 'Hello, my sweet.' Jessica's eyes moved towards the sound of his voice and she fell quiet. 'You have a pretty face, just like your mother, but you don't sing as well.'

Seth loved his children. Charlotte could see it in his eyes when he gazed at them. She'd already known he'd be a good father when she'd married him. He was not like Nick, quick-tempered and tempestuous. Seth was a calm man – a reasonable man.

Worry had caused Charlotte's first thin trickle of milk to dry up at first. She'd felt a failure when Lucian had advised her that the wet nurse should feed both of her children. But still she persevered, and had been rewarded by painful lumps.

Fanny Clark had said. 'I mean no disrespect, Mrs Hardy. It's just that you're new at this, and so is the doctor. If you place cabbage leaves on your breasts it will help to draw the milk out.'

Charlotte had scoffed at first, but had allowed Fanny to bring her some cabbage. The cool green leaves were wondrously soothing, if nothing else. Charlotte liked Fanny, who'd been recommended by Lucian. She had two children of her own. Recently, her own baby had died a few days after birth, just as she'd finished suckling the first. Her husband had left to seek work elsewhere, and she lived with her parents.

Charlotte felt sorry for her. If anything happened to her own children she knew she'd never recover. When she relinquished Major Mitchell to Fanny she felt envious. But the fact remained. The children slept well when Fanny fed them. When Charlotte tried to feed them they were fractious.

Seth handed their daughter over to her, and kissed her forehead when Jessica nuzzled into her, seeking sustenance. 'Try not to feel too bad about it, Charlotte. It can't be helped. I'll be back later. I'm going to give the clay workers their wages and I'll take John with me.'

After Seth had gone Charlotte opened her bodice and prayed for milk. Jessica nuzzled hungrily, her face going back and forth until her mouth closed round the nipple. Charlotte drew in a breath as her daughter began to suck. The sensation was so pleasurable that it was almost painful, and it seemed to reach right down into her body. She closed her eyes and savoured the connection with her daughter. She desperately wanted to nourish her own children. After a while Jessica stopped sucking.

Opening her eyes Charlotte gazed down at her, almost in despair. Then she noticed that Jessica wasn't complaining, and that her bodice was damp on the other side. With a flicker of excitement she slid her hand under it. Milk was dripping from her breast.

The surge of triumph she felt was so real that it must have transferred to Jessica, for her daughter detached, her head turned and she looked up at her. Jessica belched, and a bubble of milk was expelled from her mouth and dribbled down her chin.

She exchanged a triumphant smile with Fanny. 'It worked.'

'Of course it did. What do doctors know? Put her to the other side now for a short time, then you can try Major Mitchell on it.'

Momentarily, Charlotte forgot her worry over Marianne as she practised her new skill.

Eight

After Seth dropped John off at school, he did as the note had advised him to and questioned the fisherman called Rob about Marianne.

'As I told the other fellow...'

'What other fellow?'

'I can't remember his name.'

'Henry Smith?' Seth suggested.

The fisherman scratched his head. 'No, that weren't his name. Can't rightly remember him giving one. I think he was looking around the area. Borrowed my dinghy and rowed across to look at Harbour House, he did, though I told him he wouldn't be able to buy it. He asked about schools.'

Seth's eyes sharpened at that. 'What did this man look like?'

'A young feller, he was, younger than you. But young or not, he had a look to him that said he was no fool. He was about your height, and well set up with grey eyes.'

The stranger at the school! Seth thought. The young man hadn't offered him a name either, but how had he known his army rank? Seth hadn't given it. He put the man to the back of his mind. No good puzzling over it now. He'd just wait and see if anything developed.

He concentrated on Marianne. 'I'm given to understand that you saw a young woman board the *Samarand* two weeks ago.'

'Were it that long ago? Dressed all in blue, she were, a basket over her arm, her ribbons flying in the wind and wearing a smile on her face like she was enjoying the day. As I told the other feller, she was as nesh as a spring day. But he didn't seem all that interested in her, even when I told him she lived out at Harbour House.'

Seth smiled. That sounded like Marianne, all right, but she was stronger than her appearance implied. 'Did you see the girl again?'

'I didn't see her step ashore, if that's what you're after knowing. The *Samarand* set sail not long after. Her master went striding on board about fifteen minutes after the girl. Wake up you lazy buggers, all hands on deck, he roared, and within minutes the crew were swarming over the ship like fleas on a dog's back.' He chuckled. 'He soon had that lot jumping, I can tell you. Off she went with the tide, and she ain't due back yet.'

'Where was she headed?'

America I reckon. She didn't load enough provisions for a longer voyage. She should be back in about five or six weeks. The Thornton ships takes turn and turn about, you see. Two American to one Australian run. It happens that *Daisy Jane* – that's old man Thornton's ship, is due back about the same time.'

That information seemed fairly conclusive to Seth, and he'd learned more than he'd bargained for. Firstly, that the man who'd dropped his pencils had been snooping for information about himself. Second, that he'd probably sent the note regarding Marianne's whereabouts. He doubted that the man was called Henry Smith though.

'Many thanks. He dropped a shilling into the man's hand then turned and strode towards the rig. He was not looking forward to telling Charlotte that her suspicions were probably correct, and that Marianne was most likely on board the *Samarand.*

From what the fisherman had said, Seth was willing to wager that Nick Thornton hadn't known she was on board. The girl must have hidden herself away. Why, for the adventure of it? And why hadn't she taken any personal belongings with her? Had she gone on board intending to visit someone, and met with an accident of some sort?

He hummed to himself as he headed back to Heath House, enjoying the morning sun on his back, trying to convince himself it was the most likely explanation. Despite the bad blood existing between Nick Thornton and Charlotte, Nick was enough of a gentleman to make sure Marianne would be looked after, Seth was sure.

That thought was followed by a more worrying thought. Then why hadn't Nick turned back to port with her? He must have known that Charlotte would have worried about her sister.

He supplied his own answer by saying out loud. 'Perhaps it's *because* Charlotte would have worried about her.'

Charles Barrie was thorough in his questioning

of Adam Chapman. 'Are you certain it was my grandson with the Colonel?'

'As I stated in my report, Sir Charles, I can only be sure there was a boy of your grandson's age with a man known as Seth Hardy. I saw them for but a moment and we shook hands. The boy was introduced as his son, John Hardy.'

'But you formed an impression there was a family likeness.'

'I did form that impression.' Adam handed him the sketches. 'I drew these likenesses. That one is Harbour House, where they live.'

But Charles Barrie's eyes were scrutinizing the sketch of the boy. 'Hmm ... unless I'm imagining it there is something of Jonathan about the lad.' Charles frowned. 'Did they suspect you were investigating them? I asked you not to approach them.'

'Not at all, Sir Charles. The meeting was entirely accidental, which was fortunate because I would have never got near the house unobserved. I'm given to understand that Mrs Hardy has recently given birth to twins.'

Caustically the old man said, 'Then she won't miss my grandson when he's removed from her care. In fact, she could lose her own children for a while if she knowingly helped her husband to keep the boy.'

Adam considered it harsh to punish the woman and her children, and he found it hard to keep the displeasure from his voice when he told him, 'You didn't strike me as the type of man who'd punish two newborn infants when they rely on their mother for their sustenance.'

Shame chased across Sir Charles's face and he blustered, 'Of course, I would have taken that into account.' He quickly tried to change the subject. 'How did the boy look?'

'Happy, and well cared for. He seems to have a good relationship with his ... with his step-father.'

'His abductor, you mean.'

'No, sir, I do not mean that. Seth Hardy's story has yet to be heard. He could be completely innocent of doing any wrong. I make it my business not to judge people.'

'And I do judge them, since that's my profession. I'm an expert at it.'

'Forgive me for being outspoken, but there's a difference between making a considered judgment, and judging with prejudice, especially when dealing with somebody you've never met. I understand that you're a man who wants to do the best for his grandson, but you're personally involved. That's bound to have a bearing on your thinking, and you are jumping to conclusions.'

'And if it were you in my shoes?'

'Right at this moment I'd be thankful that the child was alive and had been well cared for, especially since you didn't know of his existence until a few months ago.'

'Would you, by God,' Charles spluttered, then he laughed. 'For such a young man you're remarkably frank. Thank you, Mr Chapman. I will not need your services any longer so you can present your account. If the boy turns out to be my grandson I'll let you know.'

'I'd appreciate that.' He reached the door and remembered the reward money. He turned back and placed the package on the desk. At an inquiring quirk of Sir Charles's eyebrow, Adam said, 'It's what remains of the reward money. I didn't need it all.'

Charles smiled at that. 'I knew you were honest the first time I set eyes on you. Keep it ... call it a bonus for a job well done. Your services may be required again if the boy and I happen to be unrelated.'

Now it was Adam's turn to smile. 'I can almost guarantee that you are.'

After Adam left Bedford Square he made his way across London to Chiswick, using the available tram service for most of the way. He turned into Sutton Court Road, where he'd bought a fairly new terrace house a year before, shortly after his father's estate had been dealt with.

Celia's face appeared at the window before he had time to take out his key. His sister beamed him a wide smile, the door opened and she threw herself into his arms. Whirling her around he set her back on her feet. 'How's my favourite sister?'

'I'm well.' She practically dragged him into the house. 'I've missed you.'

'And I've missed you ... how's our mother?'

'She's in a mood today. Seeing you might cheer her up a bit.'

Dressed in black, Florence Chapman was seated before a stretcher frame by the window embroidering a coloured bird amongst some equally gaudy flowers. He guessed it was to replace the shabby-looking panel in the fire screen. She was good at needlework. He kissed her. 'Mother.'

Peevishly, she said, 'Where have you been all this time, Adam?'

'I was employed to find someone, and it took longer than I expected.'

'I don't see why you have to work at such a demeaning profession. You should take after your father and do something in the city. At least we had a bigger house to live in with staff. And we entertained.'

His father had entertained himself by gradually losing almost everything they had at the card tables. Adam had bought the best house that he could afford from what had been left. It was of a manageable size, even though it was inconveniently far from central London. He also rented a small suite of rooms in the business district. He sometimes slept there during the week, on a sofa in the back room, which was about the size of a dressing room.

'There's no reason why you can't entertain.'

'I have no friends here.'

'Then make some, Mother. You must meet other women at church. As I recall you used to enjoy your card parties.'

'They won't be the same as my old friends.'

'How will you know if you don't bother to try and make any?'

'I want to go back to where we used to live.'

An edge of impatience crept into his voice. 'You can't. May I remind you that father died leaving us without means to pay his debts.'

She heaved a sigh. 'Oh, you always blame him ... but then, you never did get on with him.'

Neither had his mother, but it would be unkind of him to remind her of the fact.

'I suppose you're doing your best, Adam.'

Considering he'd had to give up his education in order to earn enough money for them all to survive on, yes, he was doing his best. 'We have a roof over our heads and food. And you have a housemaid.'

'But only two days a week.'

Celia broke in, 'Our housemaid is very good, and two days is enough to keep the house clean and the laundry done. I can do the rest.' She kissed the top of his head. 'If it wasn't for you we'd starve, Adam dearest. I, for one, am grateful. Mother, you should be ashamed of yourself.'

'And so should you be. If you'd accepted Edward Rayburn when your father was alive we'd all be wealthy now.'

Adam felt sick at the thought. 'Celia was only sixteen at the time and Edward Rayburn was seventy.'

'He's since died, and Celia would have become a wealthy widow. As it was, it all went to his miserable sister. What have you been doing all this time, Adam – where have you been?'

'Looking for somebody's grandson. I went to Edinburgh first, then down to the harbour town of Poole, in Dorset. It's very pretty there.'

'Did you find the child?' Celia asked.

He smiled at her. 'Yes, I did find him. I'll tell you all about it later.' He welcomed input from Celia, who was interested in his chosen profession and liked to unravel a puzzle as much as he did. At least they wouldn't be constantly interrupted by their mother's caustic comments then. She'd be in bed.

'In the meantime I have a gift for your birthday.' He pulled a small jewellery case from his pocket and handed it to Celia. Her eyes shone with excitement as she opened it to reveal a silver pendant with a garnet set in a circle of seed pearls. He took it from her and fastened it around her neck. 'I wish I could have bought you something better.'

'It's lovely, Adam, thank you so much. I'll treasure it.' She kissed his cheek. 'I'll go and make us some tea. I'm looking forward to hearing about your recent case.'

His mother looked up from her stitching. 'Well I'm not. Your father and I had such great hopes for you, Adam, and look what happened. You became an investigation agent. How can you stand working with such unsavoury people?'

He gave a faint smile. Unsavoury? His clients were hardly that. Most were discreet, well respected and wealthy – people like the judge. It had been a struggle at first, but business was picking up via word of mouth, which was the best advertising to have. Adam intended to secure a better life for them all eventually. However, he didn't argue with his mother, but decided to allow her to have the last word.

Charles fetched his hat and cane, and even though he wasn't feeling well he made his way by foot to Edgar Wyvern's chambers. News of his grandson had given him a new lease of life, and although he'd been warned that excitement was bad for a man of his age, he encouraged the feeling on this occasion.

The air outside was diffused by a thin mist that promised to become a thick fog by nightfall. On several occasions Charles was obliged to stop when it caught at his throat, and he was overtaken by a coughing fit which left his throat sore.

Edgar wasn't surprised to see him. 'From that smile on your face I imagine you've received some positive news.'

'I most certainly have. Can you take time off to accompany me to Poole, Edgar? I intend to confront this Colonel Hardy.'

'I daresay my clerk can rearrange my appointments to suit, but confrontation is not the path to take, since we don't yet know the circumstances. A letter informing the man of the situation would be the proper way to act.'

'I don't think you understand, Edgar. I intend to bring John back with me. As his grandfather my jurisdiction concerning the child is clear.' Taking a handkerchief from his pocket, he mopped the perspiration from his face.

Edgar gazed closely at him. 'You don't look well, Charles.'

'It's an inopportune moment to be taken ill. I appear to be running a fever and my throat is sore. I'm probably developing a cold.' He began to cough and held his handkerchief to his mouth.

Edgar poured him a brandy. 'Here, drink this while I go and tell my clerk to find you a cab.

Then you'd best get home to bed. A couple of weeks won't make much difference. The boy can wait until you're better.'

Nine

Marianne had never been out of England, and the sight of the gently sloping hills of Boston and the bustle of the docks was an exciting novelty.

They anchored outside. Eventually a boat arrived carrying a medical officer, and a man climbed aboard. The crew was given a clean bill of health and the *Samarand* was allowed to dock.

The ship's cargo was unloaded.

To her disappointment Nick told her to stay on board when the crew went ashore. 'I run a dry ship, and they deserve a drink. A tavern isn't the place for a woman, neither are the docks. I'd be obliged if you'd stay in your cabin. Sam can keep you company until I get back.'

He stopped to exchange a few words with the watch-keeper, and they both looked her way. When Nick waved and followed the crew down the gangplank she thought he'd be drinking with them, but he returned before too long with packages under his arm and a grin on his face that made her smile. There wasn't a trace of liquor about him. He dismissed Sam with, 'Off

142

you go, lad. You know where your shipmates will be. Behave yourself, I don't want to have to explain to your mother why I had to bail you out of the lock-up.'

Sam grinned widely.

Nick placed the packages on the table and said, 'These are for you. I've booked you into a ... hotel overnight, where you can take a bath. An acquaintance of mine will make sure you're looked after.'

Her eyes began to shine. 'A proper bath?'

He gave an odd sort of a chuckle. 'What other sort is there? And we'll have dinner afterwards. You'd best get changed, a woman wearing trousers will be frowned upon when we go ashore.'

The hotel looked like a large house, and it bore no sign of advertising itself as such. Inside it was predominantly red velvet and gold tassels, but the bath was a luxury that she appreciated. Marianne sank up to her neck in the warm, scented water and allowed it to caress her body as she gazed round at the room. It had a wide bed, and above the bedstead hung a picture of a naked woman draped in a diaphanous cloth.

'Lor,' she murmured, her eyes widening, 'the hussy is leaving nothing to the imagination.'

To her amazement a maid attended to her needs. Her hair was washed and styled. The gown Nick had bought her to wear was pretty with blue cornflowers on a cream background, the sleeves and bodice trimmed with lace. She blushed when she saw the underwear, a froth of stiff petticoats to wear in lieu of a hoop. Then there were the silk drawers, and a corset of white

143

satin and lace that was more decorative than useful, since her waist was already small.

She blushed again when Nick arrived, looking dashing in a black suit and gold patterned waistcoat. He'd also bathed and his whiskers were gone. He looked her up and down then gazed into her eyes and chuckled.

She giggled. 'Say one word about those garments you bought me and I'll strangle you with my bare hands.'

'My dear Aria, you're a delight.'

She laughed. 'Which is not something you can be accused of, Nick. You're an out and out rogue.' He looked pleased by her description of his character and she couldn't be cross with him. 'May I ask you something?'

'That depends what it is.'

Her eyes went to the picture hanging over the bed. 'Is this a proper hotel?'

'If you need to ask I think you're well aware that it's not. If the picture shocks you, I'll cover it. Let me just say this. Mrs Crawford rents out rooms and service for people in need of it. She is high class, and discreet.'

Marianne began to suspect that his attentions towards her were dishonourable. 'You mean she rents rooms to businessmen who need to meet their lovers somewhere private.'

'Sometimes she provides them with a companion as well ... but this is not something we should be discussing. If you'd prefer to go back to the ship I'll be happy to escort you. I haven't got designs on you if that's what you think. I just thought you'd enjoy the facilities.'

She felt guilty at suspecting him of having an ulterior motive, but contrarily, was miffed that he didn't. 'Why not?'

'Why not what?'

'Why haven't you got designs on me? Am I unattractive?'

He gazed at her, beginning to smile. 'Ah, you truly have the mind of a woman. You know damned well that you're an attractive baggage, as you are aware that I lied. I do most definitely have designs on you. If you think I'm not having a problem keeping my hands off you, think again.' Folding his arms across his chest he shoved his hands under his armpits. 'There, now you're safe.'

She blushed and placed her palms against her cheeks. 'Now you're mocking me.'

His hands fell to his side. 'I'll try not to. Whatever I feel, or imagine when I look at you, it's all about being a man. However, I do have some respect for you, Aria.'

'What do you imagine?'

Laughter huffed from him. 'Men's thoughts.'

Her cheeks fired up even more, though she wanted to laugh. 'I had no idea you felt attracted by me. Is that because I'm Charlotte's sister, and remind you of her?'

'Is it hell! I haven't given Charlotte a thought lately, and you're similar, but not alike. My uncle tells me you greatly resemble your mother.' Taking her hands in his, he said, 'Stop thinking so little of yourself. You have your own desirable qualities and I want you for yourself. I know you're hankering after Lucian Beresford but you don't stand a chance with him. Not then, and definitely not now. You haven't got enough money to buy his interest to start with. Besides, he's too cold-blooded and clinical for a woman like you.'

Her eyes widened. She hadn't thought much about Lucian lately. She hadn't allowed herself to think about the scandal she would have to face, either, or his reaction to it. Come to think of it she hadn't considered how Charlotte and Seth would regard it. Uneasily, she remembered Charlotte's vendetta against Nick because of something his uncle had done. What if they threw her out? She'd have nowhere to go. Nick was probably right about Lucian, too. Still, she must at least give them a chance to believe her.

'I'm sorry, Nick, I cannot be the woman you want. I might be able to convince Charlotte that I was innocent of any wrongdoing, even after what my mother did, but if I enter into a relationship with you, although it would be exciting, no doubt, the punishment would be too severe.'

'All your mother did was fall in love with my uncle, and he with her.'

'The consequence of that relationship was a child that killed her.'

He said quite gently, 'The cause of it was the abuse your mother suffered at the hands of your father. If the child had lived I imagine your father would have accepted it as his own. If he hadn't, my uncle would have given her a home.'

She forgot that Nick had been in the same situation. 'How awful to be a child born of sin – one who nobody wants or loves.'

'It is, but I was lucky to have my aunt and uncle to take me in. I'm not asking you to become my mistress, you know.'

When her mouth fell open he reached out, placed his finger under it and shut it again. There was a touch of devilment about his smile. 'Yes, that was a genuine proposal of marriage, though I planned it very quickly.'

She believed him. 'I doubt if Charlotte would allow it.'

'You're old enough to make up your own mind, Aria. We're laying over for a few days while repairs are made – we're shipping a little water and a couple of seams need caulking. We can make our vows at that little chapel up the road.'

'Is that legal?'

'We'll have witnesses, and a certificate.'

'Do you want to marry me?'

'I wouldn't have asked you if I didn't. I intend to give up the sea and open a retail establishment after my next journey to Australia. You can help me.'

'What sort of retail establishment?'

'Does it matter?'

'Well, I wouldn't like to sell food, since it attracts rats, and I hate rats.'

'No. I meant a large emporium that has different departments and sells different goods, clothing that's already made, pots and pans, nursery furniture and perambulators. My uncle scoffs at the idea at the moment, but I know he'll bring back exotic goods that can to be sold at a profit once I've started out and he's grown used to the idea. Japanese pots and ornaments et cetera.'

'Can I have a little time to think about it?'

'About what, becoming my wife or helping me to run a shop?' Nick's eyes were dark against hers, and his amusement was plain to see. He was sure of himself, expecting her to say no. He gazed at his watch. 'You have ten minutes, after which I withdraw the offer. But while you're thinking, perhaps this will help you make up your mind.' He took her face between his hands and his mouth sought hers with a persistent gentleness that took her breath away.

She'd read him wrong, she thought. He was expecting her to say yes. Then she became incapable of thinking, and the need she felt to experience physical love was almost over-whelming. It was exciting. He was exciting.

When he finished kissing her he said gruffly, 'Can I assume it's a yes, then? It will be all right, really. I'd never hurt you.'

She laughed because the only alternative was to cry, but it was a watery affair. 'You had me convinced in two minutes.'

'And you wouldn't mind being married to a shopkeeper, when being the wife of a sea captain would be a much more romantic occupation?'

She touched his cheek. 'At least I wouldn't be lonely all the time and wondering if you were safe.'

For a moment he looked vulnerable and Mari-anne saw the motherless boy in him emerge as he instinctively turned his face against her caress. 'That's the nicest thing anyone's ever said to me.'

Her heart slowly churned and a warm ember settled in her chest. At the same time she wanted to cry. Lor, how could any woman resist him?

He drew her hands against his chest and a pulse beat against her palms. 'You know, I'll make good use of those remaining eight minutes when we're wed.'

'You could make use of them now.'

His eyes flew opened. 'Now?'

'Oh, don't look so shocked, Nick. I'm curious.'

A smile played around his mouth. 'You were always curious about everything, as I recall. Are you sure this is what you want?'

At that moment she'd never wanted anything more. What was the matter with her that she could cast aside her feelings for Lucian so easily, and for someone as brash as Nick Thornton?

He gazed into her eyes, his expression unreadable. 'There's something I want to say first. We'd best keep this, and our marriage, quiet until after I return from my next voyage to Australia. I don't want to let my uncle down because he's been good to me, and won't be able to replace me at short notice. I'll tell him that I'm relinquishing command of *Samarand* after the Australian run. I'll be gone for about five months. I also don't want you to be at loggerheads with your sister and her husband because of your accident. My guess is that they'll give you a lecture about your behaviour, then pretend you were visiting your elderly aunt to try and hush it up.'

'My elderly aunt died ten years ago. Father

was furious because Constance Jarvis was left a wealthy widow, and apart from a small bequest for Charlotte and myself, she left her fortune to the orphan's home she'd founded. Our father soon lost our legacies at the gambling table.'

Nick was right though, Charlotte would probably resurrect Aunt Constance for the occasion, and they'd try and hush her adventure up. All the same, Charlotte would never forgive her when she was informed of the marriage. Nick had always belonged to her sister, she was used to his adoration and she wouldn't relinquish it happily, even if she had married Seth.

But now he'll belong to me, and I'll make him love me just as much – or even better. Marianne thought fiercely, and without any notion how she'd make such an event happen.

She smiled. 'All hell will break loose I expect, so I'd rather we told them together. I can keep it a secret for a few months. And yes, Nick ... that is what I want.'

'Then we'd best wed as soon as possible. I do happen to have a licence.'

'But—'

'But nothing, Aria my sweet. You're in enough trouble as it is. I said I'd never hurt you, and I meant it. There will be a ring on your finger before your curiosity is satisfied. Fetch your shawl and we'll go and find someone who will tie the knot for us. It shouldn't be too hard.'

The marriage was performed by a reverend who was willing to cut corners, and it was witnessed by four complete strangers.

'Will you, Marianne Elizabeth Honeyman...'

'I will.'

'Will you, Nicholas Alexander Thornton...'

He gazed down at her and smiled. 'I will.'

The ring was placed on her finger and Nick kissed her with infinite tenderness – as if he'd always loved her, instead of her sister.

They found themselves outside the chapel afterwards, gazing at each other. His smile had a satisfied edge to it as he gazed at the gold band she wore on her finger. It had two hands clasped. They'd bought it from a goldsmith's shop on the way, along with a chain to hang around her neck, with the ring attached, when they got back on board.

'Well, Mrs Thornton, shall we go back to our hotel room and eat dinner?'

She suddenly felt doubtful. What had she done?

'It will be all right, I promise,' he said again, as if he'd read her thoughts.

The champagne Nick had given her before dinner had made her head spin. He'd chuckled when she giggled, said, 'We'd better get some food into you.'

After eating ship's food for three weeks the dinner tasted delicious. A delicate soup was followed by succulent chicken surrounded with roast vegetables. There was fresh fruit, trifle and cream served as a pudding. The meal was served by a young black boy.

There came a knock at the door. It was a woman, elegant, with fair hair pulled back into a bun. 'Good evening, Captain Thornton, I'm here to enquire if the arrangements I made were satisfactory.'

Nick's smile was friendly, but impersonal. 'Yes thank you, Mrs Crawford, and the dinner was delicious. Will you join my wife and I in a glass of champagne? We're celebrating our recent marriage.'

The woman's eyes, which were as green as her gown, flicked to Marianne's ring finger. There was something amused about the smile she gave. 'Your bride has a shy innocence to her that's like a breath of fresh air. She's very lovely, and unexpected. Just half a glass for me please, Captain.'

Mrs Crawford lifted her glass in a toast. 'Congratulations to you both, I hope you'll be very happy together, Mrs Thornton.'

'Thank you. I'm sure we will.'

Mrs Thornton! The name alone would set Charlotte fuming for a year when she found out, she thought.

'If there's anything else you need for your comfort ring the bell, otherwise you won't be disturbed.' She turned to the boy. 'Clear the dinner things away, please, William.'

After they'd gone Nick filled her glass and his own and placed them on the table next to the armchair. The fire had been lit, for the days were warm and the nights chilly at this time of year. Nick made himself comfortable and pulled her on to his lap. 'Sit there and have your champagne.'

'It will make me giggle.'

He dipped a finger in it, rubbed it gently

against her lower lip then licked it off.

'How did you happen to have that licence?' she asked.

'Mrs Crawford knows a judge. She arranged it all.'

'So you arranged it in advance. Why?'

'You have a tendency to do things on impulse, so I decided it would be better to arrange things in advance just in case you said yes then changed your mind. You're a woman, after all. And that's why I only gave you ten minutes. If you'd thought past the adventure of it you might have decided against the marriage.'

She took a sip from her drink, then a gulp. She gazed at him. 'You have a strange and devious way of going about things, Nick Thornton.'

'I never promised to be perfect, and I didn't want you to slip through my fingers.'

She didn't know what to make of that statement, but smiled because it made her feel as if he cared for her. 'Oh, I see.'

She held her glass to his lips and he sipped. They finished the glass between them. Marianne felt relaxed when Nick took the glass from her fingers and set it aside. He began to undo the buttons on her bodice, then he kissed the hollow of her throat.

'I feel nervous.'

The soft chuckle against her ear weakened her knees, 'I know. You're quivering like a mouse waiting to be pounced on and swallowed by the cat.'

'You're not purring.'

'But I will be soon ... and so will you.'

153

When her gown slid down to her ankles she thought in desperation, Oh, God, she was down to her petticoats. And was that his tongue...? The ineffectual hand she placed against her bared breast was carried away and placed between his thighs.

'You have absolutely no regard for a woman's finer feelings.'

He plucked the pins from her hair and laughed. 'I most certainly do. Just tell me what those fine feelings are when I get to them. Do you want me to stop?'

'Yes ... no ... I don't know.'

He kissed the swell of her breast. 'Do you like that ... tell me.'

'Yes.'

'And this...'

She nipped the end of his ear and his hand moved down. 'What about this?'

'I love it ... don't tickle ... no, don't stop! Would you like me to pose in a wisp of cloth like the woman in the picture.'

'Later perhaps.' He laughed and swelled against her hand and she tentatively explored what she discovered. Now his purr was more like a growl. There was a dampness growing in her and her body was reacting wildly in all sorts of places. 'Yes, Nick ... yes. I like that.'

He picked her up and carried her to the bed. Before her startled eyes he stripped naked, tossing each garment aside. He was lean and well muscled, standing proud. Her eyes widened as she thought, Lor ... he's as big as a horse! Well, perhaps not quite. Well, Miss Prim and Proper, you never expected this when you stepped aboard the *Samarand*.

He unlaced her corset, tossing it with her pantalettes in the general direction of his own clothes.

He gazed down at her. She'd crossed one arm modestly across her breasts, and placed the cupped hand of the other, lower down.

He drew her arms aside and pinned them over her head with one hand. 'You didn't think that your token attempt at modesty was going to stop me, now did you, Mrs Thornton?'

She grinned at him. Being naked together was actually quite liberating. It made her feel as though she was a hussy. 'I admit, I expected you to put up more of a fight, Captain. I'm sure I'm blushing all over.'

He laughed when she gave a nervous giggle. 'Now, my delicious little morsel of woman. Let's see how long I can make you purr for,' and his head dipped, and his mouth closed over hers. He kissed her long and tenderly, so she thought she might die from that particular pleasure, alone. He moved on. Kissed her again – and again ... Her cry at the fulfillment of the most ultimate of pleasures came a little while after, and it was lost in his.

Land had been sighted. They were nearing the end of the journey. Generally the weather had been kind to them, except they'd caught the tail end of a storm halfway, a series of squalls that had sent the ship reeling, and had shredded the flying jib and the lower fore-topsail. Aria had coped easily with the storms, thank goodness.

Nick had gone to the cabin to make sure she was comfortable. She'd grinned at him, dispelling any thought he might have had that she might succumb to seasickness. The ship had canted steeply and she'd let go of the table and slid into his arms, her eyes sparkling with excitement. 'Can I join you on deck, Nick?'

Even though she seemed to be as sure-footed as a goat he couldn't risk it. 'I'm sorry, my sweet. I haven't got time to look after you and you might get washed overboard, especially if you keep sliding down the deck like that.'

He'd kissed her, and she'd clung to him for a moment, her eyes blue and intense. She'd touched his lower lip with her forefinger.

'Take care, my love,' she'd said, and those four words had sent all his defences tumbling down, and they'd painted him with such tenderness that he was warmed like a glass of amber wine.

Nick fully expected a delegation to be waiting for him ashore. He hoped it wasn't the constables, and he hoped Charlotte wasn't there. He didn't think he could stand any of her threats, or her tantrums.

It had been a lucrative run in more ways than one. His hold was full of tobacco and he had himself a wife – and Aria was a delight. He smiled when he heard her singing. Even though they'd kept up a pretence for the benefit of the crew, he'd managed to find time to enjoy what she had to offer on at least one occasion on the way back, and though it had been a hurried affair, the thought that they might get caught together had added a touch of spice to the act. Afterwards, she'd laughed, and so had he.

Six months without her suddenly seemed far too long, and he toyed with the idea of taking her with him. But sailing to Australia took far longer, and was more arduous. *Samarand* was lacking in any real comfort and he didn't want to risk it. Too, he needed this last run to earn him enough money with which to retire from the sea, and to give his uncle time to find another master for her.

Coming round Brownsea island he couldn't see the *Daisy Jane*, but that wasn't unusual. He moved the glass to the quay. A man who resembled Seth Hardy was stood there, but he couldn't see anyone else. He'd already said goodbye to Aria, but he handed the wheel to the first mate. He needed to kiss her one more time. 'Take her in. I'm going to see if Miss Honeyman is ready.'

Aria was, and she slid her arms around his neck when he entered the cabin. 'I can't bear the thought of not seeing you for six months, Nick.'

'We'll manage.' He tipped up her chin and kissed her. 'Seth is waiting on the quay. I can't see anyone else.'

On deck the first mate was bellowing out orders and the crew would be scrambling over the rigging like monkeys. Nick held Aria against him. She was trembling. He gave her a last hug. 'Hold fast. Just remember that Charlotte is your sister. Let her blame me if that's what she wants, and don't defend me too much else they'll smell a rat.'

157

'Shall I come up on deck?'

'No, wait here. I'll bring Seth down, so he can see the sleeping arrangements for himself.'

She giggled. 'I hope not. Lor ... I feel quite debauched by you. Imagine spending my wedding night in a house of ill repute. What an experience! Whatever happens, I'll never forget it. Shall I record it in my diary when I get home?'

'Do, but you don't need to record the memory of you trying to cover yourself with your hands because it will stay in my mind for ever.' She blushed when he grinned at her.

They nearly fell over as the ship scraped against something. Nick swore. 'I'd better get up on deck.' He gazed down at her, suddenly awkward. He hadn't expected it to be so hard to part with her. Running a finger down her nose he gruffed, 'We didn't even say goodbye properly. I'll miss you.'

'I'll be out on the heath tomorrow morning. We could say goodbye then. Can you get there?'

'I'll come in the dinghy. Keep a look out for me.' He turned and left, closing the door behind him.

Seth was relieved to find his sister-in-law relatively unharmed. In her usual uninhibited manner she gave him a hug and chattered on at him.

'Seth, you'll never guess where I've been ... all the way to Boston and back ... thank goodness you guessed where I was. Nick was so kind. He gave me his own cabin to sleep in, and just kept

158

the bit with the door and desk to eat his dinner at. Did he tell you about my shoulder, and about the cut on my head? There was a terrific lot of blood. It had to be stitched up and I fainted dead away.' She didn't give him time to answer. 'We sailed into a horrible storm on the way back and I was absolutely terrified. The waves were as high as a house and everything on the ship creaked and groaned as if it was about to split into pieces. Nick was an awful bully when I was discovered in the hold. He threatened to toss me overboard. Of course, he wouldn't really have done that.'

'You'll never know how close to it you got on occasion,' Nick said, making her sound like a child he couldn't wait to get rid of. 'A ship is no place for a woman.'

Seth exchanged a sympathetic smile with the captain. 'I'm sorry she was such a nuisance.'

'I understand you've become a father, Hardy. Congratulations.'

Seth felt no undercurrent of rancour in Thornton's handshake, but trod carefully nevertheless. 'Under the circumstances, that's kind of you.'

'Under the circumstances it's a waste of time crying over spilled milk. There's no reason why we shouldn't be friends.'

Seth's eyes missed nothing in the cabin arrangements, and he saw nothing suspicious. Thornton had simply divided the cabin roughly in half with a canvas wall, to afford Marianne some privacy. It wasn't ideal, but he didn't see anything that roused his suspicions under the circumstances. But had to ask. 'Where did you sleep?'

'I turned and turned about with the first mate. I can send for him if you like.'

Seth shrugged. 'I promised Charlotte I'd talk to you, Nick. Do you have the time?'

'Not at the moment. I have cargo to unload, and must pay the crew so they can go ashore. You must allow me to buy you a drink. How about the day after tomorrow in the Crown and Anchor shortly after noon? We can discuss what's on your mind then?'

Seth nodded. 'See you there.'

Marianne cut in. 'How are the babies, Seth? I expect they're grown.'

He couldn't hide his smile. 'They're a contented pair, and they're smiling now.'

'And John?'

'He's missed you, and will be glad to see you back.'

'I bought him a present in Boston to make up for it. It's a replica of a clipper ship. Oh, yes ... I've just remembered that I had to borrow some money from Nick. I needed something to wear. And I owe him for a new set of clothes he had to buy the cabin boy, since I was forced to borrow his Sunday best trousers and a shirt.'

'You wore trousers?'

'My gown got all bloody from the cut on my head, and none of the seamen wore female clothing that I could borrow. Then when we got to Boston Nick bought me—'

'You needn't explain any further,' he said with a grin. 'Tell me about it on the way home, and I'll settle up with Captain Thornton tomorrow.'

160

His sister-in-law picked up her basket, then her parcel of clothes, which she handed to him to carry along with the model ship. She turned to Nick. 'Thank you so much for your excellent care of me, Captain Thornton, and thank Sam for looking after me.'

There was a gleam in his dark eyes. 'It was my pleasure to be of service to you, Aria. Be careful where you tread on the way out. The deck will be littered with ropes.'

Various members of the crew waved and called out to her as she left.

Seth said, 'Why did Nick Thornton call you Aria?'

'It's the middle part of my name. He's always called me that. He's the only one who does.'

'You like him, don't you?'

'Yes, I've always liked him. Nick is honest and straightforward.' When he wasn't being devious and bossy, and totally adorable she thought, and grinned.

Ten

Lying to Charlotte the next morning was harder than Marianne had expected. Charlotte wanted to know every little detail, so Marianne stuck to answering the questions and avoiding the truth.

'I told you. I went on board to take his length of silk back. I was looking at the seagull on top of the mast and I tripped and fell into the hold and was rendered unconscious.'

'You were on top of the mast?'

She would have been if Nick had allowed her to go up there when they were in Boston, but he'd given her a quelling look and put his foot down with, 'Definitely not.'

She grinned. 'I was on deck with my face tipped up and fell backwards. When I woke we were at sea. My arm had been jerked right out of its socket. It hurt something cruel, and the ship's cook held me down, while Nick jerked it back in. The pain of it made me cry, and Nick was sorry he'd hurt me, but he said that was the only way it could be done.'

Charlotte shuddered. 'Why didn't Nick bring you back?'

'I wasn't found until we'd been at sea for two days. He said it was too much bother, and would cost him money.'

Charlotte frowned. 'He would have done that on purpose, just to make me worry.'

Marianne had wondered about that herself, since four days out of his life surely couldn't have cost the shipping company much. But it didn't seem to matter now, and she felt compelled to defend him. 'Nick isn't as mean as you make him out to be. In fact, he was very kind to me.'

'Oh ... you don't really know him, Marianne. He was my friend, not yours. He always considered you to be a nuisance because I had to look after you, which meant that we couldn't go where we wanted, or do what we wanted.'

Marianne knew him better than Charlotte would ever imagine, and she churned with longing for him.

'Where did you get the silk from?'

'Nick bought it for you, to make a wedding gown with. He had it with him on that day. When you sent him packing he dropped it.'

Charlotte smiled at the thought. 'Poor Nick, but it was his own fault. That was ages ago. And you had it all this time without telling me?'

'I didn't think you'd want it. He told me to keep it when I tried to give it back.'

'It was meant for me in the first place. I can use it to make some garments for the babies.'

Marianne gasped. 'It's expensive silk.'

'I don't care. Obviously he doesn't want it back.'

'But Nick gave it to me.'

'It was mine first, besides, what do you want it for? Where is it, in your room?' She rose. 'It's

163

time my babies were fed anyway. You can come up with me if you like.'

'I'll see them later. I'm going out on the heath. I've missed it so.'

'Wear something warm, then. There's a cold wind coming off the water.'

Earlier she'd packed a basket with food, and there was ginger beer in an earthenware bottle.

Marianne gazed out over the harbour, looking for a dinghy as she hurried along the path. The wind whipped colour into her cheeks and her hair unravelled. After several weeks at sea, at first the ground seemed to rise up to meet her feet, but now it was solid beneath them.

There were one or two small sailboats on the harbour, their sails fattened with wind as they skimmed over the dagger-edged white-crested wavelets. The clouds momentarily thinned out to expose a sun flash from a shiny surface. Nick's telescope perhaps?

She waved just in case, taking the precaution to look behind her first to make sure she hadn't been observed. But she'd left the house behind her. All she could see was part of the roof and the chimney tops, the fiery dragon's breath of smoke they exhaled being whipped by the wind and shredded in all directions. Harbour House didn't feel like her home any more. It belonged to Seth and Charlotte and their children.

But then, it had always belonged to Charlotte. The house was her sister's security, and she loved the place with a passion – loved it enough to have sold herself to a complete stranger and break the heart of the man who'd loved her constantly since childhood. And despite Charlotte's denials, Marianne knew that her sister would have taken Nick as a last resort.

But Charlotte's loss had been her gain. Marianne wanted nothing more than to make her home with Nick, wherever that home might be, tossed about on the stormy sea or nestled in the dusty back room of a shop while he made a success of his life in business ashore.

She began to run along the winding path as the boat began to veer towards the shore, the small company pennant at the mast fluttering. Up ahead was a small inlet that the boat was heading for. They reached the inlet together and he ran the boat up on to the sand, tied the sail against the mast, then attached the dinghy to a gorse bush, which clutched the chalky heath soil with a firm grip. Placing her basket down Marianne hurled herself into his arms, out of breath and laughing, and he held her against his warmth, swung her around, then set her on her feet and soundly kissed her.

She kissed him back as though she hadn't seen him for weeks, and realized how hard the next few days would be. She hugged him, loath to let him go. 'Have you absolutely got to go away?'

'Yes ... I must. My uncle has been like a father to me. I can't just walk away from him. The time will soon pass, my love. Then we'll be together.'

Her heart leapt at the unconsciously uttered endearment. She was like a bird, pecking up crumbs of scattered affections and gaining sustenance from them.

When she gazed up at him Marianne knew that

she'd fallen in love with him, and a smile touched her lips. She'd give him that thought to take with him. She'd brought it with her, a locket brooch – a miniature of herself as a child of six. It had been a birthday gift, gifted to her by her mother a few weeks before her death. At the back, curled round under the glass was a snip of Marianne's hair. When the locket was opened an inscription was found inside: her name etched on one side and the words 'dearly beloved' on the other.

She pinned the locket inside his waistcoat pocket and said, 'There, that's a keepsake to remember me by.'

Through the flying strands of her hair he found her scalp and nuzzled a kiss there. 'You're impossible to forget, angel.'

Another crumb, reinforcing the last one. She needed him to love her, but how much time that would take she couldn't even hazard a guess. In the meantime she'd feast on the crumbs he scattered and gain strength from them until she could have the whole cake.

'Let's go up to the copse. It's more sheltered there, and I've brought us something to eat,' she said.

'Good ... I could eat a skinned cat.'

'I'm afraid I haven't got a cat. There's some cold chicken and ham, boiled potatoes, bread, cheese and apple pie. And there's fresh water in the chalk stream to wash it down with.'

Her ear was rewarded with his chuckle whispered against it. 'It sounds like a feast.' Picking up the basket he took her hand in his and they headed for the privacy of the copse.

It was dark under the canopy of pines, and the ground was thick with rusty coloured needles, so their footsteps were absorbed into the silence and left no mark on the forest floor. The bracken was brown and ragged, its roots settling into the long sleep until spring, when it would stir to the sun and unfurl triumphant.

They settled where the undergrowth was thickest, not far from the stream, and they talked and ate. Then when they had finished talking they made love, oblivious to anything but the moment. Afterwards she laid her head against his heart and listened to it beat while he stroked her hair. Then when their tumultuous bodies were once again quiet, he braided her hair again, his fingers flying as he wove the strands in and out.

'There, you're tidy again,' he said, then stood and pulled her to her feet. 'Now I must go, before the tide leaves me stranded.'

'Will I see you again before you go?'

'We shouldn't risk it if we're to keep things quiet. The *Daisy Jane* is on the horizon and I have an appointment with your brother-in-law.'

'Go now and leave me here, because I don't think I can bear to watch you sail away.'

He didn't laugh, though his eyes told her he wanted to, and his mouth fought the tendency to smile. She supposed it was a rather melodramatic statement at that, and she giggled. 'I feel very furtive meeting you in secret.'

He laughed, then his lips touched against hers and she closed her eyes, savouring their warm

167

tenderness. When the caress was over he whispered, 'The day after tomorrow then. Same place.' She opened her eyes and through her tears, watched him stride away.

Despite her resolve Marianne did watch from her window when he left harbour. The torn sails had been replaced so they were startling patches of white amongst the grey ones.

'Fair sailing, my darling Nick,' she whispered, and waved, imagining he was watching her from the deck through his telescope.

Daisy Jane had arrived the previous day. She was a larger ship than the *Samarand*. As a result she carried more crew and was licensed to carry passengers as well as cargo. Marianne was heartened by the thought that Nick would have had time to speak to his uncle about his future plans, and once he returned he would be home for good. Then they could begin married life with everything above board. She wondered if he'd mentioned her to his uncle. And she began to count the days until he returned.

Erasmus Thornton was not happy with Nick. They had argued, and for once Erasmus had come out the loser.

He said to his sister, 'This time I couldn't change his mind. He's hell-bent on having his own way.'

Daisy looked up from the shirt she was patching. 'I don't know why you're sounding so peevish. Nick has always made his feelings about the issue clear.'

'He's a born seaman, and I can trust him with

the *Samarand*, though he cost me two sails this time.'

She snorted. 'I'm surprised you can trust him to the ship. *Samarand* has always been more trouble than she was worth.'

'She's a cantankerous bitch that needs nursing. Nick knows how to do that. I picked her up cheap, and she's brought in a healthy profit over the years. Nick's going to train the first mate to take her over this run.'

'He told me that the man scraped bottom bringing her in.'

'Touch and go often happens. The harbour is shallow, the tide was on the ebb and he was carrying more cargo than he should have been. Nick should have berthed her himself.'

The Thornton shipping company had been a legacy from their father, and had consisted of two aging packets, long since disposed of. Daisy had been left the house, which she'd been given charge of at the age of fifteen, taking the place of their mother, who'd died from typhoid. The men in the family had always come and gone, and she looked after them when they were in port and kept an eye on the accounts and their shore agent when they were not.

'You know, Erasmus, you never gave Nick a chance to be anything else but a seaman.'

'I didn't know any other trade. But a shop-keeper ... My God!'

She laughed. 'Ah, but it's to be a grand shop, Erasmus. Nick doesn't do anything by halves. You can't say he didn't give you enough warning. You'll get used to it, and perhaps he's met a woman he wants to settle down with.'

Erasmus snorted. 'After he got his fingers burned with the Honeyman girl? He won't repeat that in a hurry.'

Brother and sister were alike. Erasmus was of medium height, wiry and muscled. His face was weathered from a lifetime at sea. Daisy's face was smoother, but the Thornton features sat less easily on her and she was straightforward in her manner. Her body was thin and angular and her hair as straight and grey as a yard of pump water. She was clever for a woman, too, something her brother and Nick appreciated, but other men did not. She kept her house, went to church under protest and occupied herself with charitable causes when her men folk were away at sea.

Daisy would have liked to have wed and had a family of her own when she was younger. Erasmus had shown no interest in settling down though. He'd told her that Nick was their nephew, the son of their half-brother Dickon, when he'd brought him home, a thin, under-nourished brat who'd grabbed his food from the table like a starving rat. He'd taken it to a corner, where he'd turned his back on them and stuffed it into his mouth.

Considering that Erasmus had come ashore with Nick, and the boy only spoke a few words, none of which were English, she suspected that he'd belonged to the Greek woman Dickon had been involved with.

When she'd asked, he'd said, 'Aye, that's right. His name is Nicholas. He was being badly treated by the Greek woman's new husband and her stepsons. She begged me to take him in and bring him up.'

'You fool Erasmus, he's not your responsibility,' she'd told him.

'Aye, he is. He's a Thornton.'

Even in her spinsterhood Daisy was well aware of her brother's foibles. People gossiped. And although the Honeyman affair had been hushed up, she'd heard that a daughter had been the possible result of his liaison with her. The child had died at birth with the mother, and Erasmus had been devastated. Daisy had heard a rumour long after, that the girl had lived, but had been fostered through the orphanage run by a Honeyman relative. She hadn't told her brother that, otherwise he'd have made it his business to find out.

Erasmus was fond of Nick. So was she. But he'd been a headstrong boy, and wild at times. She'd had to discipline him more often than she'd liked when he was growing up. Thus he'd learned to respect her. She was relieved that the eldest Honeyman girl had turned him down. She'd never taken to Charlotte. Still, Daisy was hopeful that Nick would marry. If he came ashore, that would be a step in the right direction.

But then, there were the latest rumours. Not that she paid any mind to them, but she kept her brother informed. She sighed, and biting through the thread, placed the shirt to one side and gazed up at him. 'Gossip has it that Nick sailed to Boston with the younger Honeyman girl on board.'

He gazed sharply at her, said uneasily, 'I'd told

him not to take women on board *Samarand*. She's jealous, and doesn't like it. A woman was killed aboard her when she was new. The owner and his wife were looking her over when a marlin spike slipped from the sail rigger's hand and skewered her through the head. And when you came on board you nearly slipped down a ladder.'

'Because I wasn't looking where I was going. Oh, you and your superstitions, Erasmus.' Daisy began to laugh.

'Is there any truth in the rumour? Did you ask Nick?'

'I did. He roared with laughter then said that of course it was the truth. He'd taken Marianne Honeyman to Boston and he'd married her there.'

Erasmus grinned at that. 'I wouldn't put it past him to do just that. It would serve that eldest girl right for leading him on all those years then slapping him down.'

'Best you don't put such a thought in his head. But I heard Mrs Hardy tell somebody that her younger sister had been ill and confined to her bed for several weeks. I saw the girl in church the next day. She looked fine and handsome to me.'

'That one's like her mother,' Erasmus said softly and although Daisy gave him a sharp look, she said nothing.

It had taken several weeks for Charles Barrie to recover. His simple cold had developed into a severe infection on his chest, and he'd been ravaged by bouts of coughing that had exhausted him. But he'd noticed a longer period between coughing fits over the last couple of days.

His doctor smiled as he removed his stethoscope from his patient's chest and straightened up. 'If you keep this up you can get out of bed for a short while each day. I'll leave a blood tonic and instructions with your man.'

'Thank you.' Charles shrugged. 'May I have visitors?'

'As long as you promise not to tire yourself. You need plenty of rest while you recuperate.'

'Which will take, how long?'

'As long as it takes,' the doctor said smoothly. 'Take my word for it, Charles, you've been seriously ill, and if you take things too fast you could quite easily suffer a relapse. If that happened I wouldn't like to wager on the outcome. Count on being in-capacitated for several more weeks. If you have any intention of going back to the bench this side of Christmas I suggest you put it aside.'

Charles sighed after he'd gone. He swung his legs out of bed and tested them. They felt as weak as new twigs, and could hardly take his weight, so he was forced to reach down to the bed and clutch the bedding for the support it offered. He managed to shuffle precariously along the bed to the more solid safety of the wooden bed end.

'Ballam?' he bawled, and immediately began to cough.

After a few moments his man came in. Ballam's eyes mirrored his alarm when he saw him clinging precariously to the bed end, his shoulders shaking. His servant's lips pursed after he got him back into bed.

When the coughing stopped Ballam said disapprovingly, 'Sir, you should have waited for me to assist you. The doctor has given me strict instructions. Five minutes a day with my support until you grow stronger.'

'Oh, don't you give me a lecture as well, Ballam.'

'No, sir.'

'I want you to go to Edgar Wyvern's chambers and tell him I'd appreciate seeing him.'

Before his current malady Charles had rarely suffered illness. Odd how his illness had visited just when he'd been about to seize his grandson, as if God had set out to prevent him from carrying out his plan. Lying in bed, beset by fever, joints aching and attacked by uncontrollable shivering, sometimes Charles had hardly cared if he'd lived or died. But in his more lucid moments he'd had time to think about his grandson and that had determined that he live.

According to the young agent he'd hired, the lad had a good home and he looked upon Seth Hardy as his father. If that proved to be true, then John would not thank him for being abruptly removed. Charles had reached the conclusion that Edgar had been right all along, and he'd been too hasty. He would not punish the soldier's wife.

Still, Charles had every intention of retrieving his grandson and allowing him to take his rightful place in his family, as his heir.

He would give the soldier a chance to clear himself too ... get Edgar to put the situation before him and listen to his explanation.

When Edgar arrived, Charles said, 'I won't be well enough to travel for some time. I would like you to go to Dorset as soon as possible, inform the soldier of my existence, put the matter at hand before him, and bring John back if you can. And Edgar, buy the boy a gift from me. A telescope would be suitable.'

Edgar presented himself to Harbour House the day after he arrived in Poole. He asked the cab driver to wait.

The wind had a chill to it, the late November sky was grey, but the day was dry. There was no sign of the boy, but Edgar heard the lusty cry of a baby from the upper reaches of the house.

He handed his card to the maid, who allowed him inside and showed him into the drawing room to wait after he'd stated his business. There was a fire burning, and he stood appreciatively before it, warming his hands as he gazed at his surroundings.

Apart from the beaded face screens in rosewood frames there was an inlaid writing desk and comfortable, but slightly shabby chairs. A games table doubled as a sewing table. The floors were covered in blue and beige patterned rugs. Against the wall stood an upright piano with a red velvet stool. There was a clutter of pictures and ornaments, and family treasures housed in a boule and ormolu cabinet, with a large gilt mirror over the top. Inside and out

Harbour House had no pretensions to be other than it was, a comfortable family home. He crossed to the window. The view across the harbour was magnificent.

A draught alerted him to the fact that he was no longer alone. He turned to face the young woman standing there. The mistress of the house, he supposed. She was lovely to look at, but there were lines of tension about her mouth. She glanced down at the card in her hand. 'Mr Wyvern? I'm Mrs Hardy. I'm sorry to keep you waiting ... the children, you know. They're young and can't be kept waiting.'

'How many children do you have?'

'Her face lit up with love. 'I have two, a boy and a girl. They're twins, and only two months of age. Then there's John, of course. He's our stepson.'

He smiled at the touch of mother's pride in her voice. 'They must demand a great deal of your time.'

'Oh yes they do. The maid tells me you have some business with us. May I ask what it is?'

'It's with your husband, Colonel Seth Hardy. Is he here?'

The faint smile she gave wiped away the tension, as if it had been drawn there at an earlier time and her husband's name erased it. 'Seth is up at the clay pits. He should be home in about half an hour. Can I offer you some refreshment while you wait?'

'Thank you, Mrs Hardy. I'd appreciate that. I'll go and inform the cab driver that I'll be longer than expected.'

'The maid will do that. He can wait in the kitchen where it's warm, and have some refreshment too. It's a cold day.'

'He'll appreciate that.' Ten minutes later Edgar was sipping tea. There were home-made scones with jam to go with it, just like his wife used to make when he had one. Edgar thought wryly that if the woman knew why he was here she'd probably withdraw her hospitality and order him out.

The sound of laughter came to his ears.

'I won, Marianne.'

'No ... I did. I was at least an inch in front of you.'

'But you cut the corner.'

'And you leapt over the wall. So we both won, really.' Her voice was raised, but it was still as breathless as a purr from the physical effort she'd put in. 'We're back, Charlotte.'

Mrs Hardy smiled. 'That's my sister, Marianne. She's been out on the heath with John. They're constant companions when he's home from school, and she teaches him about the heath birds and the nature of our environment. I'm in here, Marianne.'

The door opened and a boy's head poked through the crack. 'You'll never guess, Mama ... we saw a dead adder.'

'Oh, my goodness! Are you sure it was dead?'

'This is the wrong time of year for adders to be abroad, it's too cold,' he said knowledgeably. 'It was on one of the rails and Marianne said a clay cart must have run over it because its head was parted from its body. It had been there a long

177

time because it's all dried up. I was forbidden to touch its head, though it was dead, because the venom was still there in the fangs, Marianne said. We dug a hole and buried the head and said a prayer over it.' He laughed. 'Though Marianne said we need only say a quarter of a prayer, because it was only a quarter of the snake, and she made me guess the words in a quarter of the prayer, and we worked the sum out on the way home so see who got it right first. And guess what?'

'You won,' Charlotte guessed.

John nodded. 'We've brought the rest home. Marianne was nearly sick when she first saw it. I'm going to ask Pa to show me how to skin it. Marianne said if it doesn't stink too much we might be able to make a belt out of it when we've cleaned the skin.'

'Ugh! How could Marianne let you do such a horrid thing.' Edgar tried not to grin. Clearly, Miss Hardy was more indulgent of the foibles of young males than her sister was.

Another head appeared. 'Don't worry, Charlotte, the snake couldn't have been any deader.' Her eyes widened. 'Oh, you have a visitor. I wondered why there was a cab outside, but it had no driver. I'm so sorry to interrupt.'

'Mr Wyvern is here to see Seth,' she said.

The door opened further and the pair advanced into the room, their faces glowing healthily from fresh air and exercise, but plainly curious to find a stranger in their home. And Edgar, who'd thought Charlotte lovely, was entranced by Marianne's appearance when they were intro-

178

duced. So delicate, Miss Honeyman's features suited her dainty body. Together, the sisters were perfection.

As for Master John Hardy, Edgar smiled as he shook hands with the boy. There was no doubt in his mind that this was Charles's grandson. The resemblance was unmistakable, especially his mossy green eyes. It would be a shame to take John away from this place, and from these people. The boy looked totally at home here, he thought.

Nevertheless, his thoughts had to take second place to the wishes of his client, and Charles Barrie, who for whatever reason had been denied access to his only grandson, had a strong case for custody of him. The friendly welcome he'd received from these people whose happiness he was about to destroy made him squirm with guilt.

The gate squeaked and Mrs Hardy rose. She sounded relieved when she said, 'That must be Seth now. I expect you'll want to speak to him privately.'

When he nodded, John and Marianne left the room with her.

Eleven

Seth was puzzled that a lawyer was here to see him. He had no surviving relatives, and couldn't help thinking that the man had mistaken him for someone else.

'Mr Wyvern?' The two shook hands, 'How can I help you?'

'I'm acting on behalf of a client of mine, Sir Charles Barrie.'

Even more mystified, Seth gazed at him. 'I'm afraid I've never heard of him. Are you sure you have the right person?'

'Yes, Colonel Hardy. We've had you investigated.'

'Investigated? I don't understand,' which was not to say he was happy about it. 'Get to the point of your visit if you would, sir?'

'I believe ... know you have the child John Barrie living under your roof.'

'There's nobody living here under that name. My stepson is called John Hardy, now.'

'It will go easier on you if you don't deny it, Colonel. The boy's mother was named Mary Barrie and he was named after his father. You formed a relationship with Mary Barrie in Tasmania.'

His brow creased, as though he was trying to

remember something. 'You've made a mistake.'

'You deny being in Australia?'

'Of course not. I was posted there with my regiment. But I married a widow called Mary Ellis.'

'Her maiden name. She was actually married to my client's son before his death. John Charles Barrie was the son they had together, and is the boy who is now living with you. It's a waste of time denying it.'

'Mary was ill ... an ailment from which we both knew she'd never recover.'

'Then why did you marry her, Colonel, for her property? Her husband had a legacy that would have been hers had she thought to claim it ... and yours if she'd married you legally.'

Seth laughed, but without humour. 'Mary had no expectations of legacy. She had nothing but the clothes she stood up in, and her son. Quite simply, I admired her courage and I fell in love with her. John took my name. And if there is a legacy from his father, then it belongs to John.'

'Even while knowing she was living off her—'

'Be very careful what you say, Mr Wyvern. If you offer one insult towards my late wife's memory I'll be obliged to take you by the scruff of the neck and throw you out, and to hell with the consequences. If you speak of Mary, do so with all respect.'

'I beg your pardon. I'm not here to fight, but to exchange facts. There is no record of your marriage in the Hobart church.'

'We said words over the family bible in front

of witnesses. It was recorded inside. Mary and John took my name, and we made it legal. That's all Mary would accept from me. She said she could never be a proper wife to me, and despite everything she'd been through, she wanted to honour her first husband, a man she'd loved with all her heart.'

Edgar gave a little murmur of approval.

'I looked after her as best I could. She put her son in my care and I promised on her deathbed that I'd bring John up as my own. She asked me to bury her next to her first husband. I dug the ground myself, and left money for a cross to be placed on the site. She is buried as Mary Hardy. Now I know why the Barrie name seemed familiar. It's on some drawings she had – her legacy for John.'

He blinked back his tears when the man asked, 'How did you get John back to England without his name appearing on the ship's passenger list?'

The investigator he hired had been thorough, Seth thought, and recalled a young man at the school with astute eyes. He shook his head to clear it.

'It was accidental, not subterfuge. John was still being fed by his mother when she died. I hired an Irish woman who had just buried her youngest child. She had another child and they were booked on board a ship returning to England. They were not well off, so I hired her to look after John until we reached England and also returned her fare to her. By the time we got here she'd weaned him. After that we lived in Scotland.'

'In Edinburgh, in the house you inherited from a relative.'

Seth was taken aback. 'Your investigator was thorough. Yes, in the house I inherited. There, I hired a nursery maid to look after John until we were able to fend for ourselves.'

'It didn't enter your head that John might have family.'

Seth drew in a deep breath. 'Yes, it did, but just before she died Mary told me her deceased husband had been disowned by his father, and he'd wanted nothing more to do with him.'

Edgar Wyvern winced. 'That might have been true once, but Sir Charles changed his mind, and blood is thicker than water, after all.'

'Is it, Mr Wyvern? In my experience, where money is concerned that isn't always the case. Mary and John were left impoverished. Where was his grandfather when they didn't have enough food to eat, when they were sleeping under the trees, and when a decent woman was obliged to beg on the street? Tell me about this man, and I'll tell you if a man who treated his own son so badly is a man who can be trusted with John's welfare. Sir Charles Barrie, I believe you said his name was.'

'I beg you not to think too harshly of him. He recently lost his eldest son, then shortly afterwards he discovered that the younger one had also perished. He had no knowledge of the existence of John at the time.'

'So having lost two sons, one of whom he'd previously disowned, he has now decided to take his grandson away from a happy home.'

183

'Sir Charles Barrie is a judge. John is his only living kin. He intends that the boy be restored to him. In fact, he has instructed me to take John back to London with me.'

'I think not, Mr Wyvern. At his mother's request I've been a father to John for several years, and by the way, you can tell him I'll be pursuing John's legacy on his behalf. Why isn't Sir Charles here pleading his own case?'

Wyvern's eyes widened. 'He's been extremely ill, and has sent me to pave the way.'

'You have done that, sir. I now know what to expect from him. I also know what I'm up against. Thank you for coming. This interview is now at an end.'

They both stood, and Wyvern said, 'You know this is not the end of it, Colonel Hardy. Sir Charles will challenge your claim to John, and he will win.'

'Not without him being shown up for the hypocrite he is. He's not thinking of John's welfare, only of his own.'

'I can understand your anger, and sympathize with it. Think the situation over carefully and calmly. Discuss it with Mrs Hardy, a young woman who seems to have a sensible head on her shoulders. See if you can come up with an alternative plan I can put before Sir Charles. I'll return tomorrow.'

'It will be a waste of your time.'

'Colonel Hardy, you're not a child. Talking is never a waste of time. John Barrie is the sole heir to a fortune, and the legacy from his father is nothing in comparison. His grandfather is fifty-five years of age. All Sir Charles wants is to spend some time with his grandchild and heir while he still has time, and make amends for what has happened. Would you try and deny him that pleasure, and the boy his birthright?'

'No, I would not. It would be good for John to know that he has a grandfather, and to meet him and to spend some time with him. But instead of him coming to me in the first place this man has investigated my background in an effort to find something to discredit me, so to remove John from my care. If he expected me to hand him over before he did me the courtesy of being given the time to investigate him, then he'll be sadly disappointed. John has already lost his father and mother. He looks on me as his parent, and it would be unfair to remove that support from him.'

They'd moved into the hall.

'Come, come, Colonel, take my word for it, Sir Charles is above reproach.'

'I can only judge you at face value, Mr Wyvern, and Sir Charles only by his stated intentions. I'll do my best to prevent John from being removed from my family, and a home where he's loved and loves in return.'

'Think about this, I beg you. Sir Charles may decide to have you charged with child stealing. I've already talked him out of it once.'

Seth laughed. 'I'm not the type of fool your client seems to think I am. I have a document signed by Mary, her signature was witnessed by two of my superior officers, men also above reproach. It's still sealed, and I'm given to understand that her wishes regarding John are contained within it.'

The lawyer's smile was unbelieving. 'And you wait until now to tell me? I'd like to see this document.'

'I daresay you would. And you will, sir. The document will be opened in court if the need arises.'

'You're bluffing, Colonel Hardy.'

'I wouldn't count on it if I were you. You may tell your client that if his concern for John is genuine and he wishes to meet his grandson, he may visit him here. We could set a day before you leave ... one that will give your client time to recover, and for me to acquaint John with the fact that he has a grandfather.'

They set a date for March.

Seth opened the door. 'Good day to you, Mr Wyvern.'

'I've left a gift for John from his grandfather in the drawing room. I chose it myself, so I do hope he likes it.'

'I'll see that he gets it. Wait a moment.' He went back into the drawing room and took a photograph from the mantelpiece. It was of them all. Charlotte was seated on the sofa with a baby in each arm. He stood proudly behind. John was with Marianne to one side. Her hand rested lightly on one of the boy's shoulders. He took it from the silver frame. 'Give this to Sir Charles with my compliments. It might help to place his mind at rest.'

'Thank you, he'll appreciate the gesture. And thank you for being so honest, Colonel.' Edgar

Wyvern held out a hand. 'Let's not part as enemies. Your quarrel isn't with me.'

'But it will be if this goes to court.'

'It will, but trust me. Now I've met you and the boy and have seen the environment in which John is living, with your cooperation I'll do my best to avoid that option, for the sake of the child. You would not object to meeting with Sir Charles in London, I take it?'

After a moment's hesitation, Seth took the offered hand. 'No, sir, I would not object.

Marianne was usually overrun with invitations leading up to Christmas, now there were very few.

'They're addressed to Mr and Mrs Seth Hardy, but I imagine you're included,' Charlotte said.

But when Marianne appeared for a social evening, she was the censure of all eyes. Women she'd known all her lives turned away from her and whispered behind their fans, some of the men stared at her with speculative eyes.

Lucian pretended not to see her, and when he couldn't avoid speaking to her, he nodded and used the formal, 'Ah, Miss Honeyman ... you'll have to excuse me a moment, there's someone I urgently need to talk to.'

Her eyes met his. 'Lucian, whatever is the matter with you? I thought we were friends.'

His eyes slid away and he mumbled, 'Of course we're friends, and can socialize later in the evening. As I said...' He made the exchange between them as brief as possible before mumbling his excuses and moving on.

Mortified, Marianne stared at her plate for the rest of the evening, and only picked at her food. Nick had warned her that this would happen, but living in isolation had buffered her against it. She should have listened to him. Such was her tension that she was sick as soon as they got home.

Charlotte was tight-lipped as she eyed her. 'Rumour must have got round about you going to America with Nick. Isn't it enough that we've got this worry over John's future, without that as well? Who have you told?'

'Nobody.'

'Then Nick must have told people. I bet that sour old spinster Daisy Thornton is putting it around. She never liked me. You'd better stay at home until it blows over, then you won't have to answer any awkward questions. Seth is trying to establish himself as a businessman in the district and any scandal about you will reflect badly on him. Really, Marianne ... you're always so head-strong, and look where it's got you. By the way, Lucian has announced his engagement to Isabelle Martin.'

'Were we invited to the engagement party?'

'There was an invitation.'

Her stomach rolled sickeningly. 'But I wasn't on it, I suppose. Will you still go?'

'Of course we will, it would be rude not to. Seth needs to meet and socialize with people. Most of the pottery owners as well as the clay producers will be there. I daresay you'd be bored by it all, anyway.' Charlotte kissed her cheek. 'Don't worry, this will all have blown over by next summer.'

By then her stomach would be as round as a suet pudding, Marianne thought. The matrons would be counting on their fingers and giving each other knowing looks, and Charlotte would have disowned her.

The fact that Nick had been right about Lucian was cold comfort to her. Not that it mattered now. 'Well, it was expected. She's an heiress and Lucian has always felt the need to accumulate wealth. Do you remember when we were young and he had expectations? He always talked about how he was going to possess a fortune when he grew up. He thought he'd inherit his grandfather's estate because he was the first boy to be born into his mother's family for fifty years. But the estate was shared between his mother and his aunts.'

'There was a time when I thought you and Lucian ... well, I know you were fond of each other. I thought you might be upset, since it was strongly rumoured that he held you in great affection. You would have made a perfect match.'

'No we wouldn't have. He's too set in his ways and I would have had to behave perfectly. You know I love to be free. Isabelle Martin will be perfect for him.' She laughed, for truly Nick had replaced Lucian in more ways than one.

'You've changed somehow, Marianne. We should invite people here, try and find you a husband.'

'Oh, I have ... decided not to marry,' she said, catching herself just in time.

'Marianne! Of course you must wed, if you can. It's expected.'

'There was a time when it was expected of you and Nick...' She shrugged. 'I was surprised when you humiliated him like that. He hasn't been here since, so it didn't take you long to forget him.'

'At least he asked me for my hand,' Charlotte snapped. 'Several times, in fact.'

Thank goodness her sister had refused him. 'You were horrid to him, you know. I did feel for him.'

'I was piqued with him, I admit. Seth tells me I went too far. They've formed a friendship, and he wants to invite Nick to dinner the next time he's home.'

Marianne's eyes widened. Perhaps they could announce their marital status then, though she doubted if her state would remain undetected. 'Nick didn't tell me that. And will you?'

'Goodness, there's no reason why he should have told you, is there? It's not as though you've seen him since you left the ship. To be honest, I don't know whether I want him here. I miss him sometimes. Sometimes I think that I might still have feelings for him.'

Marianne's heart slammed against her chest as she stared at her sister. If Charlotte turned on the charm and won Nick back she'd die of a broken heart. 'Surely not. You seem so happy with Seth.'

'I am. But he hasn't got Nick's charm. Goodness, the man was always larger than life. But he was like a dog with a bone, one he'd never let go. He wanted to own me, and I doubt if he'll ever grow out of that.'

Marianne tested the water with a light laugh. 'Perhaps he'll marry me instead if I ask him. Then we'd both be out of your way.'

'Don't be silly. Nick's always regarded you as a child, and a nuisance who tagged around after us. That's why he used to bring Lucian with him. To keep you occupied. He must have fumed when he discovered you on his ship. If you think you've got a claim there, forget it. He's always loved me, and he's too old to transfer his affections to another. Besides, even if he offered for you, I wouldn't allow such a match.'

Charlotte had no say in the matter now, Marianne thought with some satisfaction. Her sister was right about one thing though. Nick had buckets of charm, and didn't Marianne know it! He'd charmed her right into his bed ... and not even his bed, but a bed that had been used to satisfy the carnal appetites in ways she couldn't even dream about – yet! She tried not to grin. If Charlotte knew they were wed she'd take it personally, and she'd never speak to either of them again.

Marianne chewed over further worries she had. She suspected that she was carrying Nick's child inside her. Although the thought filled her with an indescribable delight, if she did prove to be with child she wondered how long she'd be able to hide her condition from everyone. It would be at least five months before he returned. Sometimes she felt sick when she woke, and she couldn't remember when she'd last experienced her menses. Just before she'd sailed away to Boston with Nick, she thought, though they'd always been erratic. If she was that way, then the infant would be born in either July or August, and by April her condition would be apparent.

Halfway through December Marianne's suspicions had become a certainty in her mind.

She heaved a sigh of relief. By now *Samarand* should be sailing into Melbourne Harbour. Marianne had become adept at concealing her sickness from her sister. Now she'd have to try and conceal her changing body shape as well for the next three months.

The weather was bitter, but not cold enough for snow, and the clouds allowed the sun through, so the pools and streams glittered with overhanging icicles.

That morning she'd taken John out on the heath. 'Always be careful of the pools, John, especially the stagnant ones, since they're full of rotting animals and leaves, and are poisonous. Best to keep away from them altogether, and from the flooded quarry pits, as well. Drink from the chalk streams if you're thirsty.'

They'd cut armfuls of holly, the berries a startling red cluster against the dark prickly leaves. And they'd gone up to the pine copse to pick up some cones to burn for the fragrance. Piled on a sack, they dragged it back to the house along with some fallen branches to burn.

Seth helped them take it indoors, and they decorated the stairs and the hall.

There was a small fir tree on the table decorated with metal trumpets, wooden soldiers and silver drums. On the top Charlotte had placed a star covered in sparkling beads, and there were quilted snowflakes. Marianne could have sworn that some of them were made from scraps of the silk Nick had given her. Taking one from the tree she held its softness against her cheek.

'What on earth are you doing?' Charlotte said from the doorway.

'It's so soft and pretty. I should have liked to have helped make them.'

'You can make the paper baskets if you like, and John can put almonds in them.' Advancing, Charlotte took the snowflake from her and placed it back on the tree in exactly the same position as Marianne had taken it from. 'It took me ages to get it looking just right. Stop fiddling with things.'

'Nick will be spending Christmas thousands of miles away from his family,' she thought to say, and Charlotte gave her a sharp look.

'Why do you keep going on about Nick? I doubt if he'll care about Christmas. He was an orphan, and he isn't very family-minded. Besides, he's a sailor. He probably has a woman waiting for him at every port.'

Jealousy squeezed a hand at Marianne's innards. Had she just become one of them?

A demanding cry came from upstairs and Charlotte smiled wryly. Her life revolved about her children now. 'I must go and feed him before they both start. Could you find some dry linen cloths and bring them up, please.'

Charlotte was feeding the children unaided now. The routine of looking after two babies was time-consuming. Marianne helped as much as she could with the washing, ironing and mending, and Seth had hired another maid, the fourteen-year-old daughter of one of his labourers. She was as thin as a bean pole and came in on a daily basis with her father, her raggy clothing covered in an equally raggy shawl. Later, he called in for her on the way home. Marianne felt sorry for her, and had already decided to give her a gift of a warm shawl for Christmas.

The laundry room had a copper boiler with a grate in the supporting bricks to set a fire. There was a wooden mangle, and racks that could be hoisted to the ceiling. The place was full of steam.

'Don't forget to rinse them properly before you put them through the mangle,' Alice was telling the girl.

Picking up the folded linens, Marianne gave the young maid a sympathetic smile and went upstairs to the nursery, where Charlotte had Major Mitchell against her breast.

Jessica was kicking up a fuss from her crib, her legs and feet kicking at the air vigorously. When Marianne picked her up she quieted and gave her a gummy smile before turning her head towards her breast and nuzzling for a teat. A tender emotion rose in Marianne at the gesture and she smiled. 'Sorry, my love, you'll have to stay hungry for a little while longer. I'll sing you a song, instead.' She brought the child up to her shoulder and gently rocked her back and forth, singing a little lullaby. This time next year she'd have her own sweet infant to care for.

'You'll be a wonderful mother when the time comes,' Charlotte said softly.

Startled, Marianne gazed at her, thinking for a moment that Charlotte had guessed. But no, Charlotte would not be either this relaxed or loving, or kind. Her babies had softened her, but not to the extent that she'd let Marianne get away with such a betrayal.

Marianne changed the subject. 'I went to our mother's grave yesterday to let her know we were both well. I talked to the Reverend Phipps, and he looked in the records for me.'

A watchful look came her way. 'For what reason?'

'To see if there was any record of an infant being buried with her.'

'And ... was there?'

'No. He said that if the child had been stillborn she might have been unnamed and—'

'There you are then. Why are you raking this up?'

'Hearing Jessica cry a couple of days ago jogged my memory. I remembered hearing the baby cry on that night she was born, so she couldn't have been stillborn.'

'I expect she died shortly afterwards. How can you remember any of the details accurately after all these years? You were young and scared, we both were. I think you remember it because you want to believe she's still alive. You always had a vivid imagination.'

'What if she hadn't died, though? What if we have a sister? Our aunt, Constance Jarvis, founded an orphanage and left most of her fortune to maintain it. What if the baby had been sent there?'

'Then it's the best place for her. I wouldn't want anything to do with a child fathered by Erasmus Thornton, especially one who'd killed our mother.'

'It's not the child's fault. Aren't you curious?'

'No, and it would be better if you weren't. There's enough scandal around us at the moment without you stirring up the past.' She grimaced as she pulled Major Mitchell from her breast with a sucking sound. He flopped in her arms as relaxed as a jellyfish, then passed wind. It woke him up, so he jumped and looked at his mother with astonished eyes before he lapsed into sleep again.

The sisters looked at each other and laughed.

'You can tell he's a male,' Charlotte said softly. 'You're a greedy little tyke Major Mitchell. I hope you've left something for your sister. Here, perhaps you wouldn't mind changing his linen while I see to Jessica.'

'As long as he doesn't repeat that performance.'

Instead, Major Mitchell belched a bubble of milk from his mouth. She caught it with a flannel when it rolled down his cheek towards his ear. When she gently ran her finger along the underside of his foot his little pink toes curled under in reflex.

He had left something for his sister. Jessica's appetite wasn't as voracious as Mitchell's, and she was soon satisfied and back in her crib, her thumb in her mouth, her eyes wide and her golden eyelashes fanning her cheeks as she began to drift into sleep.

'They're so beautiful,' Marianne whispered, so not to wake them.

'I'm so lucky to have them.'

Her own child would be dark-eyed like Nick, she thought, and its hair would curl darkly. She wanted to give him a son in his image. That would bind him to her. She would ask the gypsy to read her palm when she next saw her, and perhaps she'd buy a love charm.

The gypsies usually came in spring, and set up camp in the copse. The women would sell their pegs and tell fortunes on fair days in Wareham, which was the other side of the heath, or in Dorchester. The tinker would go round the streets of the towns to sharpen knives and scissors and repair pots and pans. He wore a battered stove-pipe hat that he doffed at the ladies.

The gypsies didn't all come and go at once. Some came early, some stayed on to work on various farms in teams, helping to bring in the harvest. After that, they went off to Somerset, Cornwall and Wiltshire to take advantage of the county fairs there.

When Marianne had been a child Jessica had woven her tales of lands across an ocean, a place where the ground looked like cream, the sea like lapis lazuli and the sun beat so hotly against your skin that it toasted it brown like the skin of the gypsies.

She and Charlotte had always been told to wear bonnets when they were out in the sun, otherwise their skin would no longer look white and delicate and they would age quickly.

As they stood together, arms around each other's waists and gazing down at the babies, Marianne felt close to her sister. There had never been secrets between them before. She should tell Charlotte about her marriage to Nick, and the coming baby. But she needed to get one thing straight first.

'Charlotte?'

'What is it, Marianne?'

'You said you still have feelings for Nick. You don't still love him, do you?'

'Of course not.' She lowered her voice to a whisper. 'I wasn't talking about love. I was talking about ... forbidden feelings. The ones you get when you look at men sometimes and wonder what it would be like with them.'

How dare Charlotte admit to having those sort of feelings for Nick when she was married to Seth? The moment of togetherness was lost when Marianne stated, because she couldn't stop herself, 'Like the feelings our mother had towards Erasmus Thornton, you mean?'

'It's not the same.'

She laughed. 'Oh, I see. When you have them it's divine, I suppose. When others have them it's sinful.'

'The difference is, I'd control mine and not allow Nick to take advantage of them. And I'd be much obliged if you'd stop bringing Nick Thornton into the conversation every five minutes. Anyone would think you were married to him.'

Marianne began to seethe, and decided that

confessing all to Charlotte might not be a good thing to do at the moment. 'Oh, do shut up, Charlotte. I'm going before we have an argument. I promised John we'd look at the stars through the telescope his grandfather sent him on the first clear night, and I want to draw a chart up.'

'Draw a chart up? Since when have you known anything about stars?'

'He who must not be mentioned in your presence taught me about them. We sat up on deck and it was pitch dark except for the stars. The sky was enchanting. The nameless one told me a story about each star. I think he made half the tales up, though. I fell asleep on his shoulder.'

'I imagine he must have bored you.'

'Far from it. If I were a man I should like nothing better than to sail around the world in command of my own sailing ship. It was wonderful, and I'll never forget it.'

Charlotte scoffed, 'You always did believe Nick's tall tales. You're a dreamer, Marianne. You think people are better than they are.'

'And you never see the beauty in life, and you always look for the worst in people.'

'That's because they usually display their worst. Oh, I know I come across as sharp and self-centred, but I had to fight with our father for things we both needed when we were growing up. He was always making promises that he didn't keep. Men do. Sometimes we didn't have enough to eat because he'd lost money at the card table. The only person I ever felt I could trust was you.'

Guilt sat heavily on Marianne's shoulders for a moment. 'What about Seth?'

'What about him?'

'Don't you trust him too?'

Charlotte laughed and a cushion hit her in the back as she left. 'Mind your own business.'

Twelve

They'd limped into Williamstown Harbour with the pumps manned, making hardly any headway, and with *Samarand* waddling from side to side like a fat sow on the way to market with a dozen piglets hanging off her teats. Her extra cargo of salty water sloshed knee high in the hold.

Luckily, the cargo was household goods, and the sea water hadn't been there long enough to do much damage. Unloading the ship didn't take long. Afterwards, Nick went below himself with some of the crew holding lanterns aloft to find where the water was coming in.

The water stank as he and his companions edged carefully along the seam. The leak was the worse place possible, the seam between the keel and the planking – aptly named the devil, needed sealing again. He cursed his uncle once again that the bottom hadn't been coppered. The same seam had been caulked in Boston. It would have to be done again. Luckily, the gap hadn't spread.

While he was down there he inspected the main mast for worm. It sounded a little hollow, as did the keel in a couple of places. All he could do was paint the patches with white lead to kill whatever was eating the ship out from under him. It had got them here, and no doubt it would get them back as long as he patched her up.

He remembered the first mate touching bottom in Poole Harbour, and cursed. The seam must have been weakened then. He should have inspected her before they left, the Australian run was hazardous enough without sailing on a ship that wasn't seaworthy.

They couldn't work on her underwater. They'd have to careen her to get at the seam this time. It was a job none would relish, so he said, 'The devil needs paying again. We'll have to careen her this time, and there will be a bonus when we get back home for those who volunteer.'

Several of the men stepped forward – a couple of them avoided his eyes and exchanged a glance. Nick suspected they intended to jump ship and join the Victorian gold rush. Not before the caulking was done, if he had anything to say about it. He'd keep an eye on them. 'You two can help as well.'

They beached her in a nearby bay, tethering her to a pole while the tide went out. She looked vulnerable with her bottom showing and covered in marine growth. Nick discovered other seams that were suspect, but they could patch her up. Quickly, the sailors began to tightly pack oakum into her seams, using marlin spikes. The tar was heated over a fire on the beach. He didn't want to wait for the next tide to inspect the other side, but his impatience was overcome by the thought that he was responsible for the safety of his crew, as well as himself.

By the time two tides has come and gone, *Samarand* was as watertight as she'd ever been. They sailed her back to the berth, pumped the remaining water from her and began to take on cargo for the homeward leg – 3,000 bales of wool.

Like most of the clippers, Nick was taking the great circle route via the South West Cape. If they survived the icebergs and made it through the roaring forties and around Cape Horn they'd enter Drake Passage. Once through that it would be a simple matter to navigate the Atlantic and home.

He hoped Aria was managing. He smiled at the thought of her, just one diminutive woman that his heart cherished. He could picture her as though she was still with him. She was different to the other women he'd known, a resourceful little baggage. He marvelled that she'd been in his life for years, and he'd only just found her.

He took out the tiny painting of her as a girl and opened the locket to read the message. Marianne Dearly Beloved. He knew the message had been intended from mother to daughter in the first place. But it must have been her most precious possession, and Aria had given it to him as a keepsake while they were apart. The thought that she might have fallen in love with him, warmed him. He ran a finger over the glass containing the keepsake of her baby hair, then kissed the locket and pinned it back inside his pocket. He didn't want to lose it, and the three months it would take before he saw her again seemed a long, long time.

He sailed short-handed, having lost four of the crew to the gold rush. He put Sam under the tutelage of the most experienced seaman, with strict instructions that the lad was not allowed into the shrouds while the ship was under way.

Nick smiled at Sam's disappointed face. Nick's uncle had sent him up the mast when he'd been about the same age, and he'd been so looking forward to it. The weather had been calm and when he'd looked down, the ship had been shaped like a small coffin. He'd been swaying back and forth on a long, thin pole that supported a large span of sails with an unimaginable weight to them and a power that owed all to the mercy of the winds and the expertise of the man standing below at the helm.

He'd been so scared by the thought that he'd been unable to move, and at the same time had realized a healthy respect for his uncle.

Someone had gone up to help him come down, but just as his feet touched the deck and he'd got over his fright, his uncle had said. 'Up you go again, lad. This time you'll either come down by yourself or you'll stay up there until we get back in port.'

He'd done it, his stomach in his mouth, the contents churning and his knees shaking with fright. The crew had cheered him on and when the deck was solid under his feet again, and his legs had nearly given out from under him, because they'd felt like jelly, Erasmus had patted him on the shoulder, said, 'Well done, lad, I'll make a seaman of you yet.' Erasmus had walked off, leaving him feeling as though he was ten feet tall.

Only then had Nick allowed himself to be sick, but downwind, as he'd been told. It had suddenly occurred to him then that he'd have to learn his craft the hard way, the same as everyone else. But this was not the career he'd have chosen for himself.

They'd hardly cleared three miles when disaster struck. It was sudden. A king wave appeared and roared down on them, a magnificent, terrifying and crippling creature with dark core and a jaunty feather on its cap, a wind-whipped foam-tipped curl that Nick had never seen the like of before. He took a few seconds to admire it before he feared it.

Samarand usually cut through the waves like a buttered knife, but the weight of this one towered over the bow then crushed them, swallowing them, sails and all. When they came staggering out of the all-engulfing cataract the ship was almost standing on her stern, and Nick, who'd clung, white-knuckled, to the nearest rope, began to slide down the deck, taking whatever he was attached to with him. A second wave reared over them. Knowing the ship was about to capsize, he released the rope. It was attached to the ship like an umbilical cord to an infant. Nick didn't want to be tangled in it when it was dragged under.

There was a splintering of wood and a ripping sound as *Samarand*'s masts and rigging were torn away. Nick was tossed about in the frothing water like a rag doll in the jaws of a dog, and battered painfully by small and large objects alike. Carried away by another wave he was hurled through the air into a trough, where he landed on something solid that drove the breath from his body. It was a raft of some sort ... the hatch cover!

His fingers scrabbled for purchase and hooked over the edge, while his toes practically dug a hole in the wood. Hurtled at breakneck speed to the top of the next swell he was spun around. He saw the clipper, keel uppermost, her planks a splintered gaping hole. Then she was there no more, borne under by the sodden wool, leaving a dirty, turbulent patch in the water as the remaining air belched from her. At least she hadn't turned over on top of him.

Oddly, the ship's dinghy bobbed about in an assortment of the debris. What luck! He couldn't allow it to get away. He waved an arm and shouted at it to stop, feeling ridiculous when it didn't. He began to paddle his raft after it, because the dinghy appeared to be unmanned. A body floated by, face down. The cook! Nick hauled Red out of the water by his hair, turned him on his stomach and pressed. Water spurted out and the man groaned, then vomited. Swooping in a deep breath he opened his eyes. 'Thank God it's you, Captain. Did you ever see the like of that water? I never learned to swim, and thought I was a goner.'

'We're not out of danger yet, and I haven't got time to look after you, so hurry up and gather your wits together.' Nick pulled his boots off. 'Guard these with your life. I'm going to see if I can get the dinghy ... and make sure you keep your eyes on me, so we don't get separated. Did you understand that, Red?'

'Yes, Captain. Don't you worry about me; nothing will keep us apart while you still owe me my wages.'

Nick chuckled, then he dived into the water. In a little while he was pulling himself up over the side of the dinghy. To his relief, Sam was lying in the water in the bottom, shaking with cold, or was it fright?

Nick couldn't afford the time to mince words. 'Are you injured?'

'No, Captain, a crack on the head, that's all.'

'Good ... so stop feeling sorry for yourself and look lively, lad. Keep an eye out for other survivors while we go back for Red.'

Sam scrambled to do what he was told, his eyes mirroring relief at finding somebody else still alive to tell him what to do.

The last time Nick had sailed this dinghy had been in the calm waters of Poole Harbour. Aria had been waiting for him and they'd made glorious love under the trees. He pressed his palm against his waistcoat and checked that he still had secure the keepsake she'd given him that day. He lifted the mast, pleased to find that the small sail was still intact. When the wind filled it he brought her round to where Red was waving his bandanna, and took him aboard.

They sailed around and picked up a few things they thought might be useful: a stone jug full of ginger beer, a torn sail with a rope attached that would serve to give them shelter if needed, and a tin can with a handle.

They saw bodies, none of which would ever breathe again, and left them to the sea that had claimed them. Most of his crew would either have been in the rigging or trapped in the hull. Their shouts across the water brought no answers. The crew had sailed together for several years and the other two survivors bowed their heads when Nick said a short prayer for the drowned souls.

Afterwards, Red said, 'Which way is the land?'

'A compass would be handy. There's a lot of water out here.'

Sam fished inside his pocket and offered Nick a brass pocket compass of the type usually given to boys for birthdays by fond uncles. It had a small magnifying glass attached that swung out. Nick had received one just like it from his uncle when he was ten. When Erasmus had quizzed him on the compass points two months later, luckily Nick had possessed a good memory to see him through.

He grinned when Sam appeared slightly apologetic at the offering. He was still young enough to indulge in hero worship, and he flushed with pride when Nick said, 'Well done, Sam, first the dinghy, now this. You may have saved our lives. If we weren't in such dire straits I'd give you your first navigation lesson as a reward.'

Keeping the tiller under his arm while he gazed at the needle quivering towards the north, Nick brought their little boat about and pointed her bow to where the land should be. She was slow to respond.

'Bale the water out of the dinghy and try and keep it down, Sam.'

'How?'

'Anyway you can. Hands ... cap ... whatever's available.'

Red smiled at the lad. 'We'll use the captain's boots here. I'll help, between us we'll make short work of it.'

'Make sure you don't lose one, else you'll be swimming after it,' Nick threatened.

The dinghy responded to the weight of water being removed, and soon their little craft was skimming over the water.

It was two days before they washed ashore, woken by the sound of surf. Their lips were cracked and dry from lack of water and exposure to the sun, and they were exhausted. They'd been carried up the coast, now they were in danger of foundering on some rocks. Turning the valiant little boat around, Nick managed to take her out beyond the breakers.

'There's a gap,' Sam croaked, his finger stabbing at an impossibly narrow, but smooth stretch of water.

'Hold tight gentlemen.' Steering the ship into the current Nick dropped the mast. His aim was unerring. Scraping over the hidden barrier of rocks below them, they were pushed through the gap by the force of water behind them, and floated with the decreasing turbulence into a small cove of calm water beyond. Water began to bubble up through split planks and Nick swore. They'd been shipwrecked for the second time in as many days.

With their remaining strength, they pulled their battered craft up the beach. Nick gazed regretfully at it. 'Even if we had the tools, she's damaged beyond repair.'

'The sand is damp up there beyond the tide mark, so there must be fresh water coming down the hill,' Sam suddenly said, rising to his feet. They staggered after him to the patch of damp and began to dig, piling the sand up behind them like three dogs digging up a bone.

They were rewarded by a handful of sandy water apiece, and it tasted like nectar. Eyeing the rocky slope above, where lush vegetation grew, Nick smiled. 'It's coming down the rock from up there. Just a trickle.'

Just a trickle was enough. After they'd licked the moisture on the rocks and had temporarily satisfied their thirst, they filtered moisture from the wet sand through their kerchiefs into the stone jar.

'What's for dinner?' Sam said.

Red smiled as he took a wicked-looking knife from his belt. 'See that rock over there? Oysters! Keep a couple of the shells apiece. They might come in handy.'

Slurping down the slimy shellfish, they washed their meal down with the filtered water, then made their way to the top of the hill and looked around them. The terrain was thickly treed and mountainous. There were several puddles to keep their thirst slaked.

'Where the hell are we?' Red asked.

'East of Melbourne, I'd say. We'd certainly gone round the promontory, but how far east I couldn't say, a couple of hundred miles at a rough guess. We have two choices, gentlemen. We can go overland across the mountains as the crow flies and hope we hit Melbourne. If we average ten miles a day in this we'll reach Melbourne in approximately three weeks. Or we can walk round the coast, which would probably take longer.'

'Which would you prefer, Captain?'

Nick would prefer to be home, snuggled into his soft bed with his soft woman. But it would be a long time before he saw Aria again. She'd worry about him, and she'd keep watch for the *Samarand* forever from her bedroom at Harbour House – a ship that would never sail into her home port again.

He cursed his romantic meandering as he gazed up at the sky. Although the sun was shining overhead at the moment, halfway towards the horizon towering flat-bottomed clouds spiked into the sky. They were painted in various shades, all of them grey and ominous. And he gazed at the tumbling water that surged against the reef, throwing spray high, and at the teeth of the rocks as the sea was sucked back to reveal their dark, rotting smile before the next wave smashed over it.

Not that the dinghy was going anywhere now.

His instinct was nudging him firmly in the ribs, and he decided to trust it.

'There's a bastard of a storm brewing on the horizon and coming our way by the looks of it. I think we'd find more shelter, more to drink and more game to eat inland. I've heard there's a way through, so there might be settlers. We might even find some of the gold that Victoria is famous for on the way.'

Red's eyes began to gleam. 'Perhaps I'll stay here in Australia and search for it once we get to civilization. It's not as if I've got anyone waiting for me back in England.'

'I'll make sure the ship's agent pays you off when we get to Melbourne, then ... not you, young Sam. I intend to deliver you back to your mother in one piece.'

Sam looked so disappointed that the cook laughed, 'Oh, go on, Captain. The boy's fifteen, and he's grown a couple of whiskers over the past couple of days, lessen it's seaweed hanging off his lip. He can be my partner, and I'll look after him. You can tell his ma that he's stayed on to make his fortune, and we'll come home as toffs. It's not as though he's got a ship to join.'

'He'll easily be able to pick one up in Melbourne. In fact, I'll give you both a written reference once we get there.'

Sam shrugged. 'But I want to dig for gold, too.'

'I'll think about it on the way. In the meantime, I'll go down and fetch the sail. Sam, you can come with me and gather together the things we rescued. We might need them.'

He rolled the canvas, tied the guy rope around it and slung it over his shoulder. 'There should be an axe stowed under the stern seat. Fetch that as well, then let's go.'

There was nothing else useful in the boat so they headed back to where they'd left Red.

As promised Nick thought about Sam's future, not that there was much to think about. Red had always been reliable, and Sam was nearly a man. It was the lad's decision whether he stayed or not, and at least Nick wouldn't have to tell his mother that her son had drowned.

They set off towards the west, and leaving the dinghy to her fate headed down into the first valley. It was tough country, filled with ferns and vegetation, and it wasn't going to be so easy to navigate as Nick had first thought. But they were all fit. At the bottom they set up camp under a moss-covered overhang of rock. Red caught a hopping creature that resembled an overgrown rabbit, cut its throat, then skinned and gutted it.

'It's a wallaby,' Sam told them. 'I saw a drawing of one in a book.'

Red laughed. 'Bugger me, if we ain't got a genius in our midst.'

'Go and see if you can find anything that looks edible, Sam. There might be some fruit or something. Take the axe to chip the bark off the trees so you can find your way back.'

Gathering some dead wood and piling it high, Nick concentrated the sun through Sam's magnifying glass to set a light under the fire. He fashioned a spit for the wallaby.

Sam came back with plants that had leaves like

a dandelion. The roots were tuberous and resembled potatoes.

'They're yams, I reckon,' Red said. 'We can cook those in the ashes. And there was a spreading plant that had pretty pale green leaves and pink berries.

Red stared at it. 'What's that?'

'I don't know, but the berries taste like cooking apples.'

By evening they were all exhausted. The wallaby had tasted vaguely of venison, and the yams had been delicious. There had been enough meat left over to keep for breakfast. Despite the heat of the day the shadows brought with them a cold night. But at least they had the fire, and they built it up to keep insects or animals at bay, and they huddled under the sail for warmth.

Before the light failed Nick took out the portrait of Aria, as he always did.

Red gazed at it over his shoulder and smiled. 'I know that face, it's Miss Honeyman.'

Nick couldn't hide his smile, and it was about time he told someone. He ran a finger over Aria's innocently childish face, which was capped by a curly mop of dark hair, and he wondered if he'd have a daughter who looked just like her one day. He said in a gruff manner, because tears were just under the surface and emotion didn't come easily to him since he'd been taught that men didn't cry, 'Actually, it's Mrs Thornton now. We were wed in Boston. If anything happens to me before we reach civilization, make sure she gets this back and tell her ... tell her that to me, she was as the inscription described.'

'Aye, I will.'

'You don't seem surprised.'

'No, Captain. We all saw which way the wind was blowing, and the only one to be surprised by that when the time came was you, I reckon.'

Disgruntled, Nick huffed, 'The devil you did.'

Red and Sam exchanged a grin when he chuckled.

Thirteen

It had been a wet winter, and the miserable days passed by slowly.

Charles Barrie had made an equally slow recovery, but recover he had, and was now building up his strength. Certainly, his energy was returning.

Not for the first time he picked up the photograph of his grandson with the family who fostered him. He understood exactly why the photograph had been sent to him. It was to demonstrate that John was happily settled with them.

Edgar had reinforced that ... had reasoned with him, had made arrangements so they could meet. Edgar had told him that the soldier was prepared to refuse his request to hand John over, and had indicated that he'd go to court over the matter rather than let John go.

Both of them had forgotten one thing. John was not related to the Hardy family. John Charles was a Barrie. His own grandson. His own blood!

He sent a messenger to Adam Chapman's house with a request that he attend him.

The young man's self-possession, when coupled with his youth was formidable as well as disconcerting. Adam Chapman stood before him, impassive, showing no trace of what was going on in his mind. His calm grey eyes had darkened slightly while Charles had put forward his proposition.

'Let me get this clear, Sir Charles. You want me to abduct the child?'

Was that how he saw it? Testily, Charles told him, 'It's hardly an abduction when the child is my relative.' He handed over the photograph. 'This is what they sent me, with the message that I could see him when I'd recovered from my illness.'

Adam smiled. 'A sensible precaution, surely, since they wouldn't want the boy to become infected. Would you do any less if you were in their position? They're a handsome family. The two women are similar in looks. I imagine they're sisters.'

Charles's only interest in the two women was the possibility that they could serve him in some way. 'Well, if you won't bring me the child, investigate the background of the family. See if you can find some juicy scandal to discredit

215

them with.' Charles sighed. He had the feeling he was going to get nowhere with this young man.

Chapman placed the photograph down on the table and engaged his eyes. The distaste in them was all too apparent, and Charles felt a twinge of shame. Nobody had looked at him that way before.

'You're not going to do what I ask, are you?'

'No, sir, I am not. I do not snatch children from their homes, and will not be used as the instrument to bring down the Hardy family. I'd strongly advise that you do not employ another to take such a rash step.'

'When I need your advice I'll ask for it, young man.'

'Nevertheless, it's offered for your own good. Can you imagine what this will do to your good name and your professional career if it gets out, sir?'

'Is that a threat, young man?'

Chapman stared at him. 'Not from me, sir, but I'd be surprised if your colleagues would support you in such an unethical scheme as you propose. But there's no fool like an old fool, they say, especially one who allows pride to rule his good sense.'

'Say what?' Charles spluttered.

'I think you understood me, Sir Charles. My integrity is not for sale to you, or to anyone. Good day.'

He had gone too far, Charles realized. 'I'm sorry,' he called after him, and he was. But the affront in the young man's eyes told him that it hadn't come across as sincere, and now was not the time.

Adam Chapman bowed, then turned and left.

Outside, Adam filled his lungs with a breath of damp air and released it slowly, allowing his anger to evaporate. He walked to the corner and glanced about the square. Odd to think he'd grown up in a similar square and had vowed to restore the family's fortune. It didn't seem so important now. Whatever the address it still stank of horseshit. Adam now realized that privilege had its price – one he didn't want to pay. He also realized that if Sir Charles turned his mind to it his career would be ruined.

'Fine for you to lecture another on pride when you've starched your own backbone with it,' he said out loud.

It began to rain. Deep in thought, Adam didn't hear the carriage come to a halt until Edgar Wyvern called him over. 'Good day, Mr Chapman. You're the very person I was looking for.'

'Mr Wyvern?'

'Don't look so bewildered. Climb in, man, you're getting soaked.'

'I've just been to your home looking for you,' he said when Adam settled himself on the opposite seat. 'Mrs Chapman offered me tea while I waited. Miss Chapman told me you'd be some time, and that you sometimes stayed in town. She suggested that you might be with Sir Charles. Are you coming or going?'

'Going.'

'I found your mother and sister to be quite

217

charming company.'

'My mother enjoys entertaining, and she gets little chance now my father is deceased.'

'You support them, I understand.'

'As best I can, since they're my responsibility.'

'Very laudable, but I wouldn't expect anything less of you.'

'Why did you want to see me, sir?'

'You have a rather distracted note in your voice. Has Sir Charles upset you?'

'I'd rather not discuss my business with Sir Charles.'

'Quite ... but no doubt I'll soon be informed of it. You remind him of his son, you know. He had a mind of his own too, and they used to have heated debates. I have a proposition to put to you, young man.'

'You should wait until you've spoken to Sir Charles, perhaps.'

'Very well, I can see you're upset about something, and a young man with his blood up is sometimes irrational.'

Exactly what Adam had told Sir Charles he was, except he'd been more to the point. An old fool was indeed an old fool, but then ... so was a young one. Adam managed a wry smile as Edgar Wyvern handed over his card. 'I apologize for being churlish,' he said.

'There's no need. Sir Charles sometimes has the same effect on me. Can you be at my chambers tomorrow at ten?'

'If you so wish.'

'I do so wish. It's raining quite hard. Take my

umbrella, young man. You can return it tomorrow.'

Adam spent the evening listening to his mother happily extolling the virtues of their visitor, something that would keep her happy for the rest of the week. He exchanged a smile with his sister, and after his mother had gone to bed told her. 'Mr Wyvern has a proposition to put before me. It may improve our lot in the long term.'

She kissed his cheek. 'Thanks to your ingenuity we are managing quite well, Adam. I know mother complains sometimes, but she's very proud of you. She was impressed by the quality of your client, and has quite changed her mind about your profession. She couldn't stop praising you to Mr Wyvern. He was a very pleasant man.'

The next morning Adam presented himself to the Wyvern chambers. There was a fire in the grate, the flames leaped and danced, keeping the shadows at bay. It was a place of warmth, of gleaming wood panels and leather chairs. Coffee was served, a small dash of brandy added to nurture the spirit and warm the blood.

'Now, young man, I've talked to Sir Charles. What do you have to say for yourself!'

'That I have thought it over and have come to the conclusion that I was right, but perhaps a little too outspoken.'

'Then you'll take on the task he offered you?'

'Certainly not.'

His host smiled. 'Good. That's what I hoped you'd say. Rest assured, Sir Charles has now been persuaded that his way is not the right path to take.'

'You assured me of that once before.'

'It's true that I've never known the man to be so headstrong, but the circumstances are exceptional. He has agreed to a proposition I've put to him.'

'What has this to do with me?'

'Sir Charles needs to see his grandson. He cannot travel at the moment. I've suggested that he should send you to Dorset, visit Captain Hardy and request that the boy be taken to London to see him.'

'Why me?'

'Because I cannot afford the time at the moment.'

Adam placed his cup in the saucer. 'I'm sorry, but Sir Charles's character has proved to be more devious than I first thought, and I no longer feel I can trust him. I want nothing more to do with this business, since it appears that I'm losing the detachment I usually apply to my cases.'

'Young man, you should remember that Sir Charles has trusted you with this important event in his life. See the matter through for him, he'll make it worth your while.'

Adam remembered Celia's shabby gown.

'The boy's stepfather can come to London with him, and a compromise has been suggested. They'll be accommodated in a hotel and the meeting will take place in Sir Charles's home with both you and Colonel Hardy present.'

'Couldn't you send Colonel Hardy a letter to

that effect?'

'He'll probably need persuading.'

'You think he'll allow me to persuade him when he recognizes me? I've already deceived him once.'

'You have a way with you, Mr Chapman, so I'm sure he will. I liked Colonel Hardy when I met him, and sense that you're kindred spirits.'

Adam had sensed the same in the brief moment they'd spent together, but he doubted if a friendship would be the result when Seth Hardy discovered that he'd been instrumental in the investigation. But better him than some felon who would snatch the child.

'Yes, I'll go, but I refuse to put any pressure on the man, and after the boy is reunited with his grandfather and I'm satisfied that all is well, that will be the end of it.'

Marianne's nausea grew worse. She went downstairs, white-faced after a particularly heavy bout.

'Good grief,' Charlotte said. 'You're as white as a ghost.'

'Aunt Marianne was sick, like she usually is in the morning. I heard her,' John said, innocently tearing a hole in Marianne's flimsy charade.

Charlotte's eyes narrowed a little. 'You didn't say you'd been ill, Marianne. Perhaps we should get the doctor in to examine you.'

'There's no need. It's nothing. I'm feeling better.'

'You don't look better.' Seth rose from the table and kissed Charlotte on the forehead. He said, 'Don't be long with your breakfast John, else you'll be late for school.'

'I'm full up.'

Marianne managed a wan smile for him. 'It's best if you eat it up. It will warm your stomach, so there's a furnace inside it to keep the rest of you warm.'

Alice set a plate with a pair of smoked kippers on in front of her. 'There you are, Miss Honeyman. Your favourite breakfast.'

Marianne's appetite fled at the site of the smoked fish. Scraping her chair back she clapped her hand over her mouth and ran, making it out through the back door just in time. The cold, fresh air began to revive her.

She heard Seth say. 'Shall I ask the doctor to visit?'

Charlotte's voice, deceptively bland. 'No. I'll see to her. I expect she's eaten something that's disagreed with her.'

'Better keep her away from the babies then.'

Waiting until she heard the horse and cart leave, Marianne went back inside. Charlotte's calm voice hadn't fooled her, and her sister was waiting in her bedroom.

'Well?' she said, her foot tapping against the floor as it always did when she was good and angry.

'Well, what?'

'You know damned well what. Whose child is it, or need I ask?'

She sighed. 'It's Nick's.'

'You slut. You're as bad as our mother. Worse!' She lashed out and her hand stung flatly against Marianne's cheek. 'You're a disgrace, and you can get out.'

'Charlotte, don't. It's not as bad as you think. Nick and I were married in Boston.'

'You liar! Nick would never had married you when it was me he loved.' This time Marianne's other cheek bore the brunt of Charlotte's anger.

Bursting into tears Marianne fell on to the bed 'Stop it, Charlotte.'

'I never thought you'd betray me like this. My own sister. God knows what Seth will say when he finds out.'

'It's none of his business. And it's none of yours. I'm old enough to decide the course my own life. I love Nick.'

'It's our business when you're living under our roof. Let me see your marriage certificate.'

'Nick's got it on board *Samarand*.'

'A likely story. You stupid little fool, Marianne. The gossips will work overtime when they find out.'

'If you don't tell them they won't know. Nick will be home in a couple of months, and we'll get married in the church.'

'So you're not married.'

'Yes ... we are. Nick got a special licence and we went to a chapel.' She pulled out the chain her ring was hanging on. 'See ... here's my wedding ring.' Hastily she dropped it back inside her bodice when Charlotte reached out, as though to tear it from her neck.

'I'll kill him when I lay eyes on him. Don't you see, you little fool, he's ruined you to get back at me.'

'Nick hasn't ruined me. You don't own him, Charlotte, and I'll make him forget he ever loved you.'

'He'll never do that.' She began to take clothes from a drawer and throw them on the bed. She stopped at the underwear Nick had bought her and gazed at it, a sneer on her face. 'I suppose Nick bought you this. She ripped the pantaloons apart and threw them in a corner, then picked up some scissors from the dressing table and slashed at the fabric of the corset before sending it after the pantaloons.

'Stop it, Charlotte. I need you to help me.'

'I am helping you.' Clothes began to fly on to the bed. 'There's another bag in the hall cupboard you can have. You can fetch a sack for the rest.'

'You're going to throw me out, your own sister?'

'You can go and knock on Daisy Thornton's door and move in with them. See if Erasmus or Daisy will give you house room, since the baby you're carrying is a Thornton bastard, you traitor.'

In the nursery the twins began to cry. 'See what you've done. I'm going to feed them now, and when I come out I want you to be gone.'

'Charlotte, you're being irrational—'

'Don't you accuse me of being irrational. Get out of my sight! I hate you,' she shrieked.

Packing her clothes as best she could Marianne picked up the two bags. The nursery door was closed as she went past.

'Charlotte,' she whispered against the panel,

because she heard the sound of sobbing.

'Get out, I said. And don't come back, because the door will be closed against you.'

Marianne went downstairs and out through the front door. The house she'd grown up in seemed alien to her now. She looked up at the nursery window and saw the curtain twitch.

As she took the pale ribbon of track towards Poole tears trickled down her cheeks. She went slowly, waiting for Charlotte to have a change of heart and call her back. But her sister didn't, and after a while she picked up speed. She realized that the only people she could turn to now were the Thorntons.

By the time she reached their home she was tired, and her shoulders ached. Her knock was answered by Erasmus Thornton. His eyes widened with surprise when he saw her standing there. His mouth formed the name Caroline then he blinked and quickly recovered. 'It's Miss Honeyman, isn't it?'

'Yes, it is. I need somewhere to stay, Captain Thornton.'

His forehead furrowed into a frown. 'Why come to me?'

What she said next obviously staggered him because his face flushed with blood. 'Because you once loved my mother, and you owe her a debt. Besides, I couldn't think of anyone else.'

He stared at her, hard-eyed, and began to close the door. 'That's in the past, and is none of your business. Go back home to your sister, girl.'

She flattened her palm against the panel and shoved her foot through the gap. 'You don't understand, Erasmus Thornton. I'm expecting a baby. You were kind to me at the ball and I thought you might help me. I have nobody else to help me and my sister has turned me out.'

He gave a short, unbelieving bark of laughter. 'Am I to believe that Nick fathered the infant you're carrying then, since I know I didn't.'

Tears filled her eyes and she sobbed, 'Of course Nick did. I'm his wife.'

Erasmus began to laugh. 'Do you expect me to fall for that? Get off home with you, girl. Nick's wife, indeed! Nick burned his fingers badly with one Honeyman female, so he's not likely to try it a second time. I'm not providing you with a roof over your head.'

Daisy appeared behind her brother and pushed him out of the way before she opened the door wide. 'You don't have to provide anything. This is my house, Erasmus and I say she can stay. Take her bags. She'll be company for me and can sleep in Nicholas's room for now, while we get this sorted out. When he comes home we'll hear what he has to say about this from his own lips. It's about time he settled down.'

'On your own head be it then, Daisy. I told you and I told him. No good ever comes of a woman stepping aboard *Samarand*. She's a jealous mistress.'

'Hush your superstitious nonsense, Erasmus, lest you want a good clout round the ear. You're not on board your ship now and you don't tell me what to do. Look at the girl, she's as pale and trembling as a ghost. Come on in, my dear. I'll put the kettle on and we'll have a nice cup of tea.

Take no notice of my brother. He's all bark and no bite.'

The woman cast her brother a scowl that sent a grin scurrying over his lips, but the unexpected kindness Daisy showed towards her brought fresh tears welling to Marianne's eyes and she gulped out, 'Thank you. I'm sure my sister will take me back when she's thought things through. It was a shock for her.'

Erasmus shrugged. 'Happen she mightn't, too. She's always been too stubborn for her own good.'

'There, there,' Daisy said. 'We'll sort this out, just you wait and see. If that rogue has got you into trouble he can put a ring on your finger. It's about time one of the damned fool Thornton men faced up to some responsibility.'

'But I told you ... we are married, and I do have a ring. Nick had bought a licence from somewhere, and we were wed in Boston in a little chapel. We spent our wedding night at a hotel run by a friend of Nick's. A lady called Mrs Crawford. She looked like a fine lady to me, but Nick said –' and she cast a doubtful glance at Daisy – 'well, never mind what he said, he has the certificate, that's all that matters.' Erasmus could barely hold back his laughter. So she and Nick had spent their wedding night in a whorehouse, and the girl knew it? Erasmus thought. Wasn't that just like Nick. No wonder her cheeks were as red as a rash on a baby's backside. And no wonder the eldest girl was spitting out a firestorm over this. Nick certainly knew how to take his revenge. He'd had his fun while he was doing it, and had planted a babe inside the girl in the process, easy to do with a girl like this, so young and impressionable. A man would find it hard to control his urges with her.

At least he'd taken her to a classy house. Eyes crinkling, and finding it hard not to guffaw with laughter, Erasmus picked up her bags and kicked the door shut behind them. The marriage was something he could check up on – and he would.

Halfway up the stairs he thought fiercely: By Lucifer, the girl was so much like her mother that she'd given him a turn when he'd opened the door. It had better not have been a bogus marriage, else he'd march Nick up the aisle himself, and with a shotgun aimed squarely at his backside. Taking revenge was one thing, ruining the reputation of a young girl was another thing altogether.

The girl would need a friend to support her in the weeks to come, and there was none better than Daisy.

Fourteen

Marianne hadn't expected to like Daisy Thornton but the two women soon became fast friends.

The older woman was unconventional in her thinking, especially for a spinster, and her comments about people were pithy and to the point. She rarely went to church. Even so, the Reverend Robert Phipps called on her from time to time.

'Damn fool, he's Erasmus's friend, and he's never going to save my soul, or my brother's, she told Marianne.

'Don't you want your soul to be saved?'

'Hah! There's nothing left of it to save. My father was a pious, hypocritical man, and he beat religion out of me instead of into me, and all before I was twelve. Erasmus too. My brother told me our souls were in our backsides, which was why our father laid his strap across it so often. Erasmus survived the beatings better because he has a hide as tough as an old wolf. We were thrashed because of Dickon's misdeeds.'

'Dickon?'

'Nicholas's father. Our half-brother from his first wife. The only time our mother was happy was when father went to sea, and I prayed that he would never come back. One day he didn't. He died, and was buried at sea. Erasmus was learning his craft, sailing with our uncle at the time.'

'What happened to Dickon?'

'Dickon went bad at an early age. Drink ... gambling, women. Dickon travelled and got into all sorts of trouble, though managing to make a small fortune for himself at the same time. He died fighting a duel over some woman.'

'Goodness.'

When Erasmus got word of it he went to Greece and came back with Nicholas. I didn't even know that Dickon had a child. At first, I thought he was a child Erasmus had fathered, but he wasn't. The boy had been supported financially by Dickon, but was being treated badly by the woman's husband and his family.'

'Poor Nick.'

There were tears in the eyes that came her way. 'You're not telling lies about Nicholas, are you girl? He's suffered enough at the hands of your family. Oh, I know he acts tough, and he brought most of it on himself by attaching himself to Charlotte in the first place. I'll never forgive—'

'Don't say anything more, Aunt Daisy. Despite the way Charlotte has treated me over this, I love my sister and I know that one day we'll be reunited.' She gave the woman a hug. 'I truly love Nick. Don't you worry, I'll be a good wife to him,' and she placed her hands over her stomach, 'I love this child that I'm carrying. Today I felt him move inside me, and it was a wondrous feeling. You'll see, when Nick comes home you'll know that I'm telling the truth.'

'Aye, well, I guess I'd better believe you then, else I'm going to end up looking the fool, which is exactly what your sister will look when the truth be known.'

'Then let that be your secret pleasure from this situation, but it won't be mine.'

Marianne missed her sister, and although she went to Harbour House to try and repair the rift between them, she found the doors and windows closed against her. No amount of door banging would gain her access.

Seth called on her a couple of times. Dear Seth, who hadn't known what a formidable adversary Charlotte could be, and who was doing his best to reconcile them.

'How are the children?' she asked him.

'Thriving.'

'And John? Is he getting on with the book for his grandfather?'

'He's doing his best. Luckily, most of the drawings are done, and I can help him with the letters. Are you all right, Marianne?'

'I'm well,' and her voice thickened. 'I miss you all so. I hate being embroiled in an argument. Charlotte is being so stubborn, but I have faith. She'll relent eventually.'

'I do hope so. She feels you betrayed her by taking up with Nick.'

'But she scorned him, Seth, and in the most cruel way. He didn't deserve being threatened with a gun. If she'd truly loved him she'd have married him. Now she's punishing me to lessen the burden of blame she carries, when all she's

231

achieving is to add to it. She's lucky to have you. Another man wouldn't put up with her moods.'

'I'm under no illusion that I was anything but second best to her. But I'm not unhappy, and she has given me two beautiful children.'

She touched his cheek, seeking to sympathize with him. 'Dear Seth. She was guided by instinct, as was I when I wed Nick. I'm sure that Charlotte will forget her injured pride in time. She's too passionate, and finds it hard to forgive a wrong. But she is also loyal, and she will soften in time.'

On Seth's second visit he tried to leave some money to help pay for her board.

Erasmus had just returned from Boston, and his curt reply was, 'The Thorntons look after their own, mister. Marianne is a Thornton now, for I've seen the registry of her marriage to my nephew with my own eyes, and have brought back a copy with me. I'm satisfied that all is above board and you can tell that sister of hers that we'll look after her.'

Marianne longed for Nick to return and help to put things right. When she lay in his bed she imagined she was lying in his arms. It was a nice room. A mahogany dresser with unadorned brass handles contained his clothing. There was an oval mirror on the top, and the small drawer underneath it contained a hairbrush, a silver card case, and several other bits and pieces. There was room in the wardrobe for most of her clothes, because she didn't have many. The rest, she placed in a trunk at the end of the bed.

'You won't need any more cupboards,' Daisy

said. 'When Nicholas returns, no doubt he'll look for a home of his own that the three of you can live in.'

There was a lace-edged handkerchief in the drawer. It had Charlotte's initials embroidered on it. Marianne tried not to feel jealous at the sight of it, but the next time she went out she threw it into the harbour and watched it bob away on the tide. Then an awful, but ridiculous thought occurred to her. What if the handkerchief sailed around the world and washed up on the shore where Nick was sitting?

She came to the conclusion that it was hard to be in love when she was uncertain that her love was returned. Marianne was under no illusion that if Charlotte snapped her fingers at him Nick would surely go to her. And that would crush her. It would probably crush Seth as well, because it was obvious that the man was smitten by Charlotte, also.

When Adam Chapman knocked on the door of Harbour House, he handed his card to a maid.

She was back in a couple of minutes. 'Colonel Hardy said he can give you five minutes, and to show you into his study.'

The house had a comfortable, lived-in feel. In the study the floorboards were covered in rugs that were worn in places where feet usually trekked back and forth. The study looked out over a garden of ragged lawn covered in fruit trees, dandelions and daisies that pushed against a thick fringe of nettles and into the tender green bracken beyond. Beyond that was a vegetable garden walled against the wind. Chickens clucked somewhere.

Adam absorbed his surroundings. Books leaned untidily against each other on the shelves, the leather chairs were worn, the panelled walls dark with years of rubbed beeswax. A fire was laid in a grate inside a large moulded iron fireplace with a brass fender and firedogs. A clock ticked on the mantle. The desk held ledgers, a silver inkwell and penholder.

There was a picture on the wall ... two young girls posed on a seat in a rose-covered arbour. One had a puppy on her lap. He went to study it more closely.

'They are my wife and her sister when they were children,' Seth Hardy said from the doorway behind him.

Adam turned.

The eyes of the man he'd come to see widened and his voice was dry when he said, 'Adam Chapman, I presume. We've met before, and I now know why you didn't give me a name outside the school. Would you prefer to be called Henry Smith?'

Hardy had a sharp mind. 'I'd actually prefer Adam. I'm sorry for the deception. I'd completed my assignment and hadn't intended to involve myself in your affairs any further. I felt the need to pass on what I'd heard to you, since a young woman was involved. I hope the fisherman proved useful.'

'He did, and my thanks.' Seth held out a hand to him, and the pair exchanged a smile. 'Why are you here now if your assignment has been completed? Do you need to meet the object of your investigation, or do you intend to scrutinize my private life as well?' He spread his hands and smiled. 'We are as you see us.'

'May I ask why you agreed to see me, first?'

'I'm curious to meet a man who discovered so much about me. You know, if you'd knocked on my door and asked for the same information, I'd have probably given it to you. It would have been quicker.'

'More likely I'd have earned myself a punch on the nose.'

Seth chuckled. 'That's entirely possible.'

'As it is I have all the information on you I needed to know. I do have scruples, and was hired to find a man's grandson, not to destroy your life. Sir Charles has since rehired me to be his envoy, something I was reluctant to take on.'

'But you did. Why?'

'I have a mother and sister to support and the pay offered was excellent. I think you know why I'm here.'

'Because of John. So much for your bloody scruples.'

'I assure you, I'm here because of my scruples. Sir Charles had a very different plan of approach than the one I'm making here on his behalf.'

Seth gave a faint smile. 'I can imagine.'

'Sir Charles Barrie requests that you take his grandson to London so he can meet the boy. He'll pay all expenses.'

'And he sent you to ask. Why didn't he write or send his lawyer again?'

'He didn't think you'd come ... and Edward

Wyvern didn't have the time. He's a busy man, and in my estimation, a man with integrity.'

'Sir Charles expects you to persuade me, after you investigated my affairs?'

'I wouldn't even attempt to persuade you. You're an intelligent man, Colonel Hardy, and well aware of the rights and wrongs of this matter.'

'Please feel free to call me by my first name. And so far it's his own rights that Sir Charles has been concerned with. I've been threatened with them on occasion and that doesn't impress me. The man lacks charm.'

'Not entirely, but he's autocratic and possesses a dogged determination. Surprisingly, he also has the ability to absorb plain speaking. You've impressed Edward Wyvern, who is about the only person Sir Charles will take advice from. You could do the same with Sir Charles if you put your mind to it. He's a crafty old fox, one who knows a lie when he sees one. Trying to humble him is not the right approach to take. I've tried it.'

'I've never employed lies with him, and I don't play games. John's happiness and his future is my only concern.'

'The boy does have the right to know he has a grandfather.'

'John does know. He also knows that he'll see him in a few weeks when Sir Charles comes to visit. In fact he's looking forward to it.' He gestured toward a drawing book on a side table. 'He's making his grandfather a book with drawings of the heath birds in it. For a lad of his age he has a steady hand and his aunt is ... was helping him.'

Adam didn't miss the nuance. 'His aunt is no longer here?'

'Marianne has married and has moved into her husband's home. She is Mrs Thornton now.'

Judging by the hurried marriage, obviously the fisherman had told the truth about what he'd seen, then. 'John must miss her.'

'Yes ... John and Marianne were good companions. She grew up in this house, and used to take him out on the heath. He enjoys learning things.'

'You have a father's pride in your voice.'

'And the same love for him that a father should have. To all intents and purposes John is my son, since his mother put him in my care from infancy.' His voice took on a slightly mocking tone. 'I concede that his artistic talent comes from his father's blood, for I have several Barrie drawings and paintings, including some of Mary ... his mother. They are John's legacy. You know, Adam, you didn't need to argue me into it. I'm quite willing to take John to London to meet his grandfather if Sir Charles is not well enough to travel here. I'll go to London on Friday and return on Monday, so John doesn't miss too much school.'

Adam smiled with relief. 'Good, I had planned to travel back on Friday myself. We could go together, perhaps.'

Laughter coloured Seth's voice now. 'Surely you don't intend to act as my escort?'

'Certainly not. You look to be more a man than

237

I could handle should you want to give me the slip, and I'm not given to violence unless it's in defence of myself. The truth is I find the journey is tedious and I would welcome your company and that of John.'

'Then you shall have it. Now, would you care for some coffee, Adam?'

'Thank you ... but I believe my five minutes might be up by now.'

Seth laughed. 'I can afford you five more, I imagine. Are you accommodated? I can put you up if you wish. We don't often have guests; we're rather isolated.'

'Your surroundings are beautiful, so that must compensate for it. You were born here in Dorset, were you not?'

'My mother was from Dorchester, and my father was a soldier. He died abroad and I can't remember him all that well. I was born and brought up in the home of my maternal grandmother. My mother took in pupils, so she saw to my early education...' Seth raised an eyebrow. 'But I imagine you know that.'

'Not that particular snippet. You were twelve when she died, and your grandmother sent you to a boarding school. There was enough left in her estate to pay for your commission ... and your Scottish relative left you quite well off when he died.'

'And I never knew he existed until then.' Seth looked him straight in the eye. 'I really must change my legal representation in Scotland.'

'It might be a good idea. I can suggest someone whom I know to be both honest and discreet,

238

if you'd wish. And thank you for your offer of hospitality. I accept, because I'd really like to explore your heath a little. You mine clay and gravel, I believe.'

'I can take you up and show you the pits if you like. The clay is conveyed in carts along rails to the loading barges, sorted, and then sold to the various potteries.'

A few days later two men and a boy were about to board a train at Poole Junction. They would change trains at Southampton, then alight at Waterloo Bridge station.

John's quick smile revealed his nervous excitement at this momentous event in his life, but he pressed hard against Seth's side and hugged a small exercise notebook, in which Seth had drawn a map of their journey and the towns they would pass through.

Before they'd left the house Charlotte had fussed. She'd checked all their buttons were attached, and that they both had clean hand-kerchiefs in their pockets. 'Make sure you're on your best behaviour, John.'

'Yes, Mama.'

'There's a picnic basket. Don't eat the food all at once in case you're sick ... that goes for you too, Seth. And you, Mr Chapman.'

The three men exchanged a grin when she said, 'Goodness, what are you waiting for then? Off you go. The cab is outside and you'll miss the train if you don't hurry. Goodbye, Mr Chapman. It was nice meeting you. You'll have to bring your mother and sister to visit one day.'

'They would enjoy that, I'm sure.'

After the other two had left the house Seth took Charlotte's face between his hands and gazed into her wary blue eyes. She'd been low in spirits since Erasmus Thornton had collared her at the church and given her a dressing down, something he knew she'd deserved. He kissed her mouth with more intimacy than she usually encouraged, and colour flooded her cheeks.

'Do something for me,' he said.

'What is it?'

'Don't think so badly of Marianne. Make your peace with her.'

Her face tensed. 'Not while she's living under Thornton's roof.'

'You sent her there, and thank God they took her in.'

'Oh, my sister always lands the right way up. People like her with her pretty ways. She didn't have to fight for anything when we were small. I did it for her. Well, now she knows what it's like to have people talking about her, and it serves her right. Running away with Nick Thornton without a word and bringing shame down on her family is unforgivable. And I don't believe they are married, whatever Erasmus Thornton said. He's just trying to save face.'

'What is it that's so unforgivable? The marriage itself. The infant she is carrying, or the fact that she has married Nick, a man who I happen to like.'

'Seth,' she murmured helplessly. 'I can't forgive her. I don't know why, because she made a fool of me, I imagine. One day, perhaps...'

'It's a pity you can't give love with a passion

240

equal to your capacity to hate.'

She flinched. 'I can ... I love my children.'

'They're not your children, my dear. They're ours, and I love them just as much.'

She took a step back, the colour draining away as if she was about to faint, her vulnerability apparent to him. 'You don't intend to take them away from me, do you, Seth? I couldn't bear it.'

He gazed at her, a frown on his face. 'Whatever put that idea in your head? I wouldn't think of depriving the children of their mother.'

'Last night I dreamed the gypsy came to me, and I heard a child calling out. It was lost, and the dream was so real that I got up and went to check on the children.'

He wanted to comfort her, but she wouldn't have welcomed it. 'It was only a dream, Charlotte. Don't let it trouble you.'

'But it seemed so real, and it has stayed with me.' She shrugged, and in a moment of unconscious self-deprecation said wryly, 'I'm usually more sensible about such things. I think I got the best of the marriage bargain we made.'

He grinned at that, said, 'I'm not complaining. You do have some good qualities, and I've learned to love you, anyway.'

Her eyes rounded in disbelief, but her smile eased the tension from her face as she murmured, 'I didn't realize.'

Neither had he until that moment. Kissing her again, he left her with that thought.

When they reached London they took a cab directly to Bedford Square. The door opened to their knock. When he saw Adam, the butler allowed them into the hall. His gaze fell on John and awareness came into his eyes. 'Is Sir Charles expecting you?'

'No, but I imagine he'll want to see us.' Seth handed the man his card.

The man was back within seconds. 'Sir Charles will see you. May I take your coats and hats, gentlemen?'

When the butler announced them Sir Charles waved him away. 'I'll ring if I need you.'

The old man rose with some difficulty, using a stick for support. The hand Seth shook had a firm grip, but the skin was dry and there was a fine tremor to it. If Seth had ever doubted this man was John's grandfather, he didn't now. The eyes looking into his could have been John's, only the gaze was much more astute. It was disconcerting.

'So, we meet at last,' Sir Charles said. 'Mr Chapman, please feel free to leave now your mission has been concluded.'

'I'd prefer Mr Chapman to stay, since his thorough investigation of me on your behalf has assured that both of you know more about me than I do. No doubt he'll be interested in the outcome of this meeting first hand. Also, he's been kind enough to accommodate us while we are here.'

Sir Charles didn't seem to be too pleased by that. 'Very well, Colonel Hardy. You won't mind if I sit, will you, and I hope you will do the same. Let the boy come forward so I can see him.'

'John, do as your grandfather requests. I'll

be here.'

'Yes, Pa.' He stepped forward and held out his hand. 'How do you do, sir. I'm pleased to meet you. And thank you for sending me the telescope. Sometimes I look at the stars through it. Aunt Marianne was teaching me their names, and she was helping me make a chart.'

'Your aunt must be very clever.'

'Oh, she is. She helped me make a belt from the skin of a dead adder. Only it didn't fit, and she said it smelled disgusting, so we threw it away.'

'One would hope it wasn't a live snake.' Sir Charles chuckled at his own joke.

'No, sir,' John said earnestly. 'I'm to keep away from live snakes. They have venom in their fangs and if they bite me I'll become very sick.'

When John gazed up at him as if seeking assurance, Seth smiled at him. 'There, that wasn't so bad, was it?'

Tears were trembling on the old man's lashes. 'Thank you for bringing the boy, Colonel Hardy. I appreciate it. Are you hungry, John?'

'Yes, sir.'

Something stated with such enthusiasm that Seth laughed. 'He's always hungry.'

'D'you know, I have an appetite too. Ring that bell over there, and when my butler comes in ask him to serve us all some tea, with hot buttered muffins and fruit cake. What's that book in your hands?'

'It's for you, sir. I made a book, so you can learn about the birds and animals on the heath

243

where I live.' He flicked over a page. 'That's a nightjar. The male has white patches on his wings and tail. If you go out at dusk and wave a white handkerchief they fly out from their nests and attack it, because they think their territory is being invaded by other nightjars.' His finger stabbed at the next page, 'That one's a woodlark. See, it has a white stripe over its eyes, and those feathers on top of its head ruffle up into a crest.'

John's stomach gurgled, and it must have reminded him of the buttered muffins, because he placed the book on the table next to his grandfather's lap and headed for the bell pull.

'Tea for four, please, Mr Butler,' he said, when the servant appeared. 'We'd like hot buttered muffins and fruit cake.'

'Certainly, Master John, and my name is Ballam. Would you like to come with me and wash your hands before tea.'

John gazed at his hands. 'No thank you, Mr Ballam ... they're not very dirty.'

Seth frowned. 'Wash them please, John. You've been on the train all day.'

'How long are you to remain in London for, Colonel Hardy?' Sir Charles said after John had followed the butler out.

'I don't want him to take too much time off from school. We return to Poole on Monday, and will be staying with Mr Chapman in the meantime. You can see him again at Easter, as we arranged.'

'I see ... would you at least consider leaving John with me until you depart. I'd like to get to know him better.'

'He's a lively child and he'll tax your strength.'

'One of my maids can take charge of him.'

'I daresay one would, but I promised my wife I'd keep him with me.'

As John returned, Charles said, 'Well, let's ask John, shall we? Edgar tells me he didn't see a dog when he visited you. I have a friend whose bitch has just produced puppies. I was thinking that John might like one. John, would you like to stay with me until your stepfather picks you up to return to Poole?'

Eyes shining, John said, 'Will I be able to take the puppy home with me?'

His grandfather gave a faint smile. 'Only if it's old enough to leave its mother ... that's if your stepfather allows you to.'

John's eyes flicked his way, and they held worry. Already he was inseparable from the thought of having a puppy, and Seth was cast as the villain who would prevent him from getting his heart's desire. As crafty as a fox, Adam had said of Sir Charles Barrie, and it was true. But Seth didn't intend to be cornered.

'Please don't manipulate John into your way of thinking, Sir Charles, or we'll be on the next train home. I'm sure we can find a puppy for you at the market in Dorchester if you want one, John, and you can choose your own. As for him staying, not tonight, Sir Charles. Perhaps tomorrow night. I'll think about it.'

'You don't trust me with my own grandson?'

'I'd rather not discuss such matters in front of John.' In fact, Seth was beginning to regret bringing him to London at all.

The next evening Seth was persuaded to leave John with his grandfather. He was loath to leave him because he had misgivings, though it was instinct more than anything.

On Monday he presented himself to Charles Barrie's house. The butler couldn't meet his eyes and said unhappily, 'I have instructions not to admit you, sir.'

Seth's heart plummeted and he pushed the butler out of the way. He could hear men's voices from the study and pushed the door open so violently that it crashed back against the wall. 'Where's my son?'

Three pairs of eyes turned to stare at him.

'Are you referring to my grandson, John Barrie?'

'John was placed in my charge by his mother. The paper was legally notarized.'

'In Van Diemen's Land, which has no jurisdiction here. I have an order issued by the British court, handing custody of the child to me. Besides, possession is nine tenths of the law, Colonel Hardy.'

The other two men there were both young and powerful and wearing police uniforms. One rose and went to stand between him and the door. The other one said, 'I'm a police constable, Colonel Hardy. Will you go quietly?'

'John?' he yelled, and lunged for the door.

The two men floored him between them. Strong as he was, they were stronger. His hands were manacled behind his back. Outside a whistle was blown. As they dragged him out on

246

to the pavement he looked up and saw John at the window.

'Pa,' the boy shouted out, though his voice was so faint that Seth could hardly hear it as he scrabbled at the window. 'Let me out, I want to go home.'

A thin-faced man appeared behind him and dragged him away.

Seconds later a horse and police cart arrived. Seth was thrown inside and the vehicle clopped off. The interior smelled of vomit.

Fifteen

The small group of survivors huddled under the overhang while the storm thrashed around them. After three days the sky cleared and the sun came up. Steam rose and perspiration covered them, along with various biting insects.

Red was the worst off. He had the white skin usually associated with red hair, and the heat turned him a shade of lobster pink. Once they'd left the coast behind there was more shade and they no longer needed the sun hats they'd made from ferns.

There was plenty to eat. Small freshwater lobsters hid under the overhangs, and fish. Game was everywhere, though hard to catch unless it was cornered, and more than once, Nick wished they'd had a gun. They discovered that the fern roots were edible.

It rained often, and the nights were so cold that they huddled together under the canvas. They all thinned down, but the activity allowed them to keep their muscle strength. After a fortnight they wore beards, even the downy-faced Sam.

Nick gazed up at the sheer mountain face towering about them. He'd overestimated how long it would take them. Certainly not ten miles a day. If they were lucky they might have covered two, and going on that it would take them several weeks. He began to wish they'd gone round the coast as he flopped down on a rock. 'Let's spend the night here. I think we're lost, gentlemen, and we need to catch some more game.'

'Oh, we'll get out of it sooner or later,' Red said cheerfully. How are you holding up, Sam?'

'All right. I could eat a whole pie crammed with stewed apples and swimming in custard.'

Nick smiled at the thought. 'A chunk of crusty bread with some ham, a wad of cheese and pickles would do me.'

'And I'd like a whole pig roasted on a spit in its own crackling with potatoes and cabbage and gravy.' Red laughed. 'Well, having tortured ourselves with those thoughts, what about lizard for a change.'

'Lizard?'

'There's one sunning itself on a rock across the river. All we've got to do is catch it.'

'It'll run like the wind before we can get to it,' Sam said.

'But which way? What if two of us sneak up

behind it and one approaches it from the front?'

Nick and Sam elected to do the catching, and set off in opposite directions so they could cross the river and circle round, while Red distracted it. Once in position they gave a soft hoot and Red approached it.

The animal stood and gazed at Red, then it came up on its back legs into the defensive position, its tail lashed back and forth and it gave a ferocious hiss.

Red hissed back and advanced through the water. The animal held its ground, then panicked when Red got within striking distance. Turning fast, the lizard headed for the nearest undergrowth and up the trunk of a tree. Nick made a lunge for it, but Sam was faster and grabbed hold of its thick tail with both hands.

The lizard held fast to the tree, its claws dug into the bark as it hissed and snarled. Nick joined him, knife at the ready, and he drew the blade across the animal's throat. As the animal dropped to the ground in its death throes, it twisted and scraped its teeth on Sam's arm, leaving a deep scratch. Nick's booted foot came down across its neck, and stayed there until it stopped moving. He hoped its bite wasn't venomous. 'You'd better clean the wound in the river right away. I'll gut the beast.'

An hour later the lizard was cooking in the hot ashes. They'd just eaten their fill when Red said quietly, 'We have company.'

They hadn't heard the natives approach, but there were half a dozen of them of various ages. Their skin was scarred, and resembled dark, polished leather. Without an ounce of spare fat on their bodies, they stood on the opposite river bank wearing little else but curls of bark to protect their bollocks from the dense undergrowth, and animal skins tied around their shoulders for warmth. Each carried a spear.

Nick and Red slid their knives in their belts where they could reach them if needed.

Red belched. 'I expect the smell of food brought them. They're probably hungry. I hope that lizard wasn't one of their gods.'

Nick smiled grimly as he picked up the remains of the lizard and held it out to them. 'We'll soon find out.'

The aboriginals gazed at each other, then began to talk amongst themselves in gutteral voices. They kept looking at Red and muttering under their breath, then seemed to reach agreement.

One of them pointed at Sam, then to the meat, and beckoned. There was nothing threatening about them, it was a request, one Nick thought it might be wise not to test by turning it down.

Nick handed the lizard to Sam. 'They want you to take it across and leave it on the rock.'

Worry filled Sam's eyes. 'What if they kill me?'

Nick thought to advise him, 'We've all got to go sometime. You'll have to try and run like hell before they catch you.'

Red laughed. 'It's me they seem to like, but they don't seem to look on you as a threat Sam, because you're young.'

'It's your hair, Red. I doubt if they've seen hair

that colour before. They seem to be in awe of you, and we can work that to our advantage. Here, Sam, and try and look confident.' Nick handed him the stick.

Nick and Red took up a threatening stance as Sam reluctantly made his way to the rock and placed the meat there. Sam spread it out in the position they'd come across it, with its legs sticking out the sides, but looking odd without its tail, which they'd eaten. He gazed at it, then placed the stick where the tail should have been.

The aborigines began to point at it and laugh and Sam turned and grinned at them.

'I'm glad they find it funny,' Nick whispered.

While Sam waded back to them, the lizard was divided up and eaten with lip-smacking appreciation.

The light was beginning to go, and the natives waded across to stare at Red. They jabbered to each other, then one of them reached out and touched his hair. Before too long they were all laughing and pulling at it.

'Enough,' Red said sharply, and they drew back.

The aboriginals withdrew across the river and melted into the bush.

'We'd better keep watch tonight. Sam, you can take first watch, Red, you do the graveyard, and I'll take the dogs.'

Nick gathered some firewood before the shadows consumed the light. The fire was a friendly warmth in the rustling and impenetrable darkness that consumed them all. The mountains loomed densely into the stars, which were reflected in the river. When he woke to do his watch he felt at one with it, like he did sometimes at sea. He was an insignificant part of something bigger, especially when the primitive sounds of the aboriginal men singing came drifting across to him.

Red snored loudly until Nick put a foot in his back and shoved him on to his side. Sam was restless and towards morning, made little moaning noises. When Sam woke he was fevered. Nick gazed at his arm, it was red and swollen around the site of the bite.

'It's infected, Sam.'

They bathed it, then Red ripped the tail from Sam's shirt and bound it.

'Can you walk?' Nick asked him.

'Yes, Captain,' he said with more bravado than conviction. 'It's only my arm.'

But he didn't last long before he collapsed, his body beset by shivers.

Nick forced some water between his chattering teeth. When they looked at the wound again it was festering and red streaks had escaped from the site. He took Red aside and said unnecessarily, 'We'll have to set up camp and wait and see if he gets over it.'

Red shook his head. 'Poor lad.'

Both of them knew it would only get worse. They rigged the sail to give him protection and prepared to wait it out, since leaving him to fend for himself wasn't an option. Red caught some of the small lobsters and boiled them in the small can they used for everything. Sam had no appetite, though they managed to get water into him, which offered a little hope.

While they were eating an aboriginal appeared silently from the bush and squatted on his haunches beside Sam. It was obvious that the man had been shadowing them. Nick made no move that could be mistaken as threatening, for the man's spear was tipped with a sharpened stone arrowhead. 'I don't think he means us any harm.'

The native looked at the wound, then gazed at Nick, his eyes both primitive and wise.

Nick touched a hand against his chest. 'Me Nick.'

The man stared at him from a moment then placed his fist against his own chest. 'Gunjinni.'

Nick pointed towards the cook. 'Him Red,' then to Sam. 'He's Sam.'

Gunjinni nodded. Going to the river bank he brought back some flat leaves, laid them on the wound then packed wet mud over them. He pointed to the sail, then made a motion of placing Sam in it and nodded towards the mountain.

'He wants us to follow him.'

Red nodded. 'They might be able to help Sam, and show us the way out of here.'

They began to pack up camp again, and soon they were heading after the native, Sam swinging between them in the sail, wandering between confused consciousness and sleep. Just after noon they reached the native camp, a clearing at the base of the mountain.

Several naked children rushed forward to stare wide-eyed at them.

When Nick smiled at them they began to

giggle.

Gunjinni pointed to them all one by one. 'Mee-nick ... Himred ... Hesam.'

Nick exchanged a grin with Red.

The man said something and a woman indicated a rough hut a little way off. Nick lifted the lad gently in his arms and carried him there. Sweat covered him and his eyes were glassy with fever. He whispered, 'Am I going to die, Captain?'

'Certainly not, I'd consider such an act to be mutiny. And if you think I intend to face up to your mother and sisters with such news, you can think again. The ladies of the tribe intend to nurse you back to health, so make sure you cooperate.'

'Yes, Captain.' Sam's eyes closed again.

As Nick laid Sam on a bed of dried rushes and bark he hoped his words had taken root.

Outside, the women had lit a fire in a small pit. In it they burned nuts, twigs and leaves that gave off a strong, piquant smell, scraping the ashes out to cool before adding more fuel. An elegant bronzed girl with small tilted breasts, fanned the smoke into the hut, while an older one mixed the burned ash to a paste. It was rubbed all over Sam, the women giggling and making soft exclamations over his naked body. One of them tended to the lad's wounded arm.

Nick could smell Sam from outside the hut. He had the same aroma as a joint of lamb, all spiced and ready to go into the oven – one that his Aunt Daisy had prepared. He had a sudden, nostalgic longing to be home, where everything and everyone was familiar. He liked his job well enough because he was competent at it, but he was not cut out to be an explorer, and he'd always known it was temporary. Just how temporary being a seaman could be, had been driven home forcibly of late.

One of the women had brewed a drink. Another knelt behind Sam and acted as a support. Her thighs were splayed either side of his lifted shoulders and she pillowed Sam's head between her comfortable brown breasts. His fevered eyes displayed his embarrassment, but he didn't have the strength to protest. The brew was fed to him drop by drop, by another woman with a shell to use as a scoop.

Nick grinned when Red muttered under his breath, 'He's a bit old to be breast fed, isn't he?'

'I reckon he's just the right age, but the lad's too ill to enjoy it.'

They pitched their sail under a tree, and the young women came to touch Red's hair and his pale skin, and to smile at him. An older women scattered them with harsh scolding. One of Red's admirers sat a little way off and began to weave a basket from reeds, sending Red sidelong glances from time to time.'

'Seems you've stolen a heart, Red.'

'My hair's a curiosity to them, that's all.'

'Be careful. She seems to be one of the elders' wives.'

But the elder didn't seem to mind the woman's attraction to Red. She was the only woman without a child hanging from her teat ... and was kept apart from the others.

That night they ate around the campfire with the men. Then it was time to retire. The girl who'd fanned the healing smoke went off with the women while the other two lay down one either side of Sam.

During the night, Nick woke briefly to realize that Red had sneaked off somewhere. The woman, he guessed.

Once, the thought of having a woman to share his bed would have been given top priority. Now he could only think of Aria, who had trusted him, and was waiting for his return. The fact that one feisty scrap of a woman could grab him so firmly by the balls astonished him. He grinned, not knowing whether to be pleased by the fact, or ashamed of himself for allowing her, just by being alive, to dictate the course of his physical comfort.

It was a week before Sam's fever broke, and his strength needed building up, so it would be another three before he'd be fit to travel.

To Sam's dismay he wasn't allowed to hunt with the men, as Nick and Red did, but was sent with the women to dig roots from the surrounding bush and to gather firewood while he recovered some strength.

They were treated as part of the tribe, except for Red, who came in for special treatment. Because of Red's glowing hair, Nick thought that the natives looked on him as a god or a spirit of some sort. They didn't seem to mind his liaison with the chief's young wife.

The day inevitably came when Nick took up a sharp stick and drew a map of Port Philip Bay in the earth with the picture of a sailing ships floating on the water and buildings around the outside.

A meeting of the old men was called, where the matter was discussed. The elder came to squat before him, and he made several marks in the earth.

'What is it?' Red said.

'A number of days, and a full moon. That's when we'll leave, I think.'

'The full moon is two weeks away.'

'I know, but it will give Sam some time to fatten up. He hasn't got his full strength back yet and we don't want him to have a relapse.'

'What's that mark he's doing now?'

'The sail we brought with us. It seems they want payment for their hospitality. Still, we won't need it any more, or the other stuff.' Nick nodded. Taking up the stick he drew the stone jar, the billy can and the other few objects they'd saved from the ship.'

Then it was the elder's turn again. He drew a man's head with corkscrew curls.

'They're not having my head,' Red said in alarm, and shook it vigorously.

The elder brought his errant woman over, and questioned her. At first she hung her head, and then she gazed scornfully at Red, then her hands went to her stomach and she began to scold him. The other women began to scold him too and they pelted him with sticks and hooted.

Standing, the elder waved his spear at the women and shouted, and they ran off in all directions into the surrounding bush. The elder drew a woman with a baby. He smiled, gently squeezed Red's penis, then tugged Red's hair.

Red sounded nervous when he said, 'Which part of me do they want, Captain, my dangler or my hair? I don't want to part with either.'

Giving a soft chuckle, Nick told him, 'He wants recompense for the use of his youngest wife. The gift of your seed has taken root, if I read the signs right.'

Red's eyes widened, then he managed an ashamed little grin. 'The woman was giving me the come on, Captain. You saw her. That doesn't equate to cutting my head or dangler off.'

'On the contrary, the elder considers what has happened to be an honour.' Nick laughed at the alarm in Red's eyes. 'And it's not your head he's after, it's your hair. They'll wear it for good luck.'

Nick smiled at the elder, nodded and pointed to Red. 'Himred agrees.'

'Do I like hell agree.'

Nick kept a pleasant smile on his face. 'Don't be difficult about this, Red. Just feel lucky he didn't demand your scalp.'

Nick marked the day before the full moon in the dirt, then he and the elder shook hands. The business was concluded whether Red liked it or not – and if needed, Nick would hold him down while they helped themselves to cook's red locks.

The woman stayed away from Red from then on, but there was much wailing going on when it was time for them to leave. Each of the men had a lock of Red's shorn hair attached to their spears, and the women wore red hair bracelets with nuts woven through them.

Sam had his cheeks pinched so many times by the women that his face went red. The elder's plump wife drew him between her breasts again in a farewell hug and the women crowded round to pat his head and shoulders, as if he were their favourite pup.

'Damn me if them women don't want to keep you here,' Red called out. 'You'd better leave him with them, Captain, else we'll never get away.'

The men began to laugh when Sam struggled to free himself.

When the women finally let him go, Nick teased him with, 'What did you get up to while you were gathering food.'

'Nothing, Captain. Honest!'

'Are you still intent on searching for gold with Red?'

'Reckon I will for a year or so, now we've learned how to look after ourselves a bit. Begging your pardon, Captain, but I've had enough of the sea. That wave fair gave me the frights. It wasn't natural, and I don't want any more adventures of that sort.'

Two weeks later the scruffily, bearded shipwreck survivors were looking at Melbourne town in the distance.

'Civilization, gentleman,' Nick said and turned to thank their hosts, who would not go any further, and waved to them as they began to descend.

They had lost track of time, but Nick's calculations determined it might be heading towards the end of April.

They headed straight for the shipping agent's office, where the astonished agent informed him. 'We'd understood *Samarand* had gone down with all hands.'

'Not quite. Four jumped ship to join the gold rush, and these two were saved along with me. I'll leave you a list of survivors and a letter for my uncle. I don't want to wait for the *Daisy Jane*. I'd rather get home as soon as possible.'

'If you want to work your passage there's a ship sailing short-handed for Southampton, via Wellington in a few days. She's carrying wool and passengers. She needs a first mate.'

'Who's the master?'

'Cunningham.'

Nick nodded. 'A good man by all accounts. He'll do me.'

Nick borrowed some money on account, shopped at the local gentleman's outfitter, and took a hotel room. The three of them visited the bath-house, dressed in their new clothes and had their photograph taken together to celebrate their survival. Red shopped for mining gear and Nick bought them a handcart and a couple of blankets as a parting gift.

'Are you sure this is what you want, Sam? It's not too late to change your mind.'

The lad nodded ... though he was no longer a lad, Nick noticed. Sam was beginning to grow his muscles and was as sinewy as his former hosts.

'You can sit down and write your mother a

letter before you go off mining. The hotel clerk will give you some paper, pen and ink. And make sure it's more than a dozen words. Tell her about the shipwreck, and how you heroically saved the life of the ship's master and cook by launching the dinghy. That way she'll feel justified in taking the reward I'm going to offer her, and bragging about you after church.'

'Aw, Captain.'

'Do it,' Red said. 'I've never had a mother, lest, not one I can recall, but I reckon yours will be grieving something cruel about you.'

Nick took Red aside while Sam laboured over his letter. 'Look after him, Red.'

'Aye, I will ... like he was my own. You wait and see, Captain.'

But time to wait was something Nick didn't have as he shook hands with the cook two days later. 'Thanks, Red. Look me up when you get back to England.'

It was hard parting with his shipmates, since they'd learned to rely on each other. Nick had thought to have Sam's name etched next to his on his knife hilt, and he gave it to him as a parting gift, along with returning Sam's compass to him.

He watched them walk out of his sight with a lump in his throat.

After they'd gone, Nick wallowed in a warm bath, ate a decent meal then had his beard trimmed. He bought himself a glass of whisky, the first he'd had in weeks. It tasted strangely bitter and left him light-headed.

A woman wearing green approached and took

the seat opposite him. Leaning forward she gave him the glimpse of her décolletage. Her skin was ruddy and wrinkled. 'Looking for company, mister?'

Nick had been celibate for such a long time that the thought of finding a woman hadn't entered his head, even though his loins had reminded him they were being neglected on occasion. Now it did enter his head, but he wasn't going to act on the impulse. He replaced the thought with the image of Aria's sweetly provocative face and her fresh young body.

There was a moment of alarm. She would regard herself as a widow now. Would she grieve? After all, it had been a hasty marriage, a union made for all the wrong reasons. But she had no proof of the marriage. His uncle wouldn't hand over the considerable legacy his father had left him without proof – though that wouldn't be hard to get. Another thought crossed his mind. Lucian Beresford would forgive her marriage transgression to get his hands on that amount of money once he learned she was not just any old widow – but a widow with a well-padded purse.

But Nick had asked Aria not to tell anyone about their marriage until he got back. And he knew she wouldn't break that promise, unless she'd needed to. Aria wouldn't give up hope on him. She'd wait for him forever, he was sure of that.

He pressed his palm against the locket, now safely pinned inside his new waistcoat, and his palm beat steadily against it. The thought of her was so warm and poignant that he couldn't wait to get home and see her.

The woman opposite him had a practised smile, but underneath he could see her weariness. He pushed a couple of coins across the table. 'Not tonight, love. Go and buy yourself a meal.'

Finishing his ale he went to his room. The mattress was too soft after his bed of bark. There were no stars above him on the yellowing ceiling, and the room smelled of tobacco rather than fresh air. Closing his eyes he imagined a dark velvety sky full of stars and Aria with her head heavy against his shoulder, and breathing gently into her ear. He smiled, wondering what she was doing at that particular moment. Watching the bracken unfurl its green fronds on the heath perhaps ... or suffering through Sunday high tea with the redoubtable Misses Stanhope...

Nick had no way of knowing how right he was – or how wrong!

'The youngest Honeyman girl married his nephew, and without them telling anyone. Erasmus Thornton himself announced it from the pulpit,' the elder Miss Stanhope said, her eyes glittering with excitement.

'I'm surprised the reverend let him into the pulpit.'

'Oh, Erasmus has been friends with the reverend for years. You could tell the sermon was planned in advance, with all that lecturing about rumour and innuendo being a sin. And Daisy Thornton was there, as bold as brass, though she never usually goes to church. There's no smoke without fire, is there, now? There's something going on there with Reverend Phipps, you mark my word.'

One of the teatime guests cried out, 'I've never seen the like of it. Charlotte Hardy tackled Captain Thornton after church, demanding to see the certificate. He told her, I saw the marriage register with my own eyes, and if that was good enough for me, it should be good enough for you. I'm not about to satisfy your curiosity, woman.'

Another took up the tale. 'Near scratched his eyes out she did. She called the captain a liar and worse.'

'Then he told her to sail off to Boston and see for herself...'

'So she said she wouldn't step aboard one of his stinking ships. He told her he wouldn't allow her aboard if they were in the middle of the Atlantic and she was drowning, since she was so puffed up with her own pride that she wouldn't sink anyway. What a to-do.' The guest fanned herself.

The beady eyes of Agnes Stanhope's sister glistened, and she lowered her voice to a death knell. 'Mrs Hardy called Thornton a murderer, accused him of causing her mother's death. Only she said it under her breath. Captain Thornton heard her though, and so did some other people.'

'Oh, that's nothing new. Nearly everyone knows Erasmus Thornton and Caroline Honeyman were once lovers. His face was flushed with anger, and I thought he was going to strike her. Then her husband arrived with their gig. When the Colonel realized what was going on he went over to her, took her elbow in his hand and marched her off.'

Lucy Stanhope gave a bit of a neigh. 'Charlotte was probably jealous. Everyone knows that she intended to marry Nicholas Thornton and he expected to marry her. She turned him down in a fit of pique after an argument, and she married the next man who came along, just to spite him.'

'Marry in haste, repent at leisure, they say.'

'He deserved better. A nicer man you couldn't wish to meet is Colonel Hardy. There was always scandal about the Honeyman family. As for the younger daughter, it's like mother, like daughter. God help the child when it's born. I wonder if they'll give it away and put it about that it died at birth, like the last time.'

The younger women tittered. 'Now, now, Agnes. We don't know for sure that the first one was sent to the orphanage.'

'You might not,' Agnes retorted, 'but I happened to be doing my day of charity work there at the time. Helping those less fortunate than oneself is so satisfying. I do know that a newly born infant was brought in, and I saw who brought it. Constance Jarvis gave the girl special attention and her own family name. Serafina Jarvis she called her.'

Eyes agog, Lucy stared at her. 'What happened to the child?'

'I don't know. She was gone the following week. Mrs Jarvis said she'd been sent out to a wet nurse, but I couldn't see any record of it. Later, when I enquired, Constance Jarvis told me the girl had died. But somebody else told me they'd heard she was bringing the girl up herself.'

'Goodness, all this intrigue. Why didn't you tell me before now?'

'You were a child at the time and it slipped my mind. Besides, one shouldn't speak ill of the dead. Oh, my goodness. I won't forget today's church service in a hurry. I hope it doesn't reach the ears of the bishop.'

'No, indeed. Do you think Marianne Honeyman is really married to Nicholas Thornton?'

'She calls herself Mrs Thornton and she wears a wedding ring.' Agnes gave a thin, malicious smile and folded her arms on her chest. 'Some man put that child inside her, and at about the time she went missing, and she's strutting about like the strumpet she is. They said she'd been visiting friends at the time. Then they said she'd been taken ill and was confined to bed. But before that there were rumours that Captain Nicholas Thornton had taken her to America with him.'

'Besides, it's hardly likely that her sister would throw her out if things were above board. I'll give Charlotte Hardy her due. She might not take any nonsense, but she's a decent woman for all that. As good Christians, we should call on her and offer her our support in her time of trouble, Lucy.'

'Quite. After all, her sister's infant must be due any day now...

266

Sixteen

It was Edgar Wvyern who posted bail to free Seth from his filthy prison cell.

Seth told him exactly what he thought of Charles Barrie. 'He's self-absorbed, full of deceit, and a liar. I'm outraged by his behaviour. As for Adam Chapman—'

'A clever young man, but blameless in this affair. I've sent word to him and said we will call on him later in the day. We'll meet with him later and discuss what can be done about the situation. I've made it clear to Sir Charles what I think of him, Captain Hardy. I've come to apologize for his behaviour, and for my part in the situation, though I acted in good faith. I have informed him, and will now inform you. I'm prepared to offer my services to you free of charge should you wish to take the matter to court.'

'Will taking it to court make any difference now Sir Charles has been granted custody of John?'

'I shouldn't think so. All it will achieve is to expose his complicity and his questionable ethics in the matter. If your motive was revenge, it would be a perfect vehicle with which to embarrass him in front of his peers. However,

I've persuaded him to drop the child-stealing charge. I do know he would not welcome the publicity the case would generate, or the stain it would leave on his character. For that reason I think the matter can be reconciled by reason and negotiation. Nevertheless, he's kin to the boy, and he has been afforded custody. You must reconcile yourself to that.'

'So, it seems that all I would stand to gain would be the satisfaction of a temporary revenge for something that would soon be forgotten. If I wanted to get John back I imagine I'd have to take a leaf from Sir Charles's book. I should abduct the boy and remove him to Van Diemen's Land, where I do have custody.'

Wyvern's eyes came up to his. 'That would be one way, I suppose. Not the step I'd expect, and advise you to take.' He shrugged. 'But then, I've been disillusioned quite often by my own judgement of late.'

Seth chuckled. 'You and me both. Rest easy. I'm not about to take such a drastic action, mainly because I'm sure that John will be well cared for with Sir Charles, despite being taken from a family he loves.'

'Good. I didn't think you were that much of a fool.'

'He must think I've abandoned him. Can I, at least be allowed to see John before I go home? I don't want him to think I've deserted him.'

'Sir Charles will not allow it at the moment. He wants time to get to know the boy and to gain his trust. Perhaps later. Be patient, Colonel.'

'Trust is something he'll have to earn with

John now. The boy's no fool and he saw me dragged into the police cart outside the house. He'll be scared on my behalf, and mistrustful of his grandfather, because he knows he was responsible.'

'If I see John I'll tell him you're all right. Write him a note if you will. I'll make sure he gets it.'

They met with Adam at his office, a rather grim-looking place with damp patches clinging to the walls. He shrugged an apology. 'It's all I can afford, I'm afraid, but at least it's central.'

Edgar smiled. 'We'll find you better premises when you decide to accept my offer. In London success is often measured by a man's accommodations, I'm afraid.'

'Some readjustment of the contract terms will have to take place. First and foremost I'm my own man, and will take cases, or not, according to my own conscience and discretion, though at the moment I'm seriously doubting my own ability.' Adam held out a hand. 'I'm so sorry about what has happened, Seth. I was hoping we could build on our tenuous relationship and remain friends.'

'We can. I don't regard this issue to be your fault, any more than it was mine. You're welcome in my home any time ... both of you are.'

It was with a heavy heart that Seth returned to Poole. Charlotte's face reflected her worry. 'Where's John?'

He told her. 'Sir Charles tricked us all. He obtained a court order for custody and refused to hand John back. He had me arrested for child-stealing, but later had a change of heart.'

Her hand flew to her mouth and she breathed, 'Oh, Seth ... how could he do such a terrible thing. You're the most honest person I know.'

She came to him then, slid her arms about him and laid her head against his shoulder, the first time she'd offered him any comfort. He savoured it when she said, 'I'm so sorry, Seth. I know how much your promise to John's mother meant to you. What will we do now?'

He hadn't given his promise to Mary much thought over the last few days, and felt a twinge of guilt. He tipped Charlotte's chin up and kissed her mouth, relishing this softer side of her nature. 'We'll have to put up with it. The most we can hope for is to be able to see John now and again.'

She grew angry, her gestures animated, her eyes sparkled with indignation and her cheeks glowed apple red. 'He had family here, a brother and sister, and parents who loved him. What can an old man offer John? He'll be lonely without us. I'll never forgive him.'

Another man on her hate list? 'Hush, Charlotte. His grandfather will give him the best money can buy, and I know John won't forget us.'

John certainly didn't forget what he'd seen. He didn't like his new life and reacted accordingly by setting out to make his grandfather's life as uncomfortable as possible. 'When is my pa coming for me?' he said to him one day.

'Your father is dead, John.'

'That was my first father, Jonathan Barrie. I can't remember him. I mean Colonel Seth Hardy. He is my father now.'

His grandfather didn't answer. Instead, he said, 'Try not to whistle in the house, please, especially so early in the morning. It's annoying.'

His grandfather became irritated very quickly. John thought that if he made him really angry, the man might send him home to his parents.

'I want you to write to my pa and my mama, and tell them to come and fetch me,' he said on another day. 'And I want to go to my proper school.'

'You have a tutor.'

'But I miss my friends. And I miss my sister and brother.'

'Stop this complaining at once, John. Those children are not your brother and sister. You're not even related to the Hardy family. The only blood relative you have is me.'

'You promised me a dog.'

'I don't like dogs. They leave hair on the furniture and will make the house smell.'

Something came over him one day and he pulled all the books out of the bookcase and piled them into a heap.

'What did you do that for, John?'

'I was looking for the book I made you. Did you like it?'

'What book was that?'

'The one with the heath birds in.'

'It's in the cupboard in the schoolroom, I expect. I haven't had time to read it yet. Now, you can put those books back on the shelves. You're not a baby, and if you do that again I'll tell your tutor to cane you.'

'My pa would never have caned me.'

'No wonder you have such appalling manners. You need discipline, young man.'

John hated his tutor, whose name was Mr Hagman. He spelled his words and did his sums wrong on purpose. He began to whistle every time he went up and down the stairs.

As he'd promised, his grandfather instructed his tutor to discipline him. A cane was used and it stung. He cried himself to sleep. He hated his tutor and he hated his grandfather.

Mr Hagman began to use the cane more often for discipline, and his grandfather didn't seem to mind. Some days he didn't even see him.

John stayed in his room as much as he could. When he was trotted out for his grandfather's friends he hardly spoke. The only one he liked was Mr Wyvern, who told him his parents sent their love, then whispered that they'd bought him a puppy for his eighth birthday.

'He's a terrier, white with a brown patch on his back, and his name is Scrap. They said you can have pretend adventures with him.'

'I want to go home,' he said. 'Will you take me there?'

'Much as I'd like to, I can't, John.'

John went to sleep that night imagining himself with his dog Scrap, with his ears pricked up, running across the heath. He even spoke to him when he was sure nobody else was listening, and could feel his body pressing warmly against his knees under the quilt at night.

One day he found Mr Hagman with the book he'd made with his Aunt Marianne, for his grandfather – the one that he'd never had time to read. John challenged him with, 'Excuse me, sir, but that's my grandfather's private property. I made it for him.'

The man was in a bad mood, and thrashed him, leaving him with stinging welts across his back and bottom. Later that evening John was looking in the book of birds and wondering why his grandfather hadn't bothered to look at it, when he came across the exercise book with the map in that his pa had made for him of the journey to London.

Although he couldn't read the longer words without trouble, he had a good memory, and remembered the name of all the towns. The yearning to see everyone he loved and to see his new puppy was overwhelming. All he had to do was get on a train at Waterloo Bridge station, go to Southampton, than get on another train to Poole. Then he could walk across the heath.

Remembering his manners, and wishing to leave a good impression, John wrote his grandfather a note.

Dear Grandpapa,
    Thank you for your hopspitality.
    I am going home to my dere papa. I do not want Mr Hagman to eat my brains or beat me any more. You may visit me if you wish to. I will show you the real birds of the Heath. They are much better than the drawings in

the book I made for you. I'm sorry you didn't like them.

Please don't put me in prison, like you did my papa.

Your grandson,

John.

John had some money that he'd received for his birthday, and some sixpences and shillings that his grandfather's friends slipped into his hand now and again. There were several florins from Mr Wyvern and a guinea from his grandfather. All were saved in his money box. John waited until Saturday morning, because his tutor didn't come on that day.

After breakfast he said, 'Goodbye, Grandfather,' and he wanted to hug him. But his grandfather didn't look up from his newspaper, just grunted.

John then waited until after breakfast when his maid took him to the park for a walk. She joined the group of governesses who were out taking the air with their young charges.

It was a nice day to travel, the air was June soft and filled with flying blossoms. The sky was a busy expanse of fluffy clouds and birds. On the heath the heather would be coming into bloom, and the gypsy caravans beginning to arrive, he thought. He felt ill with longing for home and the people he loved, that night.

It was easy to escape, since the maid wasn't watching him. John simply walked away from her, out through the gate and to the end of the road, where he knew an omnibus stopped. He'd been on an omnibus once before with his tutor, when they'd visited the British Museum to see the Elgin marbles.

John had enjoyed it at first, until he'd mentioned that some of the people curved into the frieze had their heads missing. Mr Hagman had slapped him around the head. He'd said it was a pity that John's head wasn't missing, too, and he might put a rat in his ear when he was asleep, and it would pull his brains out and eat them. John had tried to stop going to sleep in case he did, and he imagined his pillow covered in blood, and his brains spilling out and Mr Hagman eating them.

He'd been sick with relief when he woke up the next morning, but at night he found it hard to settle to sleep, and he missed Aunt Marianne or his pa telling him a story.

He sniffed back his tears as he joined the omnibus queue, jingling his money in his pocket.

The conductor held out his hand for the fare and John put a sixpence in it. He followed a man in front of him up to the seat on the top, where he clung on as the sturdy horses plodded along the street with its burden of humans. The horses reminded him of the ones that tilled the fields near his home, big, gentle beasts of burden that dragged the plough behind them all day to crumble the soil ready for planting the next season's corn crop. John was glad he wasn't a horse.

When everyone got off he said to the conductor. 'Where's the railway station?'

When the conductor jerked his thumb, John set off on foot. It was a long time before he realized he was lost.

Mr Hagman would probably give him another beating when he set eyes on him. His grandfather would be furious. Perhaps he'd even send him to jail, like he'd sent his pa to jail with the policeman. John's heart gave a little wrench. If he knew where Mr Wyvern lived he'd go there. Mr Wyvern had got his pa out of jail; he'd heard him arguing with his grandfather about it.

Then he remembered the river. If he followed that he should come to the station, and he'd soon see his mamma and his pa, and his new puppy Scrap. And he could see the river, and a bridge!

He gave a smile and set off. But when he got to the bridge he couldn't find the railway station. He gazed down the river to the next bridge, which seemed a long way away. His legs ached and he was getting hungry. He had an apple in his pocket, but he might need it later.

He remembered that his grandfather's cook had told him there was apple and rhubarb pudding for supper. His mouth began to water.

The adventure soon lost its shine. He changed his mind about running away and began to retrace his steps. After a while it began to get dark, and he became confused with all the people hurrying this way and that.

Then he saw a station in front of him, as big as a church, and he remembered there was a puppy waiting for him and decided to go ahead. He followed after a family group with several children and bags, and he scrambled on to the train, taking a seat on a wooden bench in an empty carriage.

When the train chugged from the station his stomach churned with excitement. Finally he could stand his hunger no longer. Taking the apple from his pocket John scrunched it down, wiping the juice from his chin with his sleeve.

He belched, then yawned and lay down on the hard seat. The wheels clickity clacked over the track and the carriage swayed back and forth. He felt drowsy. His eyes began to droop and within minutes he was asleep.

'My grandson has run away!' The colour drained from Charles Barrie's face as he read the note. 'Where's the girl who was looking after him?'

When Mollie Smith was found, hiding in the housekeeper's sitting room, her pale face was smeared in remorseful tears. 'One moment he was there, the next minute he was gone.'

'That's just not good enough, Smith. I'm afraid I can't keep you on after this.'

She shrilled, 'It wasn't me who frightened the poor lad by saying I'd eat his brains. It was that miserable old tutor. And it wasn't me who beat him every time he put a foot wrong. It was Mr Hagman, and it was you who told him to. No wonder the poor little sod ran way. I don't blame him. His life's been a misery since he came to live here, the poor little thing.'

Too distressed to summon up the anger her attitude deserved, he told her wearily, 'You're dismissed, and without reference. After the constables have interviewed you, you can get out.'

She sniffed. 'With pleasure. I'll go and work in my brother's pie shop. He's been nagging at me for weeks, and there will be no, Yes sir, no sir, three bags full sir, there.' She flounced off, banging the door so hard behind her that the windows rattled.

The butler coughed gently into the awkward silence. 'I've informed the constables and they will keep a look out for the boy.'

'Send for that investigator, Adam Chapman, and for Edgar Wyvern. Tell them it's urgent. Take a cab and go yourself.' And because it occurred to Charles that Mollie Smith might attempt to smear his reputation out of revenge if left alone, and his presence there might intimidate her, he added, 'In the meantime I'll sit in on the interview with that maid, and you will act as witness to the proper payment of her wages to date.'

Edgar was the first to arrive at the house.

Charles had the bird book John had made open in his lap. 'You know, Edgar, I never got round to looking at this. A lot of work has gone into it.'

Edgar seated himself and read the note from John before gazing with genuine sympathy at Charles.

'I don't need to tell you that this had been a great blow, Edgar.'

'To your pride, yes. Nevertheless, I'm not going to encourage any self-pity, and I can't say I'm altogether surprised by what's happened. It's your own fault.'

'I've been an old fool, haven't I? I took the boy away from all that he knew and loved, and in return he got an irascible old man who never had any time for him.'

'That's the truth of it, Charles.'

'You said I was too old to take on a child. But I wouldn't listen. He must hate me to have run away like this.'

'John wouldn't have invited you to visit him if he hated you.'

Charles grasped at the straw held out to him. 'Yes ... there's that. You know, when I told the tutor to discipline him that was not carte blanche permission for him to frighten the boy out of his wits, or to beat him.'

'You always had to learn from your own mistakes, Charles, but I'd prefer not to listen to you flagellate yourself over it, especially when it's motivated by self-pity. What's done is done. We must put the boy's safety first, and try to rectify the situation.'

His own stupidity in parenting the lad was so apparent to Charles that it might well have been scribbled in large accusing black letters on the red and gold wallpaper. Next time he'd make sure that the boy had companionship, and his tutor would be female.

Adam was announced, already made aware of the situation by the servant Charles had sent, and in possession of some useful information. 'On the way over I stopped and talked to one of the omnibus conductors. A boy matching John's description boarded the vehicle earlier. He asked for directions to the station when he got off. He was wearing a sailor's cap and a navy blue coat with brass buttons, over grey trousers.'

Charles confessed to himself that he hadn't noticed what John had been wearing, though the boy did have such an outfit in his wardrobe. He nodded. 'That sounds like John. Waterloo Bridge station, you say.'

'No, just the station. The driver thought he meant Paddington. I'll take a cab over there and search the station, then walk back to the omnibus stop.'

'Bring him back safely, and I'll be forever in your debt.'

'May I ask what you intend to do with John when he's found?'

Charles's shoulders slumped in defeat. 'We must learn from our mistakes. It's probable that I'll return him to the family of Colonel Hardy, where he was happy, and hope I can see him now and again. If you have any other suggestions please don't be afraid to voice them.'

Adam exchanged a look with Edgar and smiled.

Seventeen

'*Samarand* has gone down with all hands.'

Erasmus Thornton's face was grey. 'It's my fault ... I should've listened to him.'

Daisy gave a small cry of anguish.

The infant inside Marianne stretched. Goodness, it was strong, and its knees – at least, she thought it was knees – pushed a lump into her stomach under her belly button. She placed her hands over it and winced, sinking into the nearest chair with a gasp and with the colour draining from her face. She couldn't quite grasp what Erasmus was saying. Dead! Dearest Nick ... her lover ... the husband who she'd hardly known, but loved anyway. He was so strong and vital. He couldn't be dead. 'I refuse to believe it.'

'Wreckage was found—'

She didn't want to hear any more and her voice rose to a hysterical level. 'He's not dead, I tell you. He can't be dead because he promised to return, and he never breaks a promise, I won't let him be dead, do you hear me? His child will be here soon. Nick will be here to see him, just wait and see. The boy will need his father.'

Daisy's thin arms came round her. 'Marianne my dear, calm yourself. If you get upset it will be bad for the infant.'

Marianne turned to gaze at Erasmus again. 'Nick would have made it to shore ... he might be injured.'

'It happened four months ago, when *Samarand* left Melbourne. He's well overdue, and I think we would have heard something by now.' Hope filled her when Erasmus said almost pityingly, 'It's possible that he made it ashore, I suppose. There's plenty of empty coastline.'

'There, you see, that's what happened. We'll wait for a little bit longer, until we hear from him.'

'I have a ship to sail, Marianne.'

'Just another week, Erasmus,' she pleaded.

He nodded, saying reluctantly. 'I'll see if I can find out anything more.'

Daisy trotted out with her panacea for all misfortune. 'I'll go and make some tea.'

Erasmus didn't want to be penned up with two grieving women, Marianne knew. He wanted to be out on the sea where he belonged, too busy to think of anything but battling the sea, with the wind filling the *Daisy Jane*'s sails and the water hissing along the hull.

Even when he was at home his eyes constantly went to the harbour. There he'd make his peace with Nick. She wondered... 'Would you have given up the sea for my mother, Erasmus?'

'Aye, I'd have given up my life for her.' He gave a faint smile. 'After the baby was born we were going to sail away together.'

There was a nasty jolt inside her at such unexpected news. 'She would have left her children?'

282

'No, not my Caroline.'

'But my father...'

'Found out about our plans, and he wouldn't let her take you and your sister. She felt she had no choice but to stay. When she died I thought I'd die too.'

'That's how I feel about Nick. How can you stop yourself from feeling this sad and despairing?'

'You fill your life with something else. Soon you'll have a child to fill the hole in your life.'

She took his hand in hers. 'Erasmus, about the infant.'

'It will give you a reason to go on living, girl, and it will want for nothing. Nick has money his father left him. That will become yours.'

'I meant your infant ... the little girl my mother birthed that night.'

He didn't bother denying it, and his eyes clouded over. 'Aye, what about her? I can't bring her back.'

'What if you could?'

His eyes came to hers, dark and searching. 'What are you saying, girl?'

The words jerked out of her. 'What if your daughter had lived?'

The silence seemed to stretch into infinity. Eventually he gave a faint grimace. 'There is no proof. You've been listening to rumours.'

'There's no infant named on my mother's headstone. I was going to ask the undertaker if a stillborn child had been buried with her, but he'd sold his business and gone. I remember hearing a baby cry that night. It woke me from my sleep.'

He drew her into his arms and rested his chin on her head, and she felt comforted. 'You remind me so much of Caroline, you know, Marianne. If I thought my daughter was still alive I'd turn the world upside down to find her, and to hell with gossip. But I'm sure she isn't. Even if that baby had lived, we were unsure if I was the father or not, though we used to pretend...'

'The reverend said that stillborn children are often not named.'

'There you are then.'

'If I die having this baby, and if Charlotte won't give him a home, you and Aunt Daisy will look after him, won't you? He'll need a father.'

'You're not going to die, my dear. The midwife said you're perfectly healthy, and should give birth easily.'

'But if I do die, promise me you'll look after him.'

He let her go and moved up the sofa a little, taking her hands in his. 'I promise. But when I return from the next run, and if ... if Nick has perished, I'll give up the sea and marry you, if that will make you feel more settled. Then you'll have a husband and the baby will have a father. I wouldn't make any demands.'

Marianne gazed at him in surprise. 'Thank you Erasmus, that's kind of you, but I love Nick and could never marry anyone else. Not even you.'

Daisy snorted as she brought the tea tray in. 'You'll never give up the sea, and who would want to marry an old rascal like you, anyway,

Erasmus Thornton?'

He shrugged, and the moment was gone, replaced by an unmistakable expression of relief in his eyes. 'It was just an idea.'

Daisy placed a cup of tea in front of her. 'Drink that, then go upstairs and rest, my dear. You've had a nasty shock and your face looks pinched and pale.'

'I'm not hungry and I feel sick.' Her heart hammered in her chest, her back ached, her head thumped and she was dizzy. She hiccuped, and a sob tore from her. 'I can't bear the thought that Nick might be dead,' and she collapsed into uncontrollable weeping.

Marianne felt as helpless as a baby as they assisted her upstairs, and soon Daisy had her tucked into bed, with a bowl and flannel on the side table, just in case, and she was plumping the pillows under her head, making soothing noises.

Across the room the baby's crib was ready for occupancy under a dust sheet. It was a gift from Erasmus, a white painted cradle hanging from a frame. It could be swung gently back and forth. Daisy had made a little patchwork quilt, and there was a basket of baby clothes they'd gathered together ... though Marianne couldn't help thinking that she would have preferred to share that pleasurable activity with her sister.

Marianne knew she was being selfish. Daisy and Erasmus loved Nick too, and they'd loved him for longer. Their grief must be greater than hers. 'I'm so sorry to be a nuisance,' Marianne said. 'You love him too...'

'Aye ... we love him, even though he was so

285

strong-minded a rascal at times that I had to put a strap across his backside.'

She giggled at the thought of the diminutive Daisy giving Nick a flogging, but it turned into another hiccup, then tears again.

Daisy's fingers were wonderfully soothing as she smoothed the hair back from Marianne's face. 'We've got to look after you first, and the baby you're carrying. Erasmus has gone to fetch the doctor. You know ... you're probably right about Nick making it to shore, so don't go marrying Erasmus. You turning up at church with a husband on each arm would really set the tongues flapping.'

Marianne felt hope again and she propped herself up on one elbow. 'That was kind of Erasmus, wasn't it?'

'Ah yes ... Erasmus is a kind man once you get to know him.'

'And you're a kind woman, Daisy. I was scared of you when I first knocked on your door. I thought you'd turn me away.'

'Oh, I knew something had happened the last time I saw Nick. He was different, quieter and more responsible, and he seemed to have grown up. When I asked him if everything was all right, he gave me a hug and told me it was more than all right. He said I'd know about it in good time. When he told us he was coming ashore, at first I thought that was it ... but I knew there was something else he wasn't telling us. When you knocked at the door that day, I realized what it was before you told us.'

'We'd planned to keep it quiet so we wouldn't

have to put up with people speculating about it without him being here to back me up. And we'd decided to have a proper wedding when he came back, just for everyone else.' Her hands went to her rounded stomach and she smiled wryly. 'I'm afraid this rather changed our plans.'

It was Lucian who came, not his father, who'd met with an accident.

'I'm so sorry. Is he badly hurt?'

'A wrenched ankle. He should be fit in a week or so.'

Lucian was awkward, and didn't quite meet her eyes. 'I understand that your ... that Nicholas has been lost at sea.'

'Nick is my husband, Lucian. Whatever you might think of him, he is a man who has honourable intentions, and acts on them.'

'Quite.' His eyes came up to hers. 'I'm sorry, Marianne.'

'About what? Thinking the worst of me? I don't believe that he's drowned, of course.'

He gave the faintest of smiles. 'Of course you don't. You wouldn't be Marianne Honeyman if you did.'

Her voice sharpened. 'Haven't I made it clear that I'm Marianne Thornton?'

'My pardon, Mrs Thornton.' His calmness infuriated her, and she came to the conclusion that he was a cold fish. He took up her hand, felt the pulse in her wrist, and frowned. 'It's much too fast.'

'I could have told you that.' She told him the rest of her symptoms.

'When's the infant due?'

'In about four weeks. At the beginning of spring I ran into my gypsy friend, the one who delivered Charlotte's twins. She told me I'm carrying a baby boy.'

'And you believe her?'

'Of course I do. Jessica is wise beyond understanding. They were going to Dartmoor, and she said I would have my son early summer.'

Lucian looked mildly astonished. 'She would have been burned at the stake had she lived in an earlier age. You should have nothing to do with gypsies.'

'Why not? They're people, the same as us. It must be wonderful to travel all over the countryside.'

'You always see the best in people, Marianne. Gypsies are sly. They take advantage of the gullible.'

'Goodness, Dr Beresford, I know plenty of people who take advantage of the gullible, and they're not all gypsies. Some are seemingly respectable shopkeepers who'll rob an old woman of her last farthing, by pretending he's already given it to her as change, and suggesting she's dropped it. There are employers who sack their workers, then send them on their way without paying their wages. Then there are men who pretend they're in love so they can marry a woman for her fortune...'

His mouth pursed and colour touched his cheeks. 'Perhaps it would be better if we concentrated on your problem, rather than exchange pleasantries.'

Was that what they'd been doing – exchanging pleasantries?

She received the same advice as she would have given herself if she'd been doing the doctoring – only the benefit of his wisdom was offered to Daisy, who was padding around like a nervous tabby cat in the background.

Lucian raised his voice, as if he suspected her of deafness. 'Mrs Thornton has suffered a shock. She should stay in bed for a day or two and rest. No visitors, no excitement, and light meals only. She'll need to gather her strength together for her lying-in if the outcome is to be a healthy baby. A glass of warm milk will make her feel more rested.'

'I'll go and make her some.' Daisy trotted off obediently about her given task.

Lucian wore his responsibility with too much awareness of his own importance, Marianne thought. It was hard to believe they'd been children together, that their fathers had visited each other, and they'd had adventures on the heath. That he'd been a boy who'd cried at the sight of his own blood if he'd so much as scraped the skin from his knees, or who poked his tongue out at the housekeeper behind her back, so Marianne would get a fit of the giggles, then get into trouble because she couldn't stop.

Marianne felt like crying now. She wanted to shake Lucian out of his adult skin and find the boy inside him – the boy she'd loved. 'Lucian, remember when you used to be afraid when you saw blood?' she whispered.

He dropped his guard and gazed at her, the

expression in his eyes pensive and sad, as if he'd caught a glimpse of the childhood he'd left behind. 'I remember, Marianne. I had to grow up.'

'Do you think I'll ever grow up?'

'You have, beautifully.' To her surprise he stooped to gently kiss her cheek. 'I wish things could have been different between us.'

'They couldn't have been. I love Nick.'

'Your husband is dead, my dear. You must reconcile yourself to the fact.'

'He's not dead. In my heart and my mind he's still alive, and anyway, he'll live on in his son.'

'You would never have loved me that strongly, Marianne.'

'And you'd never have coped with my passion for living. You would have kept me trapped inside, stitching pretty flowers and leaves on canvas with coloured thread. They'd be beautiful, but without smell or life, and would never have been tossed by the wind, but would have been kept hidden from the sun lest they'd faded. And I'd want to run barefooted on the heath and have the wind blowing through my hair – and swim in the sea like a fish with the water cold against my naked skin, just like we used to.'

When he sucked in a scandalized breath, she whispered, 'Nick understands those feelings in me, and so did you once. Now they shock you.'

'Passion for living is best kept under control when you're an adult, I feel, since quite often it's mistaken for vulgarity, which embarrasses others. But we can still be friends, can't we?'

After telling her she was vulgar and an

290

embarrassment? She hid the smile building up inside her. The few short weeks she'd had of living with Nick was better than a lifetime of Lucian. How joyless he was now. 'Yes, we can still be that, Lucian.'

And with that lie being established by both of them, they found there was nothing left to say to each other.

Marianne had slept better than she'd expected to, though she'd cried herself to sleep.

It was almost dawn when the pains woke her. The night light Daisy had brought in just before she went to bed was guttering in a pool of warm wax, making the shadows leap and dance.

At first she was disorientated, for she'd thought she was back at Harbour House. She'd dreamed that she was small and that her mother was seated on the side of her bed, holding her hand and looking down on her with much love in her eyes. Indeed, she imagined she could still feel the warmth of her hand, and felt comforted by it.

Swinging her legs out of bed she crossed to the window. A glance showed a scape of pewter sky, water and town buildings, as if night had drained her surroundings of all colour. Soon the sun would repaint the canvas again, exactly as it had been the day before, except for a flake of paint missing here, a blossom flying there, a cloud in a different place, and a wrinkle added to an old man's face.

Downstairs, the clock chimed five. Her infant had woken her up to tell her he'd started his journey. 'You're in too much of a hurry,' she chided him softly.

Nick was dead, she'd been told. He'd never know his son. He was drowned. His lungs and stomach were filled with water, his last breath had been expelled into the deep, blue/black depth of the ocean. It had travelled fast up through the water to explode his life into the air. She wondered, how long had he hung on to that last, painful breath? Had he thought of Charlotte when he died, taken her image with him into the darkness to comfort him. She didn't mind him having the comfort of his lost love in his dying moment.

She opened the window and breathed the air deeply, captured and saved it. It would help her through the strenuous day, and if it contained any of Nick's life – help her to bring Nick's son into the world.

Beneath her window a horse and cart clopped by. It was market day in Dorchester. People would make an early start.

Another pain came, long drawn out like the one that had woken her from sleep. It was like the rise and fall of a note on a cello, exquisitely painful. Marianne welcomed it. It stopped her thinking about Nick. Going out on to the landing she turned up the gaslight and knocked gently at Daisy's door.

'The baby's coming early,' she said when Daisy poked her tousled head out. 'I just thought I'd tell you.'

'That doctor of yours said you were not to be excited? Besides, the infant isn't due for another four weeks, so you've probably got indigestion. Go back to bed.'

She smiled, remembering Boston. 'I think I may have miscalculated?'

Marianne made herself comfortable while Daisy dressed. They readied the bed, removing the blankets and spreading clean sheets.

Daisy was calm. 'I'll bring you up some warm water so you can wash.'

The pains came at more frequent intervals. They washed over her like waves on the shore, where Nick had run, his feet bare and covered with grains of sand. Erasmus was sent to fetch the midwife.

By the time the sun was overhead pain was chasing pain. Marianne panted like a dog and groaned as she stretched a little bit more. It was coming quicker than she expected.

'I can see the head, he has dark hair,' the midwife said. 'It won't be long now. This is the hard part.'

Even though exhausted, Marianne managed a smile. Of course he has dark hair, she thought, and he'll have dark eyes and he'll look exactly like his father.

Sweat coated her face and body now. Her next push widened her a bit more, so she felt as though she was stretched as far as she could go. Her water broke with a gush.

'Push as hard as you can,' the midwife urged, and she did.

'Harder.'

Marianne groaned with the effort, and wondered how the baby felt being squeezed from her

293

body. Sorry, my love, she thought.

'Rest.'

Rest, when the monster of all pains was upon her, and she couldn't resist its pulsating strength? 'I can't ... rest...' She found inside her the breath she'd captured, and it joined with her own. Nick's breath. The thought of Nick calmed her. The pain was relentless and she gripped tightly the hands that Daisy offered her.

When her pain reached a crescendo Marianne gave a long, drawn-out cry. There was a small gush of water and her infant slithered out. He began to bawl loudly.

'It's a boy,' Daisy cried out, sounding so surprised that Marianne laughed out loud.

Soon her son was washed in warm water, wrapped in flannel and placed in her arms.

As she knew he'd be, he was his father's son. Dark hair, eyes the colour of liquorice. Her son was instant love. Instant joy. She kissed his frowning forehead, his turned-up nose and the frail shells of his hands. 'You're so beautiful, and I adore you,' she whispered, and her tears fell on his face.

He turned his head towards her voice and seemed to be listening intently as she whispered words of love to him. Then his head began to move from side to side and he began to nuzzle, open-mouthed against her.

Marianne had seen enough of Charlotte's early attempts to breastfeed to know exactly what he wanted. Opening her stained and crumpled nightgown she allowed him access, then laughed when, with unerring aim, her son's mouth claimed her nipple. The practice sucks he gave before he tired and fell asleep were strong, they reached right down into her.

The midwife smiled. 'There a bonny one for you. He knows where it's at and how to go about getting in. He won't give you any trouble. I'll put the lad in his cradle so I can clean you up, Mrs Thornton.'

'I'll see to the boy,' Daisy said quickly, and gently took him up. 'The very image of Nicholas, he is,' she said, tears gathering in her eyes. She gazed down on him fondly before she laid him in his crib. 'I'll go down and make some tea. I daresay we could all do with a cup.'

Later, Erasmus smiled down on the boy with pride. 'What will we be calling the lad?'

'I thought I'd call him Dickon after his grandfather, Nicholas after his father, and Erasmus after you. Do you approve?'

'Aye, it's fitting, since they're all family names,' he said gruffly, trying not to look pleased at being included. 'I've been thinking. The boy's arrival has taken on an importance to me with regards to family matters. What if Caroline's girl did survive? Perhaps I'll make enquiries when I return – see if I can find out what happened to her.'

'Charlotte won't like it.'

'I'm not interested in what your sister likes and what she doesn't. If the girl is alive, which I very much doubt, and if she turns out to be my daughter, which is also doubtful, all to the good. If she bears more resemblance to the Honeyman family, then at least she'll have one sister who will welcome her home, won't she?'

'Yes, she will. Thank you, Erasmus.'

Erasmus was gone a few days later. Before he'd left he visited her and said, 'It's the Australian run so it will be six months. While I'm there I'll try to get some definite news about what happened to the *Samarand*. It's certain that something has. Our agent would have made some enquiries by now, and if any survivors turn up he'll know about them.'

But Erasmus hadn't sounded very positive.

Marianne was not about to observe the normal lying-in, and was up a week later. The no-nonsense Daisy didn't put up any objections, except she banned her from lifting anything heavy. Marianne wrote a note to Charlotte telling her she'd safely given birth to her son, and advising her that Nick was feared drowned.

She got no answer to her note, but there was a trickle of visitors, and Seth came with a gift of a soft shawl for Dickon. He seemed downhearted.

'What is it, Seth? Are the twins unwell?'

A brief smile touched his face. 'They're very active now, and getting into all sorts of mischief. It's John I'm worried about.'

Alarm stabbed at her, in case it was something that could be passed on to her own infant. 'John's ill?'

'He's run away from his grandfather's home. He left a note saying he was coming to Harbour House. But that was ten days ago, and he hasn't been seen or heard of since. We're worried out of our minds.'

'John's a sensible child. He's got a good sense

of direction. If he's lost, he'll find his way home, I'm sure.'

'But he's such a small boy to be wandering around on his own. Aye, but why am I worrying you about this when you have enough worries of your own? I'm so sorry to hear about *Samarand*. I liked Nick a lot.'

'I can't really believe he's dead, Seth. Sometimes I tell myself he is, then the next moment something inside me says strongly that he's alive, and will one day walk through the door. He was too alive, and had too much enjoyment of life to die. No! I refuse to believe it. And I'm sure John will get back to you. How is Charlotte keeping?'

'She's sad, and she's quiet. Things have been too much for her of late. First ... well, you know ... then John and now...' He shrugged. 'She's not coping very well. I think her conscience is beginning to bother her.'

'Charlotte has no reason to concern herself on my account. She only has to live with the guilt she feels over turning me out. And neither does she have the right to grieve over Nick. She treated him badly, and she made her own free choice. Seth, don't pander to her, else she'll never respect you. You must tell her how you feel about what she's doing, not only to herself, but to others. I do not have the generosity inside me now to share Nick with her, not even his memory. That, she doesn't own or deserve.'

'I can't condemn her for what she feels. I can only be there for her.' He rose to leave.

'You love her, don't you, Seth?'

'Aye, I do, for what it's worth.'

'If she ever stands to lose you she'll soon realize your value. You can't have Nick's ghost present in your marriage. It's not fair on either of you. Nick is part of her past, but he's part of my present, my marriage, and he's the father of my son. She has to let go of him. Tell her that.'

'Won't that be salting the wound?'

'That's exactly what she did to me, except she caused the wound in the first place. Her own is self-inflicted. As you know I've tried to reconcile our differences on many occasions, and I won't contact her again, Seth. Charlotte's taken this too far. If she wants to see me again, the approach must come from her.'

She watched him walk away, his head bowed. Seth was too nice a man to have attracted all this trouble. All he'd wanted was a home for himself and his son. She could only pray that John was safe, and they'd be reunited.

Eighteen

They were making good time. Cunningham was a solid, unflappable individual with a good reputation and a regard for safety.

He'd welcomed Nick on board, congratulating him on his survival, expressing his relief at having someone on board who knew his job.

After Nick had stowed his few belongings on board, Cunningham said, 'Take her out, Mr Thornton. We'll be heading for Wellington to pick up passengers. The usual route through Cook Strait. You've been through before, I take it.'

He smiled when Nick grimaced. 'Good, then I don't need to tell you how tricky the Strait is to navigate.'

Nick had never handled a ship of this tonnage, and said so. Cunningham stood at his shoulder without saying a word until they'd cleared harbour, then he uttered only a dozen. 'You can now handle one, Mr Thornton. Carry on, I'm going below.'

And that was the last Nick saw of him until midnight, when the man relieved him, his eyes glassy and his breath smelling of brandy. When Nick look askance at him, he said, 'Don't worry Mr Thornton. I can sail this ship in my sleep, and it won't happen again. Go and get some sleep.'

Nick presented himself to the salon the next morning, to breakfast with the sprinkling of passengers – two women and some half a dozen men. Some of them looked a little on the pale side.

Nick was not used to passengers and found the small talk with strangers tedious, especially since he was ravenously hungry.

'Captain Cunningham said you'd been shipwrecked, how exciting!' a young woman lisped.

Frightening would have been a more accurate description. Nick had been given to understand that this was Miss Garfield, and she was on her way to England to marry advantageously. 'Unfortunately, most of my crew perished.'

'Goodness ... the poor souls. Don't you think so, Miss Carter?'

Miss Carter was older, about forty, her face already lined in places with spinsterish discontent. 'Yes, indeed, Miss Garfield. I understand you were rescued by natives, Mr Thornton.'

Nick speared a sausage with his fork. 'Three of us made it to shore. My cabin boy suffered an injury, but the natives nursed him back to health then guided us back to civilization.'

'That must have been thwilling.' Miss Garfield's eyes were as round as saucers. She couldn't have been much more than seventeen, was precocious, and seemed to enjoy being the centre of attention. One or two of the men were eyeing her up. Nick couldn't decide whether her lisp was an affectation or not.

'Is it twue that they're cannibals?'

Nick chuckled. 'If they are I didn't notice. They served up wallaby and lizard for dinner, and sometimes small lobster-like creatures that live in the streams. And now and again we had snake.'

'You ate snake?' Miss Carter sounded outraged. 'How extremely bizarre.'

'There was very little choice, and actually it was quite tasty. I'm sure it was better than eating human flesh.'

Miss Garfield grinned, her eyes lit up, and she seemed quite eager to continue with the conversation. 'Oh, I don't know ... we must be quite tasty ourselves if cannibals like to eat us, don't you think so, Miss Carter?'

Her companion turned a paler shade of pale, and shuddered. 'That's a disgusting thing to say. Come, Miss Garfield, we must go to our cabin. I'm not feeling at all well. Cannibals, indeed.'

'Oh, poor Miss Carter,' Miss Garfield cooed. 'I feel perfectly well myself. Perhaps it was all that bweakfast you ate. You should have had the oatmeal. It was lovely after I'd picked the weevils out.'

'There are no weevils in my oatmeal, young lady,' Cunningham said as the two females retreated, and then, keeping a straight face, 'It was probably a cockroach.'

The man had a dry sense of humour when he chose to exercise it, Nick thought, and the Garfield girl began to giggle.

'Aye, Aye, Captain.' She turned Nick's way and simpered, 'Mr Thornton, you must teach me how to steer the ship.'

'I'm afraid the ship is too heavy for a young woman like yourself to handle.'

'Oh ... but you could stand behind me and make sure I was doing it right.'

'I'm sorry, Miss Garfield, the answer is no. If the wheel spun, the weight of it would probably crush a bone or two, or even kill you.'

'Goodness, must you be so serious, Mr Thornton?' Miss Garfield's nose went up, she took a dramatic stance, pouted, then shut the door rather forcibly. The effect was spoiled when she trapped the hem of her skirt in the door, and had to open it again to free it.

'Her parents should whack her pert little

backside with a stick,' Cunningham said under his breath.

'Her new husband will do it for her, I imagine.' Nick grinned at Cunningham then got on with his breakfast.

The members of Cunningham's crew turned out to be well trained and efficient, but they lacked the easy camaraderie Nick had enjoyed on *Samarand* with his own crew. They were given very little time to relax. They constantly varnished the woodwork, polished the brass, holystoned the deck, pumped the bilges or spliced the ropes. It was the cleanest, neatest ship Nick had ever sailed on, and bigger than his uncle's ship, the *Daisy Jane*. It also had a larger spread of sail.

'I pay them to work, and that's what they do. It keeps them out of mischief,' Cunningham said dispassionately of the crew's efforts.

They picked up more passengers at Wellington and the ship was sent on its way by a strong wind.

The voyage was generally uneventful. When they passed the spot where *Samarand* had sunk he said a silent goodbye to his crew, and thanked God he wasn't among them. Several large icebergs were sighted in the Southern Ocean early on, which afforded the crew some alarm, and the passengers some excitement. They were soon left behind. The wind thrust into the sails from behind, giving them power. The prow dipped into the waves and cut through it. Nick built up his shoulder muscles on the wheel, constantly testing the steering chains against the powerful shifting tensions of the water, and sometimes needing two pairs of hands to bring the ship back on course. She was easier to steer than *Samarand* had been though, and smoother in the water, due no doubt to the second skin of protective copper on her hull.

'*Selena Fair* lives up to her name,' Nick said to Cunningham one day.

'She'd been known to reach sixteen knots when the wind's in the right direction,' he said proudly.

Samarand had managed twelve knots at her best.

'I named her after my wife. She died a year ago on the day we sailed from Melbourne. Cholera took her off. She was a good wife and mother. Better than I deserved, I daresay.'

Which explained his drinking on that day. 'I'm sorry. Children?'

'Four, all boys and all grown, plus a brace of grandchildren I hardly know. You?'

Nick took the miniature from his pocket and handed it to him, saying slightly self-consciously, because he hadn't spent enough time with her and wasn't really used to the thought of being a married man, 'My wife, Marianne. She was only a child when this was painted.'

'She's a pretty girl.'

'She's a beautiful woman now,' and Nick smiled at the thought of her. It suddenly faded, 'She'll think I'm dead, by now.'

'The sea is no profession for a married man. It's hard on the man and his family, who might need him to turn to in times of trouble. A wife

303

needs her husband's attention, lest she stray.'

Had that happened to Cunningham? he wondered. He also wondered if Aria had strayed, and was deluged by an uneasy churn of negative emotions. No ... she'd wait for a decent time to elapse before her body convinced herself that she needed a husband and children. 'It was to be my last passage on *Samarand*, Captain. I didn't expect my career to end so badly. Twelve good men lost their lives.'

'*Samarand* was an unlucky ship, and she wouldn't have gone to the bottom empty-handed. I'm surprised Erasmus bought her. Still, he got her cheap, after her former owner and crew had suffered a series of accidents.'

'I never believed her to be an unlucky ship.'

'You had a woman on board in Boston, didn't you? I heard she tripped and fell into the hold.'

'She did, and luckily the hold was full of wool bales. Even so, we didn't find her for two days.' Nick took the locket back and pinned it safely inside his pocket. 'Marianne recovered from the accident and became my wife. I consider that to be lucky.'

'You were lucky that *Samarand* spared her and took the crew instead. That ship made a bargain with the devil at her launch. I was there, and the sky was filled with lightning and thunder and it hit the mast and danced about the rigging, hissing and causing steam to rise from her. It was a sight to behold. She didn't like sharing her master with another woman.'

Nick wanted to laugh, because Cunningham was as superstitious as his uncle was. Even so, a shiver crept down his spine. He didn't want to tempt fate by laughing at it. Although he was nearly home, for the time being the sea was still his mistress. She'd spared him once, and he couldn't bear the thought that he might have inadvertently placed Aria in any danger by sailing off with her on board – however fanciful.

'Could be that you're right,' Nick said, 'but *Samarand* has gone now, and has taken the devil with her. My wife and I intend to open an emporium.'

'An emporium?' Cunningham gave him a sharp look. 'What sort of emporium would that be then?'

'Fancy goods, and fabric. I want to incorporate local goods such as pottery, handmade lace, furnishings and works of art such as paintings and sculpture. Also a section for children's nursery furniture and toys. It depends on what's available to me as premises.'

'I could be of help if you wanted to cut out the middle man. I could supply you with the import of an occasional cargo. Fancy goods, Japanese pottery, inlaid furniture, exotic fabrics and ivories. I visit oriental ports on a regular basis and there's nothing to say you must purchase from a wholesaler.'

When he'd discussed this with uncle, Erasmus had indicated that he had contracts for regular wool and tobacco runs, and didn't have room for anything else. He wondered if his uncle would buy another ship with the insurance money, and doubted it. He would be retired himself before too long.

'It's all above board, Mister Thornton. Like your uncle I'm an independent company. But where your uncle operates under the safety of contracts, I take my cargo where I can find it. It's above board. My business is accounted for down to the last farthing by my eldest son. I sail because I love it, but my retirement nest is well feathered, and if I keep my ship well maintained, it can only add to its value when she's sold.'

Cunningham was a hard-headed businessman, something which seemed to be at odds with his love for, and his belief in, the lore of the sea, but he impressed Nick with his honesty when he said, 'If I were a young man I'd be studying architecture, like my youngest son. He wants to build houses.'

'People will always need homes.'

'None of them intend to follow in their father's footsteps. I'm away from home so much that when I look at the young men I've fathered I feel uneasy with them. They seem like polite, but familiar strangers to me, and I must appear like a stranger to them. The same with my wife. What we experienced together when love was young was gradually lost. I didn't see it disappearing until it was gone. Then there was nothing I could do about it. The sea is a hard mistress, Mr Thornton. You are wise to retire from it while you are young.'

When they battled the turbulent currents and wind gusts around The Horn, the sea and sky had combined to show him exactly what they were made of, and the ship had felt flimsy and vulnerable beneath him, as it never had before –

not even on the *Samarand*. For all her reputation, he'd felt the loss of his ship, and keenly, as if he'd let them both down by not getting them home intact.

They lost the wind for a week in the doldrums, and found time to talk. The sails hung limp. There was general cleaning to keep the men occupied. The passengers began to complain about the lack of variety in their food. Miss Garfield had lost her sparkle, and looked downright sulky and bored. She was pretty, but tedious and not very intelligent. The appearance of three more females on board at Wellington had set her nose firmly out of joint. Her companion had kept a good eye on her and the male passengers had lost interest in her as a result.

A couple of sailors did their best to entertain them, with one playing a pipe and the other dancing the hornpipe. But the men wandered off to play cards in the salon, and now and again arguments broke out.

Then the glassy surface of the sea rippled, and Cunningham smiled when a sail fluttered, then fattened with air. A moment or two later the deck planking rose to press against the soles of Nick's feet and the water lifted the ship, as if she was cradled in the arms of her lover.

'Eventually, the sea becomes part of your blood,' Cunningham remarked almost to himself, and he shouted out an order and the crew swarmed over the rigging like monkeys.

Over the next few weeks the two men reached an agreement. They parted in Southampton, after ninety-six days at sea, with a handshake.

The simpering Miss Garfield was handed over to a florid, heavyset gentleman of about forty, who gazed through bulbous eyes at her and placed his hand under her seat to assist her into a carriage. Miss Carter followed.

'I almost feel sorry for her if that's her intended,' Nick said.

Cunningham smiled. 'They look as though they deserve each other to me. I'm sorry you're not sailing with me again, Mr Thornton. Give my regards to Erasmus if you see him before I do. I'll be in Poole in a few months with your cargo. Good luck with finding suitable premises for your emporium.'

Amongst the disorderly tangle of small craft he found a fishing boat willing to earn a little extra by dropping him off at Poole Harbour.

His heart soared. Mostly, it was because he would soon be home. Added to that fact was the knowledge that he'd survived an ordeal that had strengthened him in many ways, and that Cunningham's words of wisdom had unintentionally reassured him that he was doing the right thing.

'You're becoming as fat as a piglet,' Marianne said, and tickled her son's rounded belly.

Dickon's belch produced a bubble that burst into a milky trickle. She couldn't stop gazing at him as she gently wiped it away. 'You're a disgusting creature, really, but I adore you. Isn't he handsome, Daisy? Look at his eyes, just like Nick's. And all those dark curls. He sleeps all night now. He's so beautiful, and is so good-natured, aren't you, my adorable love.'

'That's not what you called him earlier when he was having a temper tantrum.'

'He was hungry, and he's got no patience.'

When Dickon gave her a gummy smile and made a soft cooing noise Daisy smiled and said softly, 'It's a pity Nicholas isn't here to see him.'

Marianne hadn't given up on Nick yet, but sometimes she doubted so strongly that she'd see him again that she despaired. Giving up hope might be easier then having hope, she thought. Other times she cried herself to sleep, weeping into her pillow so Daisy wouldn't hear. But Daisy wept too, for often she appeared with sad eyes, and dark circles under them.

Dickon was the bright spark in an otherwise sad year. Her sister had not yet relented. Charlotte had avoided her when they'd nearly met in town. Marianne had stopped attending the early morning church service, and Charlotte had stopped attending the evening one. She'd seen Seth a couple of times in the two months since Dickon's birth, but there was no message from Charlotte. No unbending. There was a search on for John, Seth had told her, but so far there was no sign of him. Seth feared the worse.

But the gossip over the rift between the sisters had reached a new pitch, with speculation over the reason for it. Marianne knew she'd been painted as the black sheep, and now Erasmus had sailed there was nobody but Daisy to defend her.

While she changed Dickon's linens, she murmured, 'I'm sorry I've brought so much trouble down on your head, Daisy.'

Daisy patted her hand. 'It doesn't matter, girl. I know the truth, and I know you can hold your head up without shame. Besides, it helps to sort out who your friends are.'

'I notice that the good reverend hasn't deserted you.'

'More's the pity. He's renewed his efforts, if anything. I think the old fool is about to propose marriage again.'

Marianne smiled. 'Will you accept?'

'It would serve him right if I did.'

Dickon's eyelids had begun to droop. Placing him in his cradle she gently rocked him off to sleep, then the two women went downstairs.

Marianne gathered together her basket, purse and shopping list, then pulled a blue velvet jacket over the gown that Nick had bought her in Boston – one which she could easily get into again. She'd lost more weight than she'd gained with Dickon, though the bodice fit snugly across her breasts, she thought, as she set off down the hill.

The tide was out; she could smell the exposed mud in the shallows of the harbour. The crabs would be settled into their holes, their pincers ready to emerge and punish anyone who dared to tread on them. And the cockles would be creaking in the mud, the occasional bubble revealing their hiding places to those with the time and energy to dig them out.

It was a glorious September afternoon, the foliage painted in metallic colours of brass, copper, gold and bronze that blended into the landscape and tinted the sky. Marianne had a sudden urge to go on to the heath, to seek out the gypsies and listen to the gypsy tales.

Even if she didn't have to shop, she'd have to get back for Dickon's next feed. But she didn't want to see her former home, and know she was no longer welcome there. It was a place where only the child that she'd once been had lived, and then she'd been subjected to Charlotte's dictates. Now she was responsible for herself, and for Dickon. A different family was being kinder to her than her own sister.

Harbour House had always been Charlotte's. Her sister was tied to it with an invisible umbilical cord. Marianne suddenly realized that the house was her sister's security.

When she walked into the general store the talk stopped. Some of the women turned their backs.

'Good afternoon, Mrs Thornton,' the shopkeeper said, as friendly as he always was. 'How is your son?'

Daisy had told her to keep her head up, so she did. 'He's wonderful. He looks just like his father.'

'Pshaw!' someone said.

Politely, she asked the woman, 'Do you have a cold, Mrs Avery? Or is it your stomach being disagreeable? You should take some peppermint cordial for it, perhaps.' Marianne handed the store owner her shopping list, and smiled. 'Would you deliver it as usual, please?'

She'd reached the door when someone whispered loudly, 'I believe Captain Thornton the younger has perished at sea. Where is her

311

mourning dress?'

She turned, stung by the insensitive nastiness of it. 'I have no proof that my husband is dead.'

'Captain Thornton has been gone for nearly a year now. What more proof do you need?'

Her fingers curled into fists and she inhaled to steady herself. 'Certainly not as little as you need. I do not welcome your unasked for counsel, which is based on nothing more than malicious gossip. I bid you good day, ladies.'

Outside the shop she nearly walked into Charlotte, and they were too close this time for Charlotte to cross the road and pretend she hadn't seen her.

Her initial need to hug Charlotte and make good their quarrel was squashed by her misery when her sister gazed at her with disdain in her eyes. 'You should be ashamed to show yourself in public, Marianne. Go home to your bastard son.'

Marianne wanted to talk to Charlotte about so many things. John, their children, who were cousins and could grow up knowing and loving each other if this cold stranger would just allow it.

'Insult me if you wish, but don't stoop so low as to call an innocent infant such names. He hasn't done you any harm.'

Charlotte flinched. 'Get out of my way, I'm in a hurry,' she said, as if Marianne was nothing to her.

Marianne was about to obey Charlotte's demand as she was used to doing, but her mind stopped her feet before they lifted from the ground. Tears pricked her eyes.

'Why are you always so bitter and angry, Charlotte? The right of precedence is not yours to demand. You get out of my way.'

At first she thought Charlotte would step forward and push her aside, then her sister saw two of the women watching them from the shop window. Making a low, exasperated noise in her throat, she stepped round her then continued on up the road.

Marianne watched her go, willing her to stop, to turn around, come back and make amends. She hated their silly quarrel and the fact that her son might never know his cousins because of it.

It was Daisy's birthday tomorrow. Erasmus had made sure that Marianne had an allowance from Nick's estate. She stopped to buy Daisy a gift, a kashmir shawl in a soft pink, to wear over the plain grey gowns she favoured. The colour would warm Daisy's pale skin to a blush.

The fishing boats were in. Wandering down to the harbour she joined the thronging crowd and bought a cod straight from the boat. The fisherman scaled and gutted it for her, then threw the entrails to the squabbling gulls. She wrapped it in a stockinette cloth and placed it in her shopping basket.

There was another boat coming in behind it. A tall man was poised with rope in hand, ready to jump ashore and secure it to a bollard. He reminded her strongly of Nick, and she turned away as a lump grew in her throat. She'd better get back to Dickon. Although Daisy loved looking after him, she couldn't feed him, and he roared like a bull when he was hungry. Marianne didn't want to take advantage of her kind nature.

She stepped out smartly, threading her way through the crowd, and trying not to think of the confrontation she'd had with Charlotte.

Nick had spotted Aria from the boat. A smile lit up his face as he stepped ashore. He secured the boat and took off after her.

She was heading out of town at a fast pace, and not in the direction he'd expected. The heath was in the other direction. She had a parcel under one arm, a basket in the other. The feather on her bonnet bobbed. After a while the crowds began to thin out.

He could have called to her, but he was enjoying watching her too much. After a while she turned into Constitution Hill, where his Aunt Daisy lived. She slowed down when faced with the upwards climb, began to pace herself. It was late afternoon, what was she doing here? Not visiting Lucian Beresford, he hoped.

A boy of about twelve was going in the same direction.

'How would you like to earn thruppence, lad?' Nick asked him.

The boy's eyes began to shine and he nodded.

Nick took the locket from his pocket. 'See that lady up ahead. Catch her up and tell her she dropped it.' He plopped that and the thruppenny bit into his palm. 'Look lively now, lad, else you'll lose her.'

The boy was off like a shot.

Nick watched from the shadows of a spreading

tree as the lad gave the locket to her, then delivered his message and went on his way.

Marianne gazed down at the locket for a while, then opened it. He watched a smile inch across her face until it shone like a beacon. She gazed down the hill at him, her mouth forming his name. 'Nick.' Dropping her basket and parcel she came running down to where he stood. Once there she threw herself into his arms and hugged him tight. Tears tumbled down her cheeks. 'I knew you were alive ... I just knew it...' Her hands touched his face, mussed his hair. She planted a kiss on his cheeks, his mouth. His forehead. 'Oh, Nick. I've missed you so much.'

He couldn't stop smiling. 'I'd intended to go straight to Harbour House to find you, then I saw you in the crowd. What are you doing in this part of town?'

Her smile faltered. 'I live here, with your Aunt Daisy. You don't mind, do you? I know we were going to keep our marriage a secret, but it wasn't possible.'

He slid an arm around her waist. 'Of course I don't mind. But I still don't see—'

'Charlotte threw me out.'

His heart sank. How could Charlotte have done such a thing to her own sister?

They'd reached her parcel and her basket. He stooped to retrieve them. 'Has it been bad for you?'

'There was gossip. Still is, in fact. Everything will be all right now you're home. Where have you been for all this time? They said you were dead. Even Erasmus thought you were gone, but

315

he pretended he didn't. He's been so kind, and so has Aunt Daisy. I've missed you, so.'

'*Samarand* went down, but I'll tell you all about it later.' Drawing her into the shadow of a hedge he took advantage of her soft and willing mouth. He wanted to laugh. He wanted to cry. There was something different about Aria. She'd gained a little weight perhaps, but in the right place. Otherwise, she was still as slender as a sparrow.

When his glance fell to her breasts, laughter filled her eyes.

The gate gave a familiar squeak when he pushed it open. Aria had her own key, and open-ed the door. The familiar smell of his childhood home took him unawares, as did the thought that if fate hadn't decreed differently, he wouldn't be standing here now.

From upstairs there came a couple of soft yelps, and soothing noises from Daisy.

Marianne placed a finger over her mouth when his aunt shouted from upstairs, 'Is that you, Marianne?'

'Of course it is. Who else were you expecting? Come down and bring Dickon with you. I've got a surprise for you.'

Her familiarity with his aunt surprised Nick. He remembered the yelps and whispered, 'Dick-on? You've got a dog? How did you persuade my aunt?'

She gazed up at him, laughing. He'd forgotten how blue and entrancing her eyes were. 'It's a surprise for you, as well as for Daisy, Nick Thornton.'

'Who are you talking to?' Daisy said, descending the stairs. She was carrying something loosely wrapped in a shawl. She stopped dead when she saw Nick, her hand flew to her mouth and she whispered, 'Nicholas ... you're alive ... thank God! Oh dear, if I didn't believe in Him before, I do now. Welcome home, my dearest boy.'

But Nick's eyes were intent on the bundle Marianne took from Daisy, an infant with dark curls. Nick's heart turned over when she placed the child in his arms and said softly, 'This is your adorable son. Dickon, meet your papa.'

Eyes as dark as his own gazed into his, then a tiny arm emerged from the wrapping. A fist unfurled, a perfect hand in miniature appeared, and an uncertain smile came and went.

She placed a little kiss right next to his ear, one so light that it made Nick shiver. 'Well, my love, what do you think of him?'

'He's perfect.'

The boy's eyes moved to his mother. This time his smile was bigger and longer lasting. Dribble ran down his chin and his legs gave a joyous little kick.

Love for this scrap of humanity filled him. He gazed at the woman who'd produced this tiny miracle for him as a welcome home gift, and tears filled his eyes. All the time he'd been absent and he'd never given a thought to the fact that their lovemaking might have born such tender fruit.

'I think he's perfect. Thank you, my love.' He gazed at his aunt who was also crying. 'And thank you for looking after them, Aunt Daisy.'

Taking a handkerchief from her pocket, Daisy vigorously blew her nose. 'I'd better go and make us a cup of tea then. I imagine you could do with one after all this time.'

As soon as he'd gone he slid his free arm around Aria's waist. When he pulled her close she snuggled her head into his shoulder and the three of them were joined as one.

After a while her tears dampened him and he whispered, 'Don't be sad, Aria. Everything will be all right. I'll never leave you again. I promise.'

When she snuffled out, 'I'm crying because I'm happy, you idiot,' he laughed, because nobody could be happier than he was at that moment.

Nineteen

John didn't know how long he'd been in the workhouse. Several weeks had passed since he'd escaped from the man who'd asked for his ticket.

He'd run as far away from the station as he could, and had found himself in a street with shops. He'd bought himself a pie.

'Do you know the way to Poole?' he'd asked the woman who'd served him.

'And what pool would that be?'

'It's on the other side of the heath.'

318

'No, luvvy. I've never heard of it, or the heath.'

A man followed him out of the shop and drew him into the lane. 'Where are your folks, lad?'

'They live in Poole. That's where I'm going.'

'You want to go to Poole, do you, lad? It happens I'm going that way. It will cost you.'

John didn't like the look of the man. 'I haven't got much money.'

'Turn your pockets out lad and let's have a look.'

'I need it for food.'

He cried out when the man twisted his arms up behind his back. 'You've got more'n I've got, and if you don't shut up I'll break your soddin' arm.' The man's hands searched roughly through his pockets. 'Call that nothing,' he said of the florins, and pushed John face down in some rotting vegetables. By the time John stood the man was gone. So was his money, and a dog was gulping down the remains of his pie.

He'd lingered in the shopping street for several days begging for food and sleeping in the alley. One night a man took him by the collar, hauled him to his feet and threw him into the back of a wagon.

'I've had my eye on you, lad. You can't stay there any more, someone will do away with you. I was hoping you'd move on. We've got enough paupers as it is.'

The union workhouse was a few miles out of town. It was a relief to have a bed to sleep in, even though it was shared by two other boys. At first John was pleased to have regular food,

319

though he soon lost his appetite for gruel, thin pea soup with fat floating in it, and bread. Nobody took much notice of him amongst the crowd of people living there, but he attended lessons in the schoolroom, which he liked. After three weeks he caught a fever, and came out in spots.

Both of the boys who shared his bed caught it too, and the smaller one died.

'Measles,' the medical officer said, and John was placed into a room that had other cases in.

Three weeks later he was back on his ward. The place stank of urine. His head and body itched, his hair was coming out and he thought he might have caught lice.

One day he looked out of a window in desperation, and saw a couple of gypsy caravans heading for the hills. He wondered if they were going to the heath.

If he didn't get out of here soon he'd die, he thought desperately. He'd run away once, and he could do so again.

'We want some boys to weed around the graveyard,' a warder said the next day. 'You, you, and you.'

'I can pull up weeds,' John offered.

'A little minnow like you.' The warder laughed. 'All right then, come on.'

There was about twenty of them in the weeding gang. It was grand to be out of the workhouse, where the most he could hope for was to separate the tar from the oakum until he died. People died quite often in the workhouse, like the boy in the bed who'd felt cold and waxy in

the morning. John's fingers were already covered in blisters and calluses from picking oakum.
The weeding proved to be hard work, too, but
the air was fresh, and there were slabs of bread
and cheese and a barrel with ale in to drink.
Using the gravestones as cover, John gradually
worked his way over to a line of trees.

He waited there, knowing he need only to
squat as an excuse for being there if anyone
looked for him. Dusk began to fall. The boys
lined up, and John held his breath, hoping the
warder didn't count them. He didn't, and he
began to walk back to the workhouse, the warder
at the front helping to pull the cart, and the boys
in a straggling line after him.

Then they were gone from sight. Keeping to
the line of trees John began to run uphill, in the
same direction the caravans had gone. They
were a day ahead of him. He'd have to walk all
night to catch them up. The sun dipped in the
sky and long shadows spread across the land.
John crossed to the limestone track that wound
into the distance. When the moon came out he
would still be able to see his way. He'd die
rather than go back.

But despite his resolve, he quickly tired. He
made his bed behind a dry stone wall out of the
wind, curled into a ball in his coarse workhouse
clothing, and fell asleep.

The next morning the sound of horses woke
him. About to sit up, he froze against the wall
when he heard a voice. 'He wouldn't have come
this far, surely. He's too small.'

'It's surprising how far nippers can run when

they want to. I hope he's stayed on the track, otherwise he'll be lost by now.'

'Aye, well. You can't blame the boy for running away. He's probably gone back into town. There's no sign of him up ahead. Let's go back. We'll have a look round the docks.'

'We'll go as far as that copse up ahead. I can see smoke.'

'Probably the diddicoys. They passed through earlier.'

John stayed where he was, pressed against a cold wall, the long grass ticking against the back of his legs. He pulled a long tender shoot and sucked the moisture from the root end to refresh his mouth, as his Aunt Marianne had once shown him. He couldn't risk being seen. The men came back an hour later, and passed within a foot of his hiding place.

When they'd gone from sight, John rose from his bed of long grass and began to run. In the distance he could see a thin thread of smoke curling up the copse. He headed for it, frantic, in case the gypsies moved off again.

The sun reached the overhead position. It was noon, that much he knew. Otherwise, he had no idea where he was, and wished he'd paid more attention to his geography lessons. Hungry and thirsty, by mid-afternoon John's pace had long ago flagged to a walk. He could smell the smoke in the air now. He trudged on and turned into a field, where a couple of barking dogs tried to keep him at bay. He couldn't go any further and simply stayed there, swaying back and forth.

Someone shouted at the dogs and they retreated.

A woman he recognized was sitting on the step of her van. Not far from her a black kettle steamed over a fire. Unhurriedly, she rose to her feet, gazed at him then smiled. 'So there you are, Master John Hardy.'

'Jessica,' he whispered, stumbling towards her, feeling relieved that her face was familiar. He'd visited her with his Aunt Marianne and she wouldn't turn him away.

'We've been waiting here for you. What took you so long?'

He was so weary and aching he could have died from it. 'My legs wouldn't go any faster, and stones kept getting inside my boots and making blisters. How did you know I was trying to catch you?'

'Two fellers in uniform came sniffing around looking, and asked for you by name. Besides, 'tis the way of the gypsy to pass the word in the wind. We were all keeping a look out for you. Right now, I know you're thirsty and hungry and you need to sleep. You'll feel better in the morning.'

He did feel better when she took him in her arms, hugged him to her and rocked him back and forth while she soothed him with, 'Such a brave little soldier, you are, my lovely. Everything will be all right now, you'll see. Jessica will look after you until we get you home if that's what you want. Your folk will be worried, but word will get to them. There's a man looking for you though. His name is Adam, if I take you

323

back, he'll find you.'

John remembered Adam, who his pa had trusted. He might take him back to his grandfather though. 'I don't want to wait for Adam. Please let me come with you, Mrs Jessica.'

'I reckon the countryside will help take the hurt away from you, at that. Someone will pass the word.'

There was a younger man and woman, and two older children with her. They exchanged a smile.

Jessica said, 'This here is John Hardy from Poole Heath. His mama named her girl twin after me. Find him some warm clothes to wear, and feed that workhouse uniform to the flames. Roseanne, fetch the boy some water to drink.'

'He stinks something awful, ma.'

'And like as not he's lousy with it. While we still have light we'll give him a bath. I'll put some chrysanthemum and thyme oil in it. I'll rub it through his hair, too, then I'll see to his sores and crack his lice, because they'll be half dead by then and not so lively. After that he'll be ready to eat some of that nice rabbit stew you made, I reckon.'

John had never looked forward to a bath so much. It was nice to feel clean again – to feel safe. Jessica stroked soothing salve into his sores, and her fingers in his hair made him feel sleepy.

By the time John had finished his stew he was drowsy. He leaned his head against Jessica's body and she told him a story about his real mother and father who were living with the angels and kept watch over him. 'Every time you see a gold flower they would have planted it there for you, and you'll remember how much they loved you.' John felt comforted by the story and the spoon dropped from his fingers into his lap.

'There, there, my lovely, you don't have to worry any more. You're a long way from home, but Jessica will take you there eventually, and everything will be all right.'

John felt himself being lifted from her and laid on a bunk. A blanket was tucked over him and Jessica began to sing in a low voice, using words he didn't understand.

The last thing he heard was the soft hoot of an owl.

John had gone to the wrong station. He'd boarded a train at Paddington, and had got off at Bristol. Adam knew that for a fact, since the stationmaster remembered him.

'Dressed like a little lord, he was. He said his name was John. The lad didn't have a ticket when I challenged him. He told me he was going to Poole, and his father would pay for it when he got there. You're a bit young to be travelling on your own, sez me. And if you're going to Poole, what are you doing in Bristol? I threatened him with the police if he didn't hand the money over. He said he needed it for food, and when I threatened to turn him upside down and shake it from his pockets he ran off, as quick as a rat.'

Adam grinned. 'The lad was telling the truth. He boarded the wrong train in London, and I've been hired to find him. There is a substantial reward for his safe return. If you see him again I'd be obliged if you'd offer him some assistance. He's to be delivered to Colonel and Mrs Seth Hardy, of Harbour House in Poole.' Adam handed him the fare. 'Will this be sufficient recompense for his fare?'

'Yes, sir.' The man touched his cap and slid the money into his pocket, where it would probably be conveniently overlooked as belonging to the Great Western Railway. 'A reward you say. Well that puts a different light on things. I'll deliver the boy personally if I see him, and I'll treat him like one of my own.'

Bristol was a bustling port town and the chances of John going unnoticed in the crowd was strong. Adam was lucky in his inquiries that a pie seller remembered him. 'A nice young man. Polite like. Someone must have robbed him because the next time I saw him he was foraging in the alley for scraps ... sleeping there for all I know. I don't know where he came from, but he were lost and begging on the street. I told the officer at the workhouse, lest the boy be set upon. I reckoned he'd be better off there. There are lots of unscrupulous types in Bristol, and it wouldn't have taken much for him to have been picked up, taken on board one of the ships and sold into slavery.'

Thanking the man, Adam pressed some coins in his hand, booked a room for the night in the Railway Hotel. He asked directions to the workhouse. When he got there he was too late.

'John Barrie absconded from a work detail four weeks since. He disappeared into thin air.

Nobody saw him leave. We sent men into town to search for him, then up into the hills, but all they found were a couple of gypsy caravans. There were a couple of women, a man and some boys ... too old to be John. A sullen lot, the gypsies. Secretive, like. We turned everything over in the caravans, but no sign of the runaway hidden away. They didn't seem to know his name, and said they hadn't seen him.'

Adam remembered John chattering about the heath gypsies on that fateful day they'd gone to London together. His Aunt Marianne had taken him to visit them, and she'd painted a picture of the camp to hang on his bedroom wall. It was probable that John had lost his faith in men after all he'd been through, but the gypsies had been kind to him. According to Seth, one of them had brought his children into the world, when no other help had been available.

Adam gave the man the same information as he had to the stationmaster.

'I will say this, sir. If that boy went up into the hills by hisself, the poor little beggar will surely have perished by now. There are caves a grown man can get lost in.'

Not as surely as he'd perish in the workhouse by the looks of the inmates. It would be a waste of time to try and search the hills, because the gypsies knew where they were going and he didn't, and they had a four-week start on him. Adam doubted they would stay on the most used tracks. However, he knew exactly where John was now, and as certain as he was of that, he was also certain that the boy would get home safely.

All they had to do was wait.

His suspicions were confirmed when he got back to the hotel and found a note on his bed. 'John Hardy is found, is travelling with Jessica and is on his way home.' It wasn't signed and the hotel clerk couldn't remember it being delivered.

The next morning Adam took a train back to Southampton, then another to Poole, where he picked up a cab. It dropped him at Harbour House. Another cab was waiting there.

Seth met him at the door. 'You have some news?'

'Yes, I do have some.'

'Good. Come into the drawing room. Sir Charles and Edward Wyvern are here.'

He was surprised to see Sir Charles, his face haggard with worry. 'Edgar and I are staying in town until this matter is resolved.'

'An excellent idea. I have a feeling that it will not be much longer.'

'What is your news, then, Adam?' Seth said.

'I traced the boy to Bristol, where he was robbed. Several people remember him. The stationmaster, because he didn't have a ticket. And he asked a shopkeeper if he knew where Poole was on the other side of the heath, only the shopkeeper misunderstood. For a while John was seen begging on the street, but he was picked up and taken to the workhouse. He caught a fever and came out in spots. Measles the doctor in the infirmary said. He was sick for quite a while before he was sent back to his ward. When he'd recovered they put him in an

outside work gang, pulling weeds from a ceme-
tery.'

'He's too small for that type of work,'
Charlotte said indignantly.

'He requested it, apparently, and the warder
thought that the fresh air would be good for him.
He disappeared from the gang, and nobody
noticed he was missing until later than evening.
My theory is that he saw the gypsies the day
before, and that's why he wanted to join the
work party, so he could try and escape from the
workhouse and join them.'

'Why didn't you go after them and get him?'
Charlotte said.

'I'm unfamiliar with the Mendips, and I wasn't
equipped to walk across them. Besides, they had
a four-week start. It's a long way.'

'I would have crawled across them on my
hands and knees to find him,' she told him
fiercely.

'I daresay you would have done, but you're a
woman who is emotionally attached to the boy.
Think on, Mrs Hardy ... if I'd done as you suggest, I would not be here now with such encouraging news of him. Somebody left a note in my
hotel room suggesting that he was safe and on
his way home with Jessica.'

'I'm sorry, I didn't intend to criticize. Jessica,
you say. She's one of the heath gypsies.'

'You have nothing to apologize for. It's hard
waiting for news, especially where a child is
concerned. You're bound to be worried about
him. But he's a brave and resourceful little boy,
and I feel that the outcome will be favourable.'

Seth offered her a smile and turned to Adam. 'I've been working things out. The distance across is about seventy miles,' Seth said. 'Generally, the gypsies consider the welfare of their horses. The caravans wouldn't move very fast, on average about ten miles a day, and they'd camp overnight. It would take them at least a week to get here I should imagine.'

Charlotte's voice began to shake. 'But if he left the workhouse four weeks before Mr Chapman got there and joined the gypsies, where is he?'

Seth was willing to clutch at the straw Adam offered him. 'We could go out and look for them.'

'They've already been on the road for several weeks, so obviously they've detoured,' Adam pointed out.

'What if your theory is wrong?' Sir Charles asked him.

'I admit that it could be, because much of my job is based on outguessing another's actions. But this is the best lead I've had so far. We do know that John and the gypsies were in the same place at the same time. If he recognized any of them he would have asked for their help.'

Seth turned to his wife.'Which way do the gypsies usually come on to the heath, Charlotte?'

'I know nothing about the habits of the gypsies. It was my sister who was friendly with them. She had friends everywhere, some of them totally unsuitable.'

'Which might stand John in good stead on this occasion, as it did for you once,' Seth said.

Her face flamed, then paled. 'What if John didn't find the gypsies and is trying to walk here all by himself?'

'Let's prove or disprove Adam's theory before we alarm ourselves with another. Would Marianne know the ways of the gypsies if it becomes necessary to organize a search party?'

Her face closed up and she shrugged as she said to her husband, 'She might. You'd have to ask her.'

'I will ask her. Perhaps you'd come with me, Adam?'

There was an undercurrent of tension in Harbour House ... not surprising under the circumstances, Adam supposed. He nodded.

Edgar and Sir Charles rose too. Charles offered Charlotte a courtly little bow, saying with considerable charm, 'Thank you for your hospitality, Mrs Hardy. Considering the circumstances it was more than I deserved.'

She gave a faint, self-deprecating smile. 'My husband has convinced me it would be better for John if we tried to get on.'

But the woman was listening to her instinct ... and that was telling her that Charles Barrie was untrustworthy. Adam could see it in her face, which was filled with doubt.

For a moment Adam saw something flicker in the depths of the old man's wily eyes that strengthened his own suspicions that Charles Barrie was saying one thing and meaning another.

Adam had been taken in by him on more than one occasion. He no longer trusted the man an

331

inch. He suggested, 'Wouldn't it be better to get the legalities set down in writing, then all parties will know where they stand.'

'I know exactly where I stand,' Sir Charles murmured.

Edgar said unhappily, 'I've written an agreement along the lines of the sharing arrangement. We could go through it. If you agree, you need only sign it.'

'Not now, Edgar,' Charles said testily. 'I'm waiting on the outcome of other matters.'

Seth exchanged a glance with Adam, and both understood without saying that the man had no intention of signing any agreement. Not without powerful persuasion.

'What other matters is he talking about?' Adam asked Edgar when they got a private moment together.

'Sir Charles has expressed worry about the reputation of Mrs Hardy's family.'

'In relation to what?'

'Anything that can be smeared. The Thornton family. The mother's affair ... the sister's elopement ... if it was indeed an elopement. Also, there is the sister's association with common gypsies.'

'The means by which the child will be safely conveyed to the family, I imagine.'

'We can only hope.' Edgar sighed unhappily. 'I haven't said this to Colonel Hardy, but he once expressed an opinion that he should return to Van Diemen's Land with John. It was said facetiously, but perhaps it's time he carefully considered it.'

Seth was surprised when Nick opened the door. Then he grinned. 'Nice to see you again, Nick. I'm glad to see you survived.'

'So am I.'

Marianne appeared behind him, a big smile lighting up her face. She kissed his cheek. 'Lor, Seth, you look a bit worn around the edges. Has John been found yet? What's been going on? Are the children all right? Nick's return is my big news. I'm going to parade him round town later, set the rumour mill going again. How is Charlotte? I'm too happy to be angry with her any more.' She kissed her husband's cheek this time. 'I hate not having her to gossip with. Men are not very good at it, they only tell you the basic facts. Tell me what's going on!'

Giving a chuckle, Nick lifted her to one side. 'For goodness' sake, Aria. Let them in first.'

'I'll tell Aunt Daisy to put the kettle on. Them?' Her eyes went past him, then filled with curiosity. 'Oh ... who are you?'

'Adam Chapman, Mrs Thornton.'

'Ah ... the genius detective. How mysterious. Are you here to question Nick about the shipwreck? Can I listen? He hasn't told me a thing yet.'

Nick placed his finger over her lips. 'I haven't had time to talk yet. You've been doing it all.'

A blush touched her cheeks and she grinned.

'I'm here to question you, Mrs Thornton,' Adam told her.

Her eyes rounded in surprise and she squeaked on a rising note, 'Meeee?'

'We wondered if you knew where the gypsies enter the heath.'

Her eyes suddenly became bland. 'That depends entirely on which direction they're coming from. They have ways known only to gypsies, and they are secret.'

They went into the drawing room, and Seth filled them in on what had happened. He finished with, 'Seth thinks that Sir Charles is going to try and rake up some family scandal, to give him an excuse to take the boy to London.'

'He won't have to rake too far. If the people here didn't have the Thornton and the Honeymans to gossip about, they'd be struck dumb. Nick and I are the biggest scandal in town at the moment. And there will be worse to come now he's home.'

Nick gave her a pained look. 'Not if I can help it.'

Seth told them, 'I simply can't trust Sir Charles, and I'm thinking of going back to Van Diemen's Land as soon as John is returned ... if I can make arrangements without being observed.'

'I can make those arrangements for you,' Nick said. 'Nobody will think twice about me hanging around a shipping office.'

Marianne remembered her sister's attachment to Harbour House. 'Charlotte would find it hard to leave her home.'

'She'll be given a choice.'

'You'd go without her?'

'I don't want to, but if that's what she wants.'

'And your children?'

'Would stay with her. She's a good mother, and I'd make sure that they were all well provided for.'

Crossing to where he sat, Marianne placed a hand on his arm. 'Seth, to set John above your own dear children is unfair to Charlotte – and unfair to John, who's being given no choice but to part from many of those people who care about him. Indeed, it's also unfair to Sir Charles who has been cast as the villain, when all he has done is express the natural desire of an old man who wants to spend time with his only grandson and heir before he dies. In the ways of men you see each other as combatants, and are butting heads. Surely he's learned something from John running away. Surely you have.'

It crossed Adam's mind that the young woman was talking a lot of sense, and they were all listening.

'As worthy as she was, John's mother is dead. You'd place her dying wish above all that is dear to you – one that she made when she was in despair and fearful of her son's future, no doubt. Had she envisaged that you would marry and have children of your own she would never have placed that condition upon you.'

Seth shrugged. 'Probably not.'

'And what of the vows you exchanged before God with my sister? What you are thinking of doing will destroy everything Charlotte is beginning to build. She finds it hard to express affection, always has. Seeing her with her children – your children, including John, was always a joy to me. There's nothing more she wanted than a

335

family who loved her, and she would take your loss hard. Whatever has gone wrong between Charlotte and I of late, and however bad it looks to outsiders, I still love her dearly and she loves me. More importantly, she trusts you Seth.'

Seth looked uncertain then. 'What would you have me do?'

'Allow me to talk to Sir Charles Barrie on John's behalf.'

'Talk to Sir Charles?' Clearly, this was not what Seth had expected her to say.

'She's convinced me,' Adam said.

Nick gave a small chuckle. 'And me, as long as she's accompanied.'

Adam envied Nick Thornton his wife when the lively Marianne bestowed a flirtatious little smile on him. She was a peach, and if he was ever in the position to marry he hoped he'd find a woman just like her.

It wasn't until after they'd gone that he realized she hadn't answered his question about the gypsies, and wondered if it had been a deliberate oversight.

'I'm given to understand that you're worried about my character, Sir Charles,' Marianne said.

Adam and Edgar exchanged an astonished glance before they retired to the window. Nick stayed.

'I've heard idle talk.'

'Idle talk is cheap, and you don't need to repeat it to me. I don't usually feel the need to satisfy the curiosity of those who indulge in it.'

This time Sir Charles's eyes flared in astonishment. He opened his mouth and shut it again when she took from a small satchel she carried two pieces of paper. She laid them on the table. 'That is a copy of the certificate of the marriage between myself and Captain Nicholas Thornton there. And that is the certificate of the son who was born to us.' She bestowed an adoring smile on her husband, who looked bemused that anyone could feel that way about him.

Sir Charles began to look uncomfortable. 'There is no need—'

'Ah, but there is, Sir Charles. I want you to be entirely satisfied that the people surrounding John are fit and proper people to guide him. I believe you have also heard scandalous talk about my mother. She died giving birth our sister, and Charlotte and I still grieve the loss of her. Charlotte brought me up as best she could.'

'And made a good job of it, I see,' Charles murmured gallantly.

'There was talk, but I've determined that the next time I hear it repeated in public I will no longer turn the other cheek, but will consult a lawyer. That person will then be given the chance to prove their allegations in court.'

Edgar smiled, and murmured, 'Allow me to be your advocate if that ever happens.'

'Mrs Thornton, please, there is no need to go on,' Sir Charles said.

'Ah, but I feel I must, since it appears to me that you are casting about for an excuse not to honour the verbal agreement you made with my brother-in-law, Seth Hardy.'

'I'm actually trying to make sure that my heir

has a good home, as any grandfather would. I don't like the thought of him being friends with gypsies.'

'I can understand that because the fear stems from ignorance, but I've known the heath gypsies all my life, and have never come to any harm. They taught me a lot, and if John is travelling with them I can only envy him his good fortune, for it will be an adventure he'll remember forever. They know John well, and if he's gone to them for help in his journey home then it's because he's learned to trust them. Now, if there is anything else worrying you, please let's get it into the open.'

'What do you hope to achieve by this meeting, young woman?'

She smiled at him. 'My sister and her husband only have John's welfare at heart, so do I. We all love him. He loves all of us. They need to know they can trust you, and John needs to know that he can trust you. For me, I would like all those I love to be happy.'

'My word is my bond.'

She gazed at him quizzically, and he laughed. 'I never could resist a beautiful face, or a woman who pleads so prettily. All right. Edgar, pass me that agreement. I'll sign the damned thing, you can witness my signature, and Mrs Thornton can deliver it personally to her brother-in-law.'

The agreement was signed and handed over to Marianne.

Her smile warmed him. 'There ... I knew you weren't as unreasonable as you at first seemed, Sir Charles. You must come to dinner the next time you're here.'

'I will, young lady, since I'm considering taking up a lease on a house here.'

'How wonderful. Then John will be able to visit you quite often. We're looking for property ourselves. My husband intends to give up the sea and open an emporium.' When she rose to her feet so did he. Marianne kissed him on the cheek. 'Thank you, so much. You'll never regret it, Sir Charles.'

'Let's hope not.'

'Now I must go. My son will be needing me.'

Surprisingly, Sir Charles kissed her hand. 'My grandson spoke of you fondly, and often. Now I know why. Thank you for being a friend to him.'

'All of us are his friends.'

She turned to Adam. 'I'll ask Nick to take me to see Charlotte tomorrow. There's something I wish to sort out with her.'

Marianne Thornton was nobody's fool, Adam thought. She picked her moment to give her the best advantage.

As for him, he needed to think seriously about the proposition put to him by Edgar Wyvern and his associates, and the advice of the people he trusted. Who better than Seth Hardy and Nick Thornton? His own investigating agency, with his own staff. It was an exciting prospect, as long as he was answerable only to himself and could choose his own cases.

But first, he wanted to see John restored to the bosom of his family, and that day was close, he knew it.

Twenty

'I'll take you, and that's that. If Seth's not there you'll be coming home again. You'll have to get back in time to give Dickon his dinner.'

'And what are you going to do?'

'Look around for premises for the shop, amongst other things.'

When she leaned over to kiss him, Marianne's hair covered his face and he inhaled the fragrance of her. Her lips were as soft as a whisper. He pulled her gently down on top of his body, her full breasts were almost bursting from their skin when they grazed against his naked chest, and he groaned with the delight of her.

Their son was kicking vigorously in his crib, and making threatening noises.

Aria finished kissing him, gazed into his eyes and smiled with real regret. 'I'll have to feed Dickon. He's not old enough to know what waiting means.'

'But I am,' and he sounded as rueful as he felt when she rolled over and plucked Dickon from his cot. Not that he hadn't sampled Aria's delights a little earlier. But a little bit more loving never went amiss, and he had several months of abstinence to catch up on.

The infant's mouth wavered between smiles

and tears, and he impatiently moved his head as Aria teased his mouth with her knuckle, opening and shutting it like a bird and giving impatient little cries of frustration.

Eventually, Nick took his son's head and held it against her nipple. Aria allowed his mouth to close around her breast and the boy began to suck strongly, making contented little grunts. He settled down and his eyes closed as he tucked into his breakfast with serious intent.

Aria chuckled when Nick kissed her and said, 'The need in a woman to tease a male half to death is obviously inbuilt.'

Dickon held endless fascination for Nick. He'd never given fathering a child much thought, except for the children he'd intended to share with Charlotte. He remembered how angry and betrayed he'd felt when he'd heard that she'd given birth to twins fathered by another man.

He couldn't understand now why he'd felt that way, and why Charlotte had thrown Aria out when she was expecting a child. Charlotte had made her choice, and had a good husband in Seth, so to discover she was still flaming mad over his union with Aria seemed odd. It also intrigued him. Surely she didn't still harbour feelings for him, or worse, think that he still harboured feelings for her. He intended to find out, because his beloved Aria had been suffering because of it, and he wanted things put right between them.

So later, he took Seth aside and said, 'Will you mind if I talk to Charlotte? I want to repair the rift between the sisters if I can. It's hurting Aria.'

Seth nodded and gave a faint smile. 'I know ... I've been keeping an eye on her. Marianne loves you, you know. I've admired her so much over this past year. She's stayed strong through all the whispers and accusations, and she refused to despair. She kept saying that you'd return and everything would be all right again. I don't know whether she was trying to convince herself, or everyone else. She was waiting for your uncle to come back from Australia with definite news before she'd believe it.'

'Delaying what she thought was inevitable?' He gave a faint smile. 'That's typical of Aria. Negative thoughts slide off her like goats on grease.'

'Unlike Charlotte.'

Nick felt the need to spring to her defence. 'Charlotte had a lot to put up with after her mother died. She ran the house and took responsibility for Aria. Their father was a drunken bastard. Sometimes he beat them, and sometimes they had nothing to eat. You should perhaps be made aware, Seth ... I no longer have any strong feelings towards Charlotte, except for friendship. If she'd accepted me it would have been the biggest mistake I'd ever made. I think our relationship was always based on who could get the better of the other.'

'I believe you, but I'm not sure if Charlotte would. Sometimes I think she regrets her decision.'

'I doubt it. She'll defend her position to the end, and she always has a hard time letting go of things. She'd die rather than admit she was wrong.'

'Which is what she needs to do on this occasion. Marianne has approached Charlotte several times with the hand of friendship, and finally sent her a message saying that Charlotte must be the one to end the quarrel.'

'What did Charlotte say to that?'

'Her nose went up in the air and she said something like, "Humph!"'

'How did she take news of my death?'

'She cried a lot, then she went quiet, then she cried a bit more and said she wished she hadn't been mean to you because you hadn't deserved it, and she hoped you hadn't suffered.'

'I should die more often.'

Seth laughed at that. 'How about we force their hands? Come to dinner on Saturday.'

Marianne wrapped Dickon warmly in his shawl, and they took a cab to Harbour House.

Seth let them in. Of Charlotte there was no sign, but a young dog yapped ferociously at their heels.

'Shut up, you noisy creature.' Turning it on its back Marianne tickled his stomach and he writhed about in ecstasy.

'That's Scrap. I bought him for John.'

'He'll love it.' Marianne hadn't set foot in Harbour House for months. It hadn't changed, even its smell, a mixture of polish, dust and heather. She choked on her tears as she handed Seth the agreement from Sir Charles. No wonder Charlotte was so attached to it. 'Being back here makes me want to go out on the heath. How's Charlotte today?'

'Why don't you ask me yourself?'

Her sister was standing at the top of the stairs, tears were running down her face. 'Why didn't you come sooner, Marianne? I've missed you.'

On the way up the stairs Marianne scolded her, 'I did come sooner. I walked out here on several occasions, and you wouldn't let me in.'

'How could you do such and awful thing to your own sister?' Nick asked her.

'I don't know.' She gave a big sniff. 'Yes, I do. It's because I'm pig-headed and I like my own way all the time, and Marianne had married you without telling me. I'm truly sorry, Marianne. Can you forgive me?'

'I usually do, but you don't deserve it this time. However ... yes, you're forgiven.'

'And is there no welcome home for me, Char?'

Charlotte gave a faint smile. 'You have nine lives, Nick. I didn't believe for a minute that you were drowned.'

'Liar,' Seth said, which brought a grin to her face. 'Marianne talked Sir Charles into signing that agreement, so John will return to live with us.'

'May I remind you not to count your chickens. John isn't home yet.'

Marianne reached the top of the stairs. When Charlotte hugged her Dickon began to wave his arms around.

His mother placed a kiss on her son's dark head. 'But he will be home quite soon ... today.'

'How do you know?'

'I can feel it in the wind.'

Charlotte took Dickon from her and gazed down at him, smiling when he presented her with a copy of Nick's smile. She looked at Nick, as if comparing them. 'Dickon has your eyes and will probably grow up with your damned rogue charm, as well, Nick Thornton.'

Nick gave a self-effacing grin.

'Now don't you go running off, because I've got something to say to you, as well.'

He grinned challengingly at her. 'Charlotte, you haven't changed a bit, you're still the same old sourpuss.'

'Oh, but I have changed. I promised Seth that I wouldn't point a gun at you this time.'

'And I promise to take the bullet if you do. Rather that than be at the pointed end of one of your tongue lashings with my nose stuck in the dirt again,' he said gloomily.

Seth laughed. 'Come into my study, Nick, I'll give you a brandy to fortify yourself with while the ladies talk.'

Upstairs, they went into Marianne's old room, which was exactly as she'd left it. Placing Dickon on the bed, Charlotte hugged her tight. 'I cannot tell you how sorry I am. I should never have thought such awful things about you and Nick. It doesn't matter why Nick married you, as long as you're happy. At least he did the right thing.'

The right thing? 'Lor, Char, you do like to think the worst of people, don't you? Of course I'm happy. I didn't expect to fall in love with him, though.'

'But does he love you? I mean, it was always

345

me he expected to marry.'

'Whether he loved me or not, I'm going to make him so happy that he'll never want to leave me. You hurt him badly, Char. You led him on, then cast him aside as if he was worthless.'

'So you married him because you felt sorry for him.'

'Sorry for him?' Marianne giggled. 'It was probably the other way around. He knew people would talk about us after I went to Boston, and they'd come to the wrong conclusion. Nick swept me right off my feet. I adore him.'

Dickon gave a demanding little cry.

'He needs a feed.'

'Then let's go into the nursery, because the twins will need one too, and it's time the cousins were acquainted. It's warmer there, and we can leave them with the maid afterwards. You'll be surprised at how big the twins are now, and they're both walking. Jessica first, then Major Mitchell, though he has to hang on to the furniture. They're on solids now, but they still need milk...'

If there was one thing Charlotte had never lacked, it was courage. But even Marianne was astounded when she made her apology to Nick in front of her husband and herself.

'I need to apologize to you, Nick. Although I loved you, it wasn't the type of love that would sustain a marriage. That's something I've unexpectedly found with Seth. I should have told you earlier that I didn't care for you in that way.'

'It's all right, Charlotte. I'm sure you did. I

was too stupid to listen, anyway, and I forgave you for that a long time ago.'

'I didn't expect you to marry Marianne when you still felt affection for me. And then it was kept a secret and I learned she was having a baby. It upset me because I knew you'd found a perfect way of taking your revenge and I didn't want Marianne to be hurt.'

'Enough, Charlotte. Let's get a couple of things perfectly clear. I didn't marry Aria to take revenge on you. When I met your sister I had already fallen out of love with you, except I was thinking perhaps we could be friends again.'

Marianne felt his hand slide warmly round hers, and as their fingers intertwined he smiled at her. 'I admit that both things crossed my mind when I discovered you were on board, Aria, which was why I didn't turn back to port. But something happened.'

'What? You said you wanted to marry me to protect me from any gossip that would arise.'

'Who gives a damn about women's gossip? Put simply, I fell in love with you. It was almost immediate, and it was nothing like I'd ever experienced before. I remembered you'd been hankering over Lucian Beresford, who was totally unsuitable for you, so I decided to grab you for myself.'

A smile sped across her face. Her heart thumped and her stomach felt like a sack of leaping frogs. 'Oh, Nick,' she said, and burst into tears.

He smiled at her expression, 'What are you crying about? Didn't you realize?'

When she shook her head, he smiled, but

rather smugly.

'I nearly died of grief when you went missing, and if it hadn't been for Dickon I would have done. Your uncle offered to marry me himself if you didn't come home, and Daisy used to cry herself to sleep on the nights I didn't cry myself to sleep.'

Nick's grin grew wider. 'Erasmus proposed to you?'

'Sort of.' She laughed. 'He looked rather relieved when I turned him down. Can we go out on the heath for a little while, Nick?'

'Oh, you and that heath, Marianne,' Charlotte said with a certain amount of exasperation.

'Come with us, just for an hour. I'll show you where the gypsies camp ... Seth, you too. I have a feeling...'

They donned their coats and set out. The day was a cool one, the water from the harbour was slapping against the shore, the gulls wheeling. Soon winter would set in, mists would creep across the heath and lock the house inside it. The banks of the streams would be hung with icicles.

Marianne slipped her hand into Nick's and thought about him and their son. She was full to bursting with happiness and had never felt so contented.

The gypsies had arrived, she knew. There was a smell of smoke in the air, one that hadn't been there when they'd arrived at the house.

They'd made camp in the pine copse, which was on a rise, with the chalk stream flowing in a groove the water had worn through the heath cover. They'd probably stay for a week then move on to a more sheltered spot for the winter, if the weather remained good. They'd be back again in spring.

The dogs approached first, bellies low to the ground and tails wagging when they recognized Marianne. Hackles were raised for the others. Scrap set up a juvenile yap from the safety of Seth's arms.

There were six vans and six sturdy horses, fires were going and there was an air of togetherness amongst the inhabitants of the camp.

Jessica came towards them, a smile on her face. 'You'll be after having the boy, then. I would have brought him back to where he belongs earlier, but I needed to earn my living along the way, and he needed to heal. The lad had troubles going on inside his head. He's there, with the horse. Allow him to finish his chore first. It will only take a minute or two.'

They sat on a fallen pine and watched him. John was astride the broad back of Jessica's horse, brushing the tangles from its mane. The horse had its eyes closed and seemed to be drowsing.

Charlotte gazed at Seth with tears in her eyes and Seth kissed her forehead.

Nick took Marianne's hand in his. 'Let's leave them to it and go back to the house now, my love.'

Marianne gave Jessica a hug and whispered. 'Thank you, Jessica.'

'How did you know we were here?'

She told Jessica the same as she'd told the

others. 'I heard it on the wind.'

The gypsy took Marianne's face between her work worn hands and kissed her forehead. 'I reckon you did, at that, my lovely. You have some gypsy blood in your veins; it came through your mother. Would this be your man?'

'He is my husband. His name is Nicholas Thornton.'

'She has a soft heart, but a brave one. Look after her, Nicholas.'

'Always,' Nick said.

As they walked away they heard John call out, 'Pa! ... Ma! I knew you'd both come. Is that my dog, can I play with him?'

As Nick and Marianne headed back across the heath the wind scattered the last of the autumn debris before them, clearing a path.

Ahead of them, Harbour House came into view. There, Marianne's ancestors had lived, fought and died. There, she and Charlotte had been born, and there, her mother and father had breathed their last. It had not been a house of happy memories for Marianne, but nevertheless it was in her blood and in her past. Nick was her future.

The sound of a name seemed to be whispered on the wind as it combed through the tough heath gorses. Serafina...

Marianne gazed up at Nick, at his profile, which was strong and loving, and the hairs on the nape of her neck, prickled. 'Nick?'

A dark, liquid glance came her way. 'What is it, my love?'

'Did you hear anything?'

Taking her in his arms he tipped up her chin and whispered against her mouth, 'I thought I heard your heart sing ... then again, it may have been mine.'